IN THE DEMON'S DOME...

Quiet, Eerie quiet. All Daniel could hear was his own breathing whispering through his face mask. He took a few steps and his footfalls rang very loud in the hollow stillness. The dome was a cavernous museum where time had stopped 100 years before. Everything lay just where it had been dropped on its final day. The leaving had been panicked flight.

Apprehension crept over Daniel like a chill in the air. His heart was galloping. And he became aware that there was something there. Something unseen. A presence. Fear! This was a monster!

Daniel ran, echoes of his footsteps clapping close behind him like something in pursuit. He dove in through the ship's hatch which he'd left open in case of the need for a quick exit.

But open hatches were open to other things as well. . . .

WIND CHILD

by
R. M. Meluch

A SIGNET BOOK
NEW AMERICAN LIBRARY

SIGNET, SIGNET CLASSIC, MENTOR, PLUME, MERIDIAN AND NAL
BOOKS *are published by New American Library,*
1633 Broadway, New York, New York 10019

FIRST PRINTING, MAY, 1982

3 4 5 6 7 8 9 10 11

PRINTED IN THE UNITED STATES OF AMERICA

PUBLISHER'S NOTE

Prologue

Lady in mourning. Lady in wait. A slender figure dressed in black, standing at the window in stoic sadness, she was too young to be a widow. The room was mostly dark, the deep colors of the carpet broken only by a solitary shaft of sunlight that crossed before the lady and fell at her feet in a bright patch bordered in the patterned shadow of the lace curtains. A breeze disturbed the crystal wind chimes hung from the lintel and sent flecks of color shifting through the room as sunlight danced rainbows off the pendants, prisms as perfect as drops of rain. Or tears.

Laure had never waited for any man. That she chose to do so now worried the lord LaFayette. He hoped that the inevitable disappointment would not fall on her too hard, for he had seen enough of his daughter's hurt rage in the past few days to last him the rest of his life.

Why, of all men, had she chosen to wait for this one? An ex-bodyguard she had not seen or heard of in three years. Her acquaintance with him had lasted a total of three months—in which time he had saved her life, but, as the man himself had said, that was what he was being paid for. This time, however, he was offered no money. Laure had just asked a very expensive favor of him—for passage to Aeolis cost dearly—and that kind of man did not grant favors. She had not even told him why. She had simply bid him come.

"*Chérie*, please. You give him too much faith," said Lord LaFayette. The man would have arrived by now if he were coming. "Walk in the garden with me. You have been in this house too long."

"He will come," Laure said calmly, without her usual wrath on being disbelieved. This was simple affirmation, as certain and unanswerable as "The sun is shining."

And before the lord could sigh, there came the muffled sound of running footsteps on thick carpeting. Laure's maid appeared, bobbed a curtsy just inside the door, and said breathlessly, "Milady, milord, he's here!"

Laure, who had never once missed a chance to gloat over a victory, did not so much as cast a prideful glance at her doubting father this time. She turned from the window and walked out of the room.

There he was, in the same place she had first seen him, and from the same angle—she at the head of the stairs, he in the parlor.

East.

Three years had not done much to him; at his age, three years wouldn't. He was still silver-haired, hard and lean, ugly/handsome. Even standing in his customary careless way, masked in his customary loose-fitting, shabby clothes, it was apparent he still retained a serpent's quickness. Blue eyes were still fierce and bright; his face sunbeaten, too rugged, and sagging. He still needed a shave. Perhaps there was another scar, another wrinkle. And he was not carrying a gun this time.

Laure walked down the stairs. The first time, she had skipped and she'd been smiling.

East looked up. An expression of surprise crossed his face to see the lady dressed in black.

On the last stair, she halted. Her eyes narrowed. "Your hat," she said.

East looked at the hat in his hand, puzzled, not sure what she meant. "You gave it to me," he said.

"You sat on it," she said, no expression in her voice.

"I sat on the old one," said East.

"I threw the old one out," said Laure.

East held the hat behind him. "No." Not again. It had taken him too long to get this one looking comfortable.

She nodded slightly, acquiescing—for now.

She had not mellowed—that much he could see, despite her calm. She was the kind of lady for whom hurricanes were once named, with that kind of fury and the stillness of a storm's eye—and she knew what those were like.

Yet she was so much older somehow. She was only twenty-six. Thin, she had always been; imperious, that too; in black, never.

"Laure, who died?"

"Stephen."

East's former employer. Laure's husband. A lot of questions came to mind, but this was the time for only one. "What do you want me to do?"

"Just be here," she said, and she walked back up the stairs.

2

East retired to the small room he had occupied three years before when he used to guard the lady.

There was a deck of cards and a bottle of beer waiting for him on the table.

It was in the evening when East was losing at solitaire that the late Lord Remington's niece Corinna happened into East's sanctuary and gasped. She had never seen an unrejuvenated old person before. Offworld, he would be called rugged. On Aeolis, he was hideous.

Corinna hesitated in the doorway, staring, and slowly it occurred to her who this was. This was the man Laure had been waiting for.

Recovering from her initial shock, Corinna decided to tell Laure's man what sort of lady cousin Laure actually was.

"Do you know what she did?" Corinna said.

East was not interested in whatever it was this pale, sweet-scented belle wanted to tell him. Instead of answering, East said, "Tell me how Stephen died."

Stephen Remington should have lasted a good hundred years more. His death could not have been natural.

"Oh, I'll tell you," Corinna began, gathering up her nerve and stepping farther into the room with the ugly man. She told her story.

Stephen had been on the stairs when Corinna's little pet cauchauna darted out and wrapped its forepaws around Stephen's ankle ("affectionately," said Corinna), and Stephen fell. Laure ran down after him, kicking aside the cauchauna, which had let go as soon as Stephen had lost his balance. Corinna screamed and ran to gather up her gentle, mewing pet and comfort it. Then she saw Stephen lying at the foot of the stairs and heard Laure shrieking into the phone for medics, who arrived moments later and pronounced Stephen dead. The medics took Stephen away, and Laure's gaze landed on Corinna cuddling her cauchauna. Laure flew at Corinna, tore the mewing animal out of her arms, and ran to the kitchen.

"And do you know what she did?" Corinna asked, the pitch of her voice rising to a squeak.

East had a general idea.

"She *boiled* it!"

Yes, that would be in character.

"Alive!" Corinna added unnecessarily, not getting the proper horrified reaction from East.

3

"I grant you it was a mistake," said a calm voice from the doorway. "It was much too merciful."

Laure was gazing levelly at Corinna, who backed away, edging behind East's chair and speaking in his ear. *"And* do you know what else? The police are investigating her."

"For offering bribes to a physician," Laure explained, still with little emotion. "I tried to have Stephen resurrected."

East spilled his beer.

"Don't look so shocked, Mr. East," Laure said sternly. "I did love him."

Then why the hell did you call me? East thought.

Laure glanced back to Corinna and spoke as she would to a servant, "Leave us."

Corinna stared at both of them in horror, both so cool toward the murder of her pet. Feral, both of them. Corinna fled as from a wild animal's den.

Laure sat across from East, looked at his beer, and said, "Where's mine?"

East set a drink in front of her.

She was looking strained, weary of being stately and gracious to the constantly arriving mourners, vultures, and those offering sympathy. But she showed tears to no one. East had begun to think he was the only man ever to see her cry.

"East, would you drive my car?"

East had borne no fondness for Stephen Remington, had even thought of murdering him once, and he wondered if he could in clear conscience take part in Stephen's funeral. Hypocrisy was not among East's many vices and faults. He could not mourn for Stephen. But he supposed he could genuinely express sadness for Laure's grief and wish very sincerely that Stephen rest peacefully dead for eternity.

He nodded.

"Thank you," she said softly.

East could not recall her ever saying those words to him before. But he was no longer her hired man; she no longer commanded him.

Which was not to say he was free from her.

In the morning East brought Laure's car around. He was going to get out and open the back door for her, but she opened her own door and jumped in beside him in the front seat.

They rode in silence for a while as the car skimmed across the lake and into deep woods where there was no road, the way to the cemetery indicated only by a long straight clearing of trees, wide enough to admit the silent train of vehicles.

Laure spoke finally without looking at East, her eyes locked straight ahead on the hearse preceding her car.

"What is your name?"

Legally he was simply East, for his given name was not registered in the Universal Bank Computer. Only two other people in the galaxy knew his name.

"Jonathan."

Three people.

"Is that all?" she said. "How common."

"It's *my* name," said East, irked. She had no reverence for a gift, probably the only one he had to give.

As if reading his thoughts and acknowledging that she was careless, she asked, "Why did you tell me?"

"You asked."

From the moment he'd met her, he could deny her nothing.

By evening Laure had rid the house of all her guests, including her father, and shut the door, leaving only herself, the servants, and East.

Formal relationship gone, East was not sure what he was to Laure—no longer a hireling, not exactly a friend, and never a lover. He could not tell how long he was needed here, and she gave no indication.

She was silent for nine days, nine days in black. The house was tomblike. The servants crept through its halls like monks in a church and spoke in whispers. Laure's mood reigned. She never came to East to talk, and he rarely saw her, but he heard her sometimes pacing the floor of the room above his at hours gentlefolk seldom saw.

On the morning of the tenth day East stepped from his room and came abruptly to a halt.

Laure stood at the foot of the stairs, wearing a knee-length dress of pale blue, her dark hair loose upon her shoulders. East remembered that it was springtime here.

She did not move, but stared at him—almost terrified—as if she'd been caught at something, frozen like a deer struck full in the eyes by a sudden bright light. East stopped breathing.

She blinked, started to say his name, suddenly broke from her place and ran the distance between them, into his arms, and held on tight.

East had a question for her that came out an order, for he

5

would not, could not, tolerate refusal. And even though Laure never took orders, it did not occur to her even to question this one.

By nightfall the lady LaFayette-Remington was Mrs. East.

PART ONE: Daniel

I.

A brittle silence seeped into the afternoon and became fixed. Crickets and cicadas refused to sing, and birds puffed out their feathers as if bracing for a storm, their heads tucked under their wings. Wild creatures returned to their dens or crept up to houses like rabid things, and even dogs stopped barking their warnings, until it seemed nothing that lived would stir, except for the horses that would pace at a restless trot, stop, cock their heads to the southwest, snuff the air and let it out with a snort and a stamp of hoofs, sensing evil on a summer day.

And it came.

The sky went suddenly dark as an orange cloud swept across the Texas plain, leaving a wake of acid burns wherever it touched down, and those heedless birds that had not found shelter in time were knocked out of the sky in midflight, falling to earth in a rain of dead insects and withered leaves.

The swarm, the *cuyane*, gathered and darkened, orange to black, billions, each the size of a dust speck and as formless, scorching land and city, whistling into cracks and skittering through buildings like trapped flies with acid wings.

The great cloud billowed aloft, then plunged down, a roiling, mindless mass. It tumbled and splattered headlong into obstacles, trying to get through, to get past—

—and slapped against Laure's window, then slid off—upward like trapped bees, not downward as would something that was not alive.

Laure watched with fascinated revulsion. Then she stepped away from the window and rolled lazily onto the bed. Kicking off her sandals, she stretched out her bare legs, threw one

7

arm behind her head, and pouted at being alone. She wondered if she could will her husband to her. Some people thought she was telepathic.

She had not seen Aeolis in fifteen years—not since her only child had been born—and she did not miss it, not even on days like this when the alarm sounded and she was confined to the small house while the living mud-rain of the *cuyane* whipped at the windows. She seldom thought about the idyllic, weather-controlled, disease-free aristocrats' paradise she had left behind, and not even the duke himself could make her return. He had tried. He wanted her to be an ambassador.

The planet of Laure's birth had two names, for it wore the faces of two worlds. One was the Earth colony now called Aeolis, founded nearly 250 years ago; the other was the alien world called Kistraal, died 10,000 years ago. There was hardly anything Kistraalian left on the planet except for a few natives that still lingered to haunt the Earthling colonists of the new world.

The Duke of Aeolis needed an intermediary between the Earthlings and the Kistraalians. The Earth Service had failed to provide one, for there was a severe problem in communicating, which was that no one could figure out *how*.

At one time not long ago, the Kistraalians could be talked with face to face, human to humanoid. Each Kistraalian possessed three separate forms assumable at will. One form was humanoid; one was animal; and one was an inorganic living form that could only be called wind because it manifested itself as currents in the air and would not sit still to be analyzed further. But now the species was dying out, and the Kistraalians appeared in one form only, the wind form. These were the creatures the Duke of Aeolis had to contend with.

The creatures had no detectable way of communicating with Earthlings or even with each other. And the Kistraalians did not seem to be making a great effort on their part, for it was known that they must have a way of speaking with Earthlings. There had once been a young Earthwoman who talked with the winds.

But Laure was not coming back to Aeolis. Nor would she tell her secrets. It suited her to be thought a telepath, and she would not sit still to be tested. The Kistraalians, she said, could make themselves known if it pleased them, and evidently it did not.

She rolled over and rested her chin on her hand, still pouting.

East was looking for his wife. He was never sure anymore what Laure would do when the *cuyane* descended. He used to be able to trust her to run for cover, but now that their son Daniel was old enough to look out for himself, Laure was less cautious. She'd once had an affinity for danger, and it was back now.

He found her upstairs on the bed. He was not surprised to see a row of wild birds perched atop her mirror, a mockingbird, a crow, a wren, and two young grackles, which Laure had coaxed in through the skylight in the face of the living storm. The birds were subdued and frightened in this strange sanctuary, but not panicked, somehow knowing that the woman was their safety. Laure had a way with wild things. East dismissed the idea of any psychic power and attributed it instead to sensitivity and an openness to things strange.

Laure was more kin to God's creatures than to humankind. She never lost a sense of life, of youth, of grace, of ferocity. And she was still as slender as a girl. East was feeling— besides relief on seeing her safe—something a little too quiet for lust, a little too sexual for love. He still felt as strongly for her as he ever had.

Laure heard him come in, but she did not look up. She had her chin propped on her hand and forearm and was intently regarding the grounded birds.

"East, take me flying," she said.

East glanced at the window as another wave of sludge slapped the pane and oozed upward. "In this?"

The *cuyane* struck the window again with an emphatic smack. Laure got up slowly and pressed her palm to the glass. "Yes," she said quietly.

"Anywhere in particular you want to go?" East asked.

She turned to him. "I want to go where it's going."

The house was in the way of where the swarm wanted to go. And, mindless as it was, it did seem to *want* to go somewhere, though everyone knew that the *cuyane* wandered in an ever-changing direction like a random wind.

But this time the direction did not change, for it was not random.

The ship was a converted guerrilla fighter, a spaceship with atmospheric capabilities, built to withstand wars, repeated reentries—and a buffeting by a cloud of inorganic alien parasites. East piloted the ship into the middle of the swarm where the *cuyane* clustered so densely as to be opaque, and the ship's sensors could detect nothing at all beyond its immediate surroundings—the swarm itself.

Though East could not see, he was not much worried about crashing into another ship. Anyone with any sense would fly around, above, or below a *cuyane* swarm.

Laure stood behind him, put her arms loosely around his neck, and gazed at the viewport. "It looks like hell," she said.

The billions of *cuyane* had multiplied from a few specks accidentally imported in the potting soil of an alien plant. Being inorganic, the creatures had slipped past traditional bioscanners, and they resisted traditional pest controls.

The *cuyane* traveled for hours on a never varying course. Laure was asleep. East and the *cuyane* never slept.

Then finally the swarm changed—and not in the way East was expecting. It was not a change in course.

He woke up Laure. "They're slowing down."

Laure got up and returned to the viewport. "Let's see where they've brought us."

East took the controls. "Nebraska is a good guess," he said and eased the ship downward.

Gradually the swarm thinned, and at last, still nearly a half kilometer above the ground, the guerrilla ship dropped out of the cloud, into dimmed daylight.

"Oh, East."

"My God."

The terrain below for miles around was desolate and lifeless as if they were not on Earth but some dead world of another sun. The land was completely stripped.

"Did the *cuyane* do all this?" Laure whispered.

East took her hand without thinking what he was doing—it had become reflex—and gave it an unconscious squeeze. "I don't think so, sweetheart."

The *cuyane*, which had continued traveling above the hovering ship, passed clear, and, as it did, the guerrilla fighter was abruptly flooded with sunlight. On the land below, the dark shadow of the swarm retreated, leaving the stark plain exposed with horrible clarity.

Ahead, on the dark horizon where the *cuyane* were going, was a tower. The swarm stopped and clustered there—with other swarms that were coming from all directions, from far and wide, forming one huge mass towering miles high like a thunderhead.

The silver hair on the back of East's neck pricked and stood on end.

He spotted something else on the plain, not far away, glinting in the light—a small structure not even the size of a house. He squinted, and nodded toward it for Laure to look.

A small hand smoothed the back of his neck. "Put us down and let's go see."

Laure stood under East's arm in the shade of the guerrilla fighter a short way from the structure they had seen from the air. The base was rectangular, metal, not new. The superstructure was very recent, mostly plastics, with a tangle of wire net and rigging above. The whole queer building seemed in counterpoint to the tower over which the *cuyane* swarmed.

It felt odd to be out in the open air with a giant mass of *cuyane* in sight. But the swarm was not going anywhere, as if it was where it wanted to be.

There were no other signs of life, not even flies. The air smelled dusty.

East shook his head. Laure had a talent for finding trouble. She'd done it again. Whatever all of this meant, it could not be good.

East unwound Laure's arm from around his waist. "Stay here."

Those words rarely had any effect on Laure, and he didn't know why he bothered saying them. She might obey for as long as ten minutes.

He walked up to the structure, which seemed inert enough. Whatever it was designed to do, it was not doing it.

He stepped up on the platform, scanned the horizon, and saw what looked like two more structures the same as this one, all the same distance from the tower where the *cuyane* gathered. His uneasiness grew.

He looked down at the platform beneath his feet. There were letters cast into the metal: UNITED EARTH SERVICE.

Of course. That confirmed a strong suspicion. This area had to be a military zone. Only the Service would have access to so much uninterrupted land—and only the Service would reduce something so precious to this condition. The plant life had no doubt been exterminated by previous experiments. And this experiment—for East knew that was what he and Laure had stumbled into—had something to do with the *cuyane*.

He looked to the tower and all the orange parasites congregated there.

Well, damn. East grinned. They had been *called*. All the parasites were responding to some kind of signal sent by the Service.

11

That was what the tower was for. What the structure East was standing on and its two clones were supposed to be doing, East had no idea.

Then he saw something in the incomprehensible gadgetry that he recognized. A Service timer. No mistake. And it was running.

They would clear the area, wouldn't they, if . . . ?"

East's first impulse was to run back to the ship and get out fast, but there was no time. The timer had just passed the minus-one-minute point and was approaching the red zone. One minute to what?

He searched quickly for some kind of sign, found a hatch in the metal platform—locked—and kicked at it loudly with his heel.

It opened and an urgent voice from below said, "Get in!" as someone else in the background was cursing and saying, "I *told* you I heard a ship."

East climbed down a seven-foot ladder into a dark bunker. There were five men, sort of in uniform, looking fittingly subterranean. The one who had let East in was closing the hatch.

Warnings were sounding inside East's head. He had been in the Service once upon a time, and he immediately knew the situation.

"You were lucky, friend," the first man was saying. He glanced at the chronometer. "Another fifteen seconds and we fry the surface like—"

"Stop it."

"Can't."

O my God. "Laure."

Laure stayed under the fighter's wing until she lost sight of East, then she ventured out to look. She hopped onto the curious structure and wandered over the metal base. She did not see any sign of her husband.

"East?"

She made a complete circuit. "East?" She frowned. Something beneath her feet hummed. The structure vibrated.

"Jonathan?"

East started up the ladder, but many hands dragged on him and held him back. "Are you crazy?" one said. "You can't go up there." But East lashed at them, trying to climb the ladder, hands holding him down. Overhead he could hear

12

a light footstep. Tearing free, he thundered, "I've got to get my *wife!*"

His hand reached the hatch. Five seconds.

"You go out, you don't come back in!"

The hatch flew open and East was out. "Laure!"

"East."

He swept her up, kicked the hatch open as it was closing, ignored the ladder and jumped. He heard the hatch slam overhead before he even hit the ground. An alarm sounded, and all the panel lights flashed from green to red.

Laure did not struggle, even when rough hands seized her and the ground disappeared and she fell a long drop from bright sunlight into darkness, tumbling onto concrete, and rolling. Her face was pressed against East's chest by his big hand shielding the back of her head. She could hardly breathe, smelled tobacco, was jostled, thumped, and hurting.

When all was still again, East loosened his hold, and Laure lifted her head. It took her eyes a few seconds to adjust. The first thing she saw was East's hand bleeding. He had taken most of the bruises.

Then she heard a whistle and a voice, the tone of which was an assault in itself. "We-ell."

She saw the man, a lecherous leer on his face to match the one in his voice. "I'd like some of that," he said to East.

"I bet you would," East growled.

The Service was composed seventy-five percent of criminals working off sentences. East himself had been inducted that way decades ago and could tell that this crew belonged to the seventy-five percent.

Laure's skin crawled under five pairs of hungry eyes, and East held her close. Should anyone touch her, East would kill him—if she didn't first.

"She's a damned pretty woman," one man drawled.

Another one came more directly to the point. "Share?"

"Not on your life." East could feel her muscles move and tense, like a cat with all its claws out, ready to bolt, scratch, and bite.

But though she seemed a cat, she was more something infinitely precious. Were it to come to a choice between the galaxy and her, then the galaxy, mankind, and all sentient life with it would be ransomed, left to perish, all for her.

East was outraged that he had come so close to losing her. He spoke angrily to the Servicemen, "If you're testing some kind of weapon—"

13

"No weapon," one interrupted too quickly, with much too much emphasis. "Just a device."

Hair-splitting semantics did not concern East, and he continued, "If you're testing a device—a *deadly* device—why didn't you make sure this area was cleared first?"

"We thought we did. Why did y'all trespass into a military zone?"

"We couldn't see through the—" And he suddenly realized he was answering his own question. Opacity worked both ways. The guerrilla fighter had flown in undetected in the heart of the *cuyane* swarm.

The Servicemen shut down their device and examined the monitors. "Zero, zero, zero," said one. "They is dead." And they all laughed and whooped, and toasted their success with cheap wine and worse liquor.

East and Laure stayed right where they were—under the hatch.

"Only one thing missing from this party," one of the Servicemen said loudly.

His friend answered even louder, "Yeah, what's a pretty young thing like her doing with an ugly old man like that?"

Laure looked even younger than she was, especially next to East.

"He's gotta be the far side of a hundred. She can't be half that. I think we should rescue her." He looked to Laure. "What say, darlin'? Aw now, don't look up at the hatch. We're gonna be here awhile. It's gonna take some time for all those dead *cuyane* to drop out of the air." He leered.

Another of the Servicemen walked over, and Laure tensed. In a broad Texas accent he offered her a plastic cup of wine.

Laure knew what primitive men were like—she had married one—and she knew their types. This one was a clod but meant no harm. She spoke to this one. "Was it a steray?"

"What? That?" he jerked his thumb upward.

"What you used to kill the *cuyane*," said Laure.

"No, ma'am. It's a brand-new kind of machine. Works just as well."

Laure was chilled. "Why?"

"Why what, ma'am?"

"Why did you invent a new kind of machine?"

"To kill the *cuyane*. They're not like regular life. They're in-or-gan-ic."

"But a steray kills them. That should have been sufficient." It would have been sufficient if the Service would only *use* it. But killing the *cuyane* had never been a priority. Now this. A

14

whole new device, totally without purpose. Unless there was a kind of life that sterays could not touch. Laure knew of one.

The young man shrugged and backed away from her dark expression.

East took Laure's head between his hands and made her face him, his palms on her smooth cheeks, his fingers in her dark hair. She was afraid. East looked at her questioningly.

"East, take me home." she said.

He had never heard her call Aeolis home, yet he knew that was where she meant. He had guessed what she feared. He had seen her summon the winds of Aeolis, the Kistraalians, by the thousands. "But the winds don't die," he said very low.

"Take me home."

II.

A lonesome cry, a raw sexual wail, a quiet evensong, another voice for Daniel's harmonica to sing with. It was *his* harmonica by default; he had found it in a mud puddle and cleaned it out, and was teaching himself to play.

He sat on the back porch, sounding out distracted snatches of this and that. He squinted, partly because the sun was high, partly because his father's eyes were narrow and fierce, and Daniel wanted his own eyes to look like that even if they were not blue. He had a handsome face ("Are you sure he's mine?" East had asked Laure), which was still smooth except for a few wisps of a very sorry beard. Brown hair bore a reddish blaze in too long bangs that fell across his sunburned nose. He was wearing his shirt tied around his waist by the sleeves and had managed to get himself sunburned across the shoulders as well.

He did not talk much; East had always been spare of words, but, more than that, Daniel's voice still squeaked at the worst times, so he maintained his silence, and when he did talk it was softly. The harmonica was heard more than Daniel was.

Laure came out on the porch to kiss him on the head and say goodbye. She and East were going on a trip to Aeolis.

Daniel grunted and kept playing.

He had no idea what his parents could possibly be going to Aeolis for. Aeolis was a world of aristocrats and land and more wealth than Daniel could conceive of. What had his family to do with any of that?

But Daniel was too preoccupied to give it much thought. He had only one thing on his mind these days. As soon as his parents' ship left, he called up a girlfriend and invited her over—not the one he really wanted, but an easy one. He was at an age when just about anyone would do, and though he preferred another girl—the one he had those kinds of dreams about—he had hurt one virgin already and could not face that again just now.

16

The direct route between Earth and remote Aeolis was thick with pirates, and private vessels were strongly advised to avoid it. East and Laure took the direct route. Their ship, having once been a guerrilla fighter and still looking like one, was not a tempting target for brigands.

They were not far into pirate space when a warning signal kicked off, energy screens blazed to life, and the ship went into automatic deceleration. Laure, who had been sleeping on East's shoulder, woke up.

"Mine field," said East. Guerrilla ships were designed to detect such things and programmed to take immediate defensive action.

The mines were pirate set, a zone of them spread out like a net to entrap unwary private vessels that blundered into it. The presence of mines meant that pirate scavengers would be lurking not far off, waiting to board their disabled prey.

In this case, East did not expect the pirates to show themselves. The fighter was still undamaged and looked very military. The mine field would merely be an annoying delay while a jagged course was wound through it at a sublight crawl.

But the pirates did appear—two ships—and began to move in.

East was slow to believe, and, when he did, he was astounded. "Well, damn."

He got up, took Laure by her shoulders, and sat her in his place at the helm. "Fly for me, sweetheart."

Laure had piloted under fire before, and she plunged the ship into a stomach-wrenching evasive course among the mines. She glanced aside to her husband, who had moved over to the gunner's seat. "East, are you licensed to arm this ship?"

"No," said East, opening fire.

One pirate ship flew straight into the invisible fire and broke apart.

"Strange," East muttered.

"What is?"

"They weren't expecting that. He dove right into my sights. And look at that one." He pointed at the retreating second ship. "*Now* he runs. They didn't think we were armed."

"We aren't supposed to be," said Laure.

"But how did they know that?" said East.

There was nothing about the guerrilla fighter to indicate that it was now civilian and required to be disarmed.

17

Laure was gazing after the running ship, a hunter's gleam in her eyes. She looked to East.

"Do you want him?" he asked.

There was no law against shooting pirates, and, once attacked, Laure was fully capable of killing without regret. "Yes."

"You're the pilot."

Laure broke into pursuit as fast as she dared amid the mines.

The fleeing ship, growing frantic as the distance between them closed, fired a desperate spray of shots behind him, unaimed and missing his pursuer, but one did detonate a mine just off the port side of the guerrilla fighter. The fighter's screens hummed sickly as the mine glowed and spread like a small nova, while the pirate ship cleared the zone and shot away faster than the speed of light.

Laure stopped the fighter and pouted.

East was scowling, but for another reason. Dark brows met over fierce blue eyes. He rested his rough chin on a fist that had been broken many times and brooded. "How did they know we were civilian?"

"Maybe the ground controller who cleared us from Earth is getting a percentage of this operation," Laure suggested.

East nodded. *"Somebody* must be."

East swung the guerrilla fighter off course and stopped at a space station to check the ship over, afraid the hull had taken a scoring from the mine detonation. An eager young man in the hangar offered his services, but East worked on his own ship, not wanting anyone poking around the fighter's guns and accidentally discovering that they were still operative. Trust was not East's long suit.

He and his wife stayed the night inside their ship rather than seeking more comfortable quarters in the station. East did not want to return in the morning to discover some expensive part had suddenly and conveniently gone bad and needed replacing. The young man in the service hangar had been a little too eager to help; there were more pirates in this area of space than the ones that flew in ships.

Laure sat on the bed in the dark, her arms loosely draped around her knees, which were drawn up almost to her chin. She was holding a rose in one hand, rolling the stem between her thumb and forefinger, pensive. She was supposed to be sleeping.

Lying beside her, her husband reached up and touched her

18

cheek, his rough hand tender, and his voice something she felt as much as heard, deep, sometimes a rumble. "What's on your mind, woman?"

She sighed, started to speak, stopped, started again. "All things can die. Maybe they can all be killed too."

She was thinking of the Kistraalians, the immortal winds, and of the device in the desert that killed inorganic life.

"I know what that machine is for, and it's not to kill *cuyane*," she said. "And even if they never use it, still, it's immortality yanked out from under me—the idea of Forever—gone, just like that." She snapped her slender fingers. "I've known the winds all my life. They played songs on the wind chimes over my cradle. Forever was always there. Now Forever is only a candleflame, and something that was always there suddenly is not. Am I making any sense?"

"Just a little." He took her hand.

She looked beautiful tonight. He was always amazed. She held the rose to her smooth cheek, her dark hair loose on her bare shoulders. After all these years she still was not half his age. But women older were crones, and women younger were shallow children. There was only Laure.

"East," she began, plaintive, then stopped.

He gave a light tug on her hand for her to continue, but she shook her head and made a small noise as to say it was nothing.

"Tell me," he insisted gently.

"I don't ever want you to leave me. That's all."

When Laure and East resumed their journey, it was not toward Aeolis. On impulse Laure decided to extend their detour and go to the place she and East had run away to after they were married.

East had taken her from the shelter of Aeolis, where she could not even catch cold, to an untamed world of stings, bites, warts, blisters, and gales, where the rain did not stop at her command. She had been afraid she would wither in the world outside like a fragile tropical flower transplanted, for people aged outside Shangri-La, but she thrived. She had never been rejuvenated, but she was still young. The lines around her eyes were from smiles and only made her look impish. She had scars like a commoner—though she had never even seen a scar before she'd met East—and stretch marks of which she was excessively proud. As for hardships, she loved them. She loved East's showing her his world, loved being in it, loved where he had been.

19

They had returned to Aeolis for a visit only once after three years when she had become pregnant and had had to give up her nomadic life. Her father had been wonderstruck at how she glowed and what she told him. "Oh, Daddy, we climbed a mountain and I shot a stalong—it ate all our supplies—and we paddled down a river on a raft we built with our own hands." She proudly showed calluses on her once aristocratic hands. "And East must think I sound like a child."

East smiled, remembering. They were on the same mountain now, under the open sky, still as wildly in love. She kissed his chest and watched him, enthralled by his face. She caught him smiling at the stars, light catching on his lashes, as if sharing a secret with them, and she wanted to know. She punched him lightly on the chest to make him talk. "What?" she demanded.

Blue eyes smiled at her, winked. "You."

And late in the night they fell asleep on the mountain.

East woke when Laure jerked back into him. She had been sleeping on her side, her back nestled against him, her head under his chin, his arms around her, so she could not move without waking him. When she flinched, her head rapped his jaw shut and he bit his tongue.

She quickly took his arm from around herself and said, "Move back."

He did, half awake, his tongue smarting, his mind fogged. East rarely slept, and when he did it left him groggy.

Laure stood up, backing away from something, and as she did, East saw what it was that had prompted the rough awakening, and he became suddenly aware of the urgency that had been in her voice and her making him move away.

Where they had lain, where his arm had encircled her, there coiled a small valley snake, its venom the most quickly and inevitably fatal natural poison in the galaxy. They were never seen at these altitudes. It raised its head at East like the specter of a much larger snake he had once killed for Laure. East drew the gun from his pack and shot it several times until there was nothing left of it.

He turned to Laure, took a step toward her, and froze.

She had pushed her blouse off her shoulder and was staring at two red wheals.

No!

She spoke. "Just like that . . ." She looked up at him, bewildered. "East—"

Never so panicked, so helpless, so disbelieving, he held her in his arms, sank to the ground with her when she could no longer stand, and searched all his memories for an answer that did not exist.

Overhead he saw the distant lights of a ship, without hope. Even had he been able to contact it, there was no cure swifter than the poison.

Laure murmured very softly, eyes shut, "Always thought I would be the one left alone."

That was the way they had assumed it would be. East was nearly half a century older than she and was suddenly facing his final half-century without her, she who had become his whole life.

"Talk to me," she said, fainter. "I always loved your voice. . . ."

He did not know what he said. Words of love, things he had always wanted to say but somehow never did, and her name again and again, until he could not speak, could not breathe, could only hold her and blink hard. East never cried. He was crying.

Laure opened her eyes. She lifted her arms, clasped them around his neck, pulled herself up, and kissed him. "I've always been mean to you. I love you, Jonathan. . . ."

III.

Daniel sent his girlfriend home. He slid his harmonica into his pocket, too upset to play it, and mumbled to it, "I think we're in trouble."

He went to the funeral parlor expecting to see a stranger and to wonder at the foul, morbid joke, but the back of his mind pricked, and by the time he arrived he knew that in that box would be one of two people.

It was Mother.

"Any message?" Daniel asked thickly.

"None."

Daniel stared. Father must have gone mad—if he hadn't killed himself. Of course he would not be able to word a message. *Dad, where are you?*

The only clue as to where East might be was where the delivery had originated—not Aeolis. They had never made it to Aeolis.

Dad, please don't come home in another box, please—

Daniel's eyes misted over, then recovered. He scratched his sun-peeling nose. He tried to think what he was supposed to do next.

The disposal. There were two choices. "Um . . . how much does it cost to . . . um . . . cremate or annihilate?"

"Why would you want to do either of those?" the funeral director asked, surprised.

Daniel was confused. "Doesn't everybody?" What other way was there?

"Well, yes, but your mother has a plot of land—"

"She has a *what?*" Daniel's voice cracked and slid up an octave.

Only the very wealthy—the unbelievably wealthy—owned land in any amount. It could not be bought, only inherited. And to own it during one's lifetime was one thing, but to rest in it for eternity—that was for aristocrats. How Daniel's mother had ever acquired a grave plot, he could not think.

Then *they* arrived. A whole unfamiliar flotilla of ships de-

22

scended, and out *they* came. It was clear from first glance that here was wealth, wealth in its aristocratic extreme.

A mature, profoundly sad man named Jean-Marcus, Lord LaFayette, came to Daniel, took his shoulders, and said, "Say it is a foul computer error. The UBC told me my daughter was dead." Then he saw that the boy was in black. "It is true. Oh my son, I am sorry."

Laure's father.

Laure's kin.

Aeolians.

Daniel's whole existence reeled, and he discovered who he was. He had known his mother would bequeath everything to him, but he had not known that she owned anything—least of all land and a title. Suddenly Daniel was LaFayette-Remington, lord of two estates.

"She was so young. Like her mother. Why do LaFayette women die so young?" Jean-Marcus LaFayette lamented. Then he spoke to Daniel very sadly. "We've come to take Laure home."

Daniel stared stupidly for a moment, then said, "She *is* home."

"Son, you don't understand. We want to give her a *burial.*" His tone was condescending. "On Aeolis."

Daniel spoke very quietly through his teeth. "She's going to be buried in Texas."

And there was no peace after that. Daniel had prayed for someone to take all this from his hands, but now that Jean-Marcus was here, Daniel wished he would go away, for suddenly Daniel was fighting to keep what he had tried to pass off.

Lord LaFayette meddled in everything. He objected to Daniel's plans for a Christian burial, because Laure was not Christian; then Daniel found him talking to the funeral director and giving instructions for the headstone design to read: Laure Eva Aeolia Lorelyn Phillips DeForêt Delmar DeLaCruz LaFayette-Remington.

"Do what?" said Daniel.

"Her name," said Lord LaFayette.

"My mother's name is East." *Dad, where the hell are you?* Lord LaFayette grudgingly added East to the end.

"Now get all that garbage out of the middle," Daniel told the director. "It's Laure East—and for cryin' tears, write this in American." He pointed at the inscription.

"Laure's native tongue is French," said Lord LaFayette.

"My dad doesn't read French," said Daniel.

Jean-Marcus LaFayette drew himself up like a swelling volcano. "Your father—" he began, then exploded, spewing forth outrage and insult, "Your father was an opportunistic, self-serving—"

"Look, Mr. LaFayette—"

"—barbarian *swine*. Just a cheap American roué as old as *my* father, who seduced my little girl, submerged her good name in his mongrel one, and *where is he now?* He killed her, then—"

Daniel punched him in the mouth, and Jean-Marcus LaFayette folded to the floor.

"That's for my father. And as for my mother, *she wasn't your daughter* and you're no kin of mine!"

Daniel did not know who Laure's real father was, but she had once told him a secret, so Daniel knew it was not this man.

Lord LaFayette slowly picked himself off the floor and moved to a chair. He sat heavily. "I know."

Daniel became aware that the room was totally silent. Snakes wound around his nerves. *O God, Dad, help!*

Lord LaFayette looked up at him from his seat and spoke without presumption but from firm conviction and undercurrent of deep emotion. "But no matter the bloodline, I was her father. Whether she chose to be my daughter, that's her affair. I loved that little girl and I will not call her my stepchild."

Daniel cleared his throat, swallowed the frog that was in it, blinked. "Well, when she mentioned 'Daddy' I think she was talking about you, not . . ."

The lord nodded gratefully.

Daniel made it through the funeral, but then stumbled into the empty ship's hangar beneath the house to be alone, feeling ready to break. He turned his harmonica over and over in his hands, set it down, fidgeted.

He remembered an exchange between his father and himself:

"If you're ever in trouble, and your mother and I aren't here, go to my father. My father has been around forever. He can live through anything. My father was on the Ark— stowing away as one of the goats or one of the mules, I'm not sure which."

"Goats, Dad. Mules don't come in pairs."

"In that case my father was *the* mule on the Ark."

Daniel could hear Aeolians moving about in the house

above him, and echoes of his father's words in his mind. He grabbed his harmonica. "C'mon, we're getting out of here."

East's father lived out by the Navaho nation in a windowless hogan. He was 120 years old, more or less, tall, tough, and wiry. His skin was leathery, almost mummified by the dry Arizona heat. His hair was perfectly white, very long, usually worn braided. He had arthritis, which did not slow him down much, just made him swear a lot. He would have nothing to do with modern cures and firmly believed that a Navaho Singer could cure anything. Himself, he looked somewhat Navaho, but was not.

As Daniel approached the hogan on foot, he saw an old Navaho woman outside, seated at a large loom. Beside the loom, cross-legged on the ground, sat Old East. Daniel had never met him, but knew from report that this must be the man. Surely there were no two men like this.

Old East looked up and saw Daniel coming, and Daniel took heart, breaking into a run for a few steps. Then the old man looked away again, and Daniel slowed to a walk, then to a halt. The old man was ignoring him completely.

Daniel was confused and embarrassed, but he could not turn back now. He walked up to the old couple and stopped a few steps away, bewildered. The old woman met his eyes, and Daniel spoke to her. "Doesn't he see me?"

The old man muttered to the woman in warning tones, but the Indian woman got up from her loom, ignoring the warning, and walked right up to Daniel. "He sees this." She tugged on Daniel's black mourning jacket. "He thinks spirits followed you here. Humor him."

But Daniel burst into tears. *"I can't!"* He shouted at the old man, "My mother is dead, I don't know where my father is, and I'm your grandson, goddammit!"

"Shhhh!" Old East shrank from the announcement shouted to all evil spirits far and wide.

But the woman snapped at him, "Well, they know you're here now, so you may as well greet your kin." She put a maternal arm around Daniel and spoke confidentially. "This is the twenty-fourth century, I don't believe in spirits"—her eyes glanced covertly left, right, and up—"during the day. Come in and cry, child."

The woman's name was Maria, or that was what she called herself. She was Old East's second wife—maybe. Neither of them could recall if they had ever actually gotten around to becoming legally married.

There were no chairs inside the hogan, so Daniel sat on the floor. Maria fed him, not talking much, humming to herself, and just being Maria, with her matron's shape, laborer's hands, and voice like running water. Daniel felt comforted already, somehow.

At length Old East came inside, in no great hurry—nothing was hurried here—and sat. Daniel wondered if the old man had been getting rid of the spirits Daniel had brought with him. "He probably sent them to Mexico," Maria whispered to Daniel with a wink. When Daniel reacted with puzzlement she clarified, "Anyone who follows his road directions, no matter where he's going, always ends up in Mexico."

After ignoring his grandson for another interval, Old East turned his eyes to Daniel with great attention and intensity. The eyes were the same as Daniel's father's—slits of blue, keen as a hawk's, set in wrinkled, sagging lids. His voice was low and strong, but very quiet. "Now tell me what happened," he said to Daniel, just loud enough to be heard. "Tell me *quietly.*"

Daniel told him without tears, and the old man's face became very grave. Daniel sensed that death was a great evil to him.

When Daniel finished, Old East shook his head in disbelief. "It can't be." Then, more quietly still, "How did she die?"

"Snakebite, they told me," said Daniel. "A valley snake."

White eyebrows raised, and Old East nodded with great significance. "Oh."

Another superstition, Daniel guessed.

"Was your father with her when it happened?" Old East asked.

"I don't know. I don't know." Daniel felt himself close to crying again and he bleated, "Where is my dad?"

"Probably gone crazy," said Old East with resignation. "He'll turn up when he's ready. Be patient. You're a man now."

"I don't feel like one," said Daniel, a lump in his throat.

Old East let out a puff of breath, a kind of sigh. "Neither, I suppose, does Jonathan."

The heavens broke open that evening, and the dry land was flooded with rain. Daniel ran for cover in a shed a short ways from the hogan and decided to wait out the storm there. He squatted in the doorway, watching rivers of mud flow and merge as the big drops pelted down. He took out his harmonica and started to play.

He tried to remember the last time he had seen his mother alive. He had been playing his harmonica. A kiss on his head, a grunt from him, that he remembered. He had not stopped playing. He hadn't even looked at her.

Daniel's song died with a few wavering notes, and he started to shake. He looked at the instrument with sudden loathing. "Damn you," he breathed. "Damn you."

Anger grew like the muddy streams. Daniel got up and hurled the harmonica as far as his strength would allow, and screamed against the storm in a cracking voice, "Ashes to ashes, mud to mud, go back where you belong!"

He stood and shook and stared. And a feeling grew in him that he had thrown away his only friend. He bit his lip, pushed back his bangs, and looked up at the hostile sky, which showed no sign of lightening. He fidgeted, lost patience, and ran out into the rain to search.

His clothes were quickly soaked, and rivulets streamed down his face. He could not find the harmonica; he could not see his own feet for the brown water coursing over them, and he started to cry, a sobbing bleat full of terror and loss. He felt no older than two. "I want my harmonica," he whimpered, feeling stupid and not caring.

He got down and crawled, hands grasping into puddles, and coming up empty. His motions became jerky and frantic, horrified that what he searched for might have washed away and might be gone forever, till at last fingers touched metal, and he seized up the harmonica and clutched it to him as if someone were going to take it from him.

Finally he recovered himself and got to his feet, feeling very foolish but calmer and lighter. He cleaned the mud out of the metal reeds and walked back to the hogan in the rain, playing a lonesome song.

It was a good place for putting oneself back together, and Daniel almost forgot that there was anywhere else or ever had been. No one kept time here. Maria was ever at her loom beneath a tarp that was as much to keep off the harsh sun as the desert rains. Sometimes there was a young girl of indeterminate age beside her, winding yarn, matching colors, and looking on like a master's apprentice.

The girl was Maria's great-granddaughter by her first marriage, and Daniel tried to figure out his relationship to her. *Step half second cousin once removed?* Anyway she was suffi-

27

ciently distant bloodwise and clanwise for Daniel to proposition her, since there was no mistaking the look in her eyes when she stole shy glances at him from beneath thick black lashes, and a rose blush touched her brown cheeks. She wanted him too. But she did not trust him as far as she could throw him. "Give me time, if you have it," she answered. "If not . . ." There was no need to continue, and she was not one to keep talking after all had been said.

Daniel stammered awkwardly, not wanting her to think badly of him—for that suddenly mattered very much. "I *don't* have time—I wish I did." He remembered he had a home and that he had to go back.

The girl shrugged. "Some things just aren't meant to be." She went back to work, and Daniel was furious with himself.

He went into the hogan, where his grandfather was braiding his long white hair with aged hands and muttering about his joints.

"I've got to go home," said Daniel, taken by a sudden urgency, as if he had wakened from a lazy dream and found that he'd overslept and was very very late for something. "What will my dad do when he comes home and finds me gone?"

"He'll come here," said Old East without haste. "He may even come here first."

Daniel sat down on the floor next to him. "What if he never comes back at all?"

At first Daniel thought Old East would be angry, but the old man spoke in a low calming voice. "There's no love like that of your woman, especially the mother of your children. You live for her, you might even die for her, but you can't die with her or you're no kind of man at all. You live, and you might even love again." He nodded toward the door to the outside—toward Maria. "But whatever comes, life is all you've got and it's short enough. He knows that. He'll come home. After he's done being crazy. He'll have to come here to have the spirits driven away."

"But my dad doesn't believe in spirits."

"He may say. He may think. But down here"—Old East indicated his gut—"he knows. That's how it is out here. He may go to the stars, but one's children come home. When a man doesn't know where to go, he goes where he starts. In times like this, one's children come home."

"The child is ninety years old," said Daniel.

"Big fucking deal," Old East said sagely, and that was *that*.

A month, then closer to two passed. Daniel was missing school but did not care. Truant officers could not extradite him from the U.S.A. back to Texas, and if they'd tried, Old East would have beaten them about the ears—or sent them to Mexico.

Daniel wanted to talk to the girl, Maria's great-granddaughter, but became flustered and his voice broke, so he deemed it best to shut up.

The girl was called Two Braids. It was not her real name, just a name she had been given because she had them—the braids—and they were very long.

Real names were rarely used around the hogan. Old East attempted to explain that in one's name was strength and it could be worn out with careless use. That was why Daniel's father was called simply East and not even the all-knowing Universal Bank Computer knew that he was Jonathan.

Two Braids' birthday came. Daniel was not sure how old she was and was too embarrassed to ask her. She was sweet-faced like a child, but the wisdom in her eyes was not childish. Daniel decided to ask his grandfather about her.

It was her twelfth birthday.

She's just a kid! Oh my God, I propositioned a kid! Daniel gulped, horror on his face.

"What is it?" said Old East.

Daniel tried to be casual. "Oh, I just thought . . ." He cleared his throat. "I thought she was . . . a little . . . older."

He hurriedly went to apologize to her.

She was distressed, her bell-like voice sweet and hurt. "If you take back wanting me I will be very upset. You didn't mean it?"

How one tongue could be tied in so many knots Daniel could not figure. He stuttered, he froze, his face burned. He apologized. He apologized for apologizing, and kicked himself a thousand times and felt like shrieking.

I botched it. Oh God, why did you let me botch it?

He walked back to the hogan. The phone rang as he stepped inside. Daniel had not been aware before that there was a phone. It had no hologram nor even a video to show who was trying to call. Old East answered it.

"Yeah, he's here. Where the hell have *you* been?"

Daniel jumped, heart suddenly racing.

There was a cross exchange of words over the phone. The old man's voice was gruff but not unkind, and Daniel had

29

lived under this roof long enough to see past it and hear the deep love that was there.

"Well, where are you now?" Old East was saying. Then, "How did you end up in Mexico?"

IV.

Coming home did not feel like home. The house was strange now, half empty, and Father was a total stranger, thin, aged, his face drawn and unevenly suntanned from just having shaved after being in the sun unshaven for many days. A sense of world-weariness hung on him, and he was drunk. He was sitting in a chair, bottle of whiskey set on one chair arm, shot glass on the other.

Daniel sat on the sofa and pointed down at the end table next to him. East set a glass there and filled it. Daniel drank it.

East never said where he had been, only, "I'm sorry I wasn't here when you needed me."

Daniel shrugged, brushed it aside, assuming it was the natural result of breaking in half.

"Why were you going to Aeolis?" Daniel asked after a long silent interval.

East rested his half-pale cheek against a dark, badly battered fist. He began slowly. "Do you know what kind of natives are on Aeolis?"

Daniel nodded. "The Kistraalians. I've done some reading on them . . . lately. They're wind."

"That's all they are now. What's left of them," said East. "What is different about the winds is that they don't die and you can't kill them. They're inorganic and they will live forever, or else get bored and quit when they feel like it. Now it looks like the Service might be trying to develop a weapon that will kill the winds." He told Daniel about the weapon test in the desert. "Laure wanted to warn them."

"But I thought we didn't know how to communicate with the winds," said Daniel.

"*We* don't," said East, returning his attention to his shot glass. "*She* did."

Daniel shuddered, drank another whiskey, and stared at the wall a long long time.

31

Admiral Czals was a handsome vigorous man of middle years, with a profile like an idealized Caesar. Streaks of white blazed at his temples, while the rest of his hair was dark. A stormy expression crossed his eyes of pale steel.

The admiral was feeling soiled. Assassination was a nasty business to begin with, but this particular one had left a tarnished taste behind it and, worse yet, a feeling of being unfinished. The ghost was haunting him, and Admiral Czals liked his targets thoroughly dead.

What the admiral disliked most about killing was that it was a last resort. Admiral Czals hated being left with only one choice. It gave him a sense of powerlessness, of being driven into a corner.

And worse of all, to be forced to resort to cyborg snakes!

The thin, ascetic-looking scientist who had designed the abominable creature-weapon was regarding the admiral curiously, trying to divine the source of his disquiet. "Did the murder not go as planned?" the scientist inquired in an almost singing voice.

"Assassination," Czals corrected irritably. "She was a lady."

Admiral Czals had a saying: That which is least expected is most apt to happen. But of all people to cross his path, Laure Remington East!

A woman stumbles onto a secret weapon test, and she just happens to be the only woman in the galaxy who can communicate with the weapon's intended target. She immediately takes off for the target's homeworld, a planet she has refused to visit for seventeen years. What else was there to be done?

Making her death appear accidental had been a masterwork—and Czals despised the scientist for it.

Two months had passed since the woman's death without repercussions. There had been a few tense weeks when the trackers had lost the husband's trail, but at least he had not tried to go to Aeolis. And when East finally had resurfaced, it had been on Earth and he'd gone home.

Under such circumstances, Czals should have taken the priority rating off the case and considered the matter settled, but something prevented him, something unresolved.

As the Officer in Charge of Aeolian Affairs, Admiral Czals had much to consider. He reviewed the whole matter step by step, searching for what was kicking at the back of his mind.

Ten thousand years ago, an advanced civilization had existed on the planet Aeolis, then called Kistraal. Each Kistraalian appeared in three forms—humanoid, animal, and wind—and each form was an independent *life*, each form aging only while the creature existed in that particular form. The humanoid form had a life expectancy of forty to fifty years, but the Kistraalian could spread that time out over an indefinite period by simply not assuming his humanoid form for long intervals; and so it was with the animal form. But once the life spans of the humanoid and animal forms were exhausted, the Kistraalian dared not assume those forms or he would die. The wind form, however, lived for as long as the Kistraalian cared to stay alive.

And only the winds had survived the catastrophe that had destroyed all organic life on Kistraal and left it barren for ten thousand years.

Then, 250 years ago, Earthlings rebuilt Kistraal, renamed it Aeolis, and settled it, only to discover when the planet's natives rematerialized out of the winds that the land they had tended so carefully belonged to someone else.

But instead of entering into a war for possession—Admiral Czals shuddered to consider it—the Kistraalians had obligingly crossbred themselves to the brink of extinction. The Kistraalians were divided into twenty castes according to their twenty different animal forms, for, although only the humanoid form could produce children, parents of unlike castes produced sterile offspring. And the birth of too many such sterile children had signaled the end of the Kistraalians as a species. The last Kistraalian to retain a physical form had exhausted that life five years earlier—to Czals' great relief. Now only the winds were left, and the winds produced no heirs.

Even so, Admiral Czals wanted to be sure that this was indeed the end of the Kistraalians. He had ordered the development of the secret weapon against the winds because things that lived forever disturbed him and because he had to make certain that there was no chance of Earth's ever losing her precious colony Aeolis to aliens. The winds were harmless enough now, but in case they became greedy, Admiral Czals would be ready.

So it seemed that all contingencies were covered. Yet there was a loose end. Admiral Czals turned to the scientist. "Winds are the only natives of Aeolis left now," he began. "But for two hundred and forty years there were Kistraalians in humanoid form on the planet along with our Earthlings."

"Yes, Admiral," the scientist acknowledged in his singing voice.

"I have a very wild question," the admiral continued. "Could they crossbreed—the Kistraalians and the Earthlings?"

"Not so wild," said the scientist. In fact he was pleased with the question and eager to answer it. "You see, long ago, even long before the Kistraalian civilization was destroyed, the Kistraalians used to be human as we are—*exactly* as we are—with differences no greater than the variations between the several races on Earth."

"You mean they were *Homo sapiens?*" said the admiral.

"Yes. Exactly."

The admiral's steel eyes darkened. "Then how did they come to have three lives?"

"Only through the rather brilliant and fantastic engineering of the Kistraalian scientists did they become as they are. A convenient lack of religious strictures allowed the Kistraalians to experiment with themselves. The Kistraalians as we know them are man-made." He smiled, proud of science and what scientists could do given the opportunity. "But it is conceivable, even probable, that even after the Kistraalians had made themselves tri-lived, they were still capable of producing the reproductive cells of their original form—an occasional random human egg, an occasional human sperm."

"How often would that happen?" asked the admiral.

"Impossible to say for certain. I can work only from theory. One might guess every, oh, one in a million gametes might turn up purely human."

"Then it's a long shot," said Czals. "The crossbreeding."

"Depends on how you look at it," said the scientist. "The Kistraalian female would have produced one egg per menstrual cycle, and chances, according to my guessed odds, are only one in a million that the egg would be completely human. So, given an Earthling male and a Kistraalian female, yes, it's a very long shot."

"But?" said the admiral.

"But," said the scientist. "The Kistraalian male would have produced two hundred million sperm at a time, and two hundred of those would be human. And, of course, the male would not be restricted to one time at a time, if you know what I mean." The scientist grinned. He was beginning to grate on the admiral. "So, given a frisky Kistraalian male and a willing Earthling female, in any one month you might have, oh, as many as forty-eight hundred possibilities of a human offspring—out of forty-eight hundred million gametes, of course."

34

The admiral was not going to figure out exactly how frisky the Kistraalain would have to be. He was troubled. He had come here for reassurance. This was not what he'd wanted to hear at all. "Then it *could* have happened."

"Yes."

"Which immediately brings up another question."

"That being?"

One woman in the whole galaxy talks to the winds.

"*Has* it?"

"Dad, can I go to Aeolis?"

East raised his dark brows in an expression that was mildly surprised and clearly not pleased. Here was an old fear—his son becoming one of the effete, overrefined rich that East despised.

East set down his shot glass. Blue eyes were shiny with alcohol and very narrow. His voice was a low rumble. "And why would you want to do that, your lordship?"

But Daniel did not want to go to Aeolis to inspect his inheritance. "I want to take Mother's message for her. It was what she was doing when she died. I thought I ought to finish it."

East's fears fled, and so did the scowling expression, but he could not be optimistic. "Danny, those winds don't talk to everyone. Matter of fact, they don't talk to anyone but Laure."

Brown eyes avoiding East's, Daniel spoke very softly. "Well, one of them was her father."

After a thunderstruck split second, East found his voice and roared, *"What?"*

Daniel was standing perfectly still, fists jammed into his pockets, shoulders hunched, face lowered so that his eyes were all but obscured by his long red-streaked bangs. His voice was just above a whisper. "She told me a couple of years ago that her real father was an alien from the planet where she was born. But she never told me where she was born."

"She told you—" East had a great deal of trouble speaking. He could barely think. His face grew very dark as the blood gathered there under his unevenly tanned skin, seeming darker for his silver mane that bristled at the neck, wolflike; and all the muscles on his lean frame knotted hard and stood out as if he would spring to his feet and kill someone. "Why the hell—why the—why in the name of Almighty God didn't she tell *me?*" He was shouting.

35

Daniel spoke in his same quiet voice. "Because sons can't divorce their mothers."

For a minute East could not talk at all. His mouth would open but he could not speak. His eyes were at their widest and still barely wider than slits, still blazing. Hurt, bewildered, furious, sorrowful, and unable to express what he was going through, he spoke. "Is that what she was afraid of?"

Still quiet, Daniel answered, "You're one of the most bigoted and pigheaded men alive. Of course she was afraid."

East was speechless for what seemed like a very long time. Then, recovering his ability to think, East's reason rebelled against all he'd just heard. "Daniel, it's impossible. Even the most Earthlike aliens can't have children by Earthlings. The Kistraalians are so genetically different from us. *How?*"

Daniel shrugged. "I don't know. But she said it was so, so I believe it."

East sank back in his chair. He believed it too, against all logic. Whatever Laure said was so. And she had talked to the winds.

Laure, I didn't know you were afraid of me.

He closed his eyes. The creases in his face seemed very deep. He spoke wearily. "Keep in touch."

"Aren't you coming with me?" said Daniel.

"I have no ties with Aeolis but you," said East. He sighed and looked empty. "I'll be in Arizona."

V.

Lord LaFayette received Daniel with profuse apologies, then both quickly let past differences be past.

Daniel did not say why he had come to Aeolis, and no one questioned it, for it seemed obvious that anyone who *could* come to Aeolis naturally *would*. Leaving the paradise world was what raised eyebrows, not coming to it.

But now that Daniel was on the planet, he could not think how he was to contact a Kistraalian. He had assumed an idea would come to him by the time he arrived. One hadn't.

Now what?

Find a wind and start talking to it, hoping it was a live one? Talk to it in what language? Where did one find Kistraalians? A world was a big place to search for something invisible.

To begin, he had a cousin take him to his mother's estate, and there he spent the night.

He was lying awake, deep in self-pity, when he thought he heard soft, garbled voices on the edge of his awareness. He sat up in the bed.

There *were* voices in the room.

"Who's there?"

The voices stopped.

Daniel waited and the voices started again, tentatively, like crickets, whispering very low.

"Who's there?" Daniel said again.

Again the voices stopped, abruptly. The curtains at the window moved with a passage of outgoing air, and Daniel sensed he was alone.

Later the winds returned, more of them, whispering in a rushing incomprehensible language, till one voice, startlingly clear, said "Laure."

"Laure," said Daniel. "She was my mother."

The whispers became frenetic, repeating "mother" questioningly.

The winds brushed him, buffeting him, wanting him to do something, but Daniel could not figure out what that was.

"Laure," they said.

Daniel tried to ask questions, but they did not seem to understand.

"Laure," said Daniel.

"Laure," said the winds.

Then Daniel's cousin opened the door and stuck his head in. "Daniel, who are you talking to?"

"Do you hear that?" said Daniel. The whispers had not ceased, paying no heed to the newcomer.

"Hear what?" said his cousin curiously.

"Forget it," said Daniel.

His cousin paused. "Daniel, are you all right?"

"Just thought I heard something," Daniel mumbled. He fancied the winds were laughing at him.

His cousin withdrew.

Alone again, Daniel spoke—this time in whispers—in every language he knew or half knew. He wished he had a language nodule as his father did, but then he suspected that having the knowledge of every language on Earth would not be much help in this situation.

Suddenly there was a new whisper, perfectly articulated and in English. It said, "Thirty-two degrees fifteen minutes three seconds north, sixty degrees fourteen minutes nineteen seconds west."

Coordinates. Daniel assumed he was supposed to go there. "When?"

"Oh five hundred."

Daniel groaned and lay back in the bed. It was going to be a very short, very long night.

The sky was turning from black to deep blue, the stars beginning to fade, but night still held the forest where Daniel had to walk. He was frightened once by a scream like a banshee, then a whimpering like something being murdered. Daniel gasped and spun around to face the demon, but it was only a gray fox cringing in a tree, trying to scare Daniel to death with its voices—or at least make him go away. Daniel laughed weakly in relief and continued down the narrow winding path of weeds and red brick.

At last a clearing broke under a still starry sky, and Daniel stared at the place he had come to.

It was a cemetery.

He felt a breath of age, of something primeval, but no

38

ghosts—only a sense of rest after a long long journey. It was the graveyard of Aeolis' first builders. They had been commoners, and their two-hundred-year-old monuments had been left to weather, forgotten. But there was a secret, wild beauty about the place, more peaceful for being neglected. There was no sorrow here. Those sleeping in this ground slept serenely under tangles of vines and growing grass as year by year the forest slowly closed in to reclaim it.

The sky grew steadily lighter, the forest colors appearing but still muted with morning mist held in the tree branches.

A horse nickered.

Daniel looked beyond the weathered monuments of the clearing to a shadowed glen where stood a carriage and two gray mares. There was no driver; the horses were untethered as if they had run away from somewhere and come here, dragging the carriage with them. Now they stood quietly, at peace in the wild, akin with the gravestones.

Daniel stepped off the weedy path down into the shallow glen, the rustle of old leaves making his footsteps sound loud to his own ears—like coughing in a church.

He walked up to the carriage, which was made of polished wood with brass fittings. Black velvet curtains were drawn shut over minutely decorated and inlaid window frames. There seemed to be no one else around.

Daniel circled around the back of the carriage to the other side and halted suddenly, stifling a cry.

He did not know why he had been so startled. The man had not moved, only stood at the carriage door—one foot up on the step, one elbow resting on the seat—waiting; but even motionless something about him commanded instant attention. A young man, yet not young at all. His skin was smooth as unflawed marble, his dark eyes aged and ageless as a sphinx. He seemed tall, but was not; his build was slender yet powerful. His clothing was aristocratic, simple, and mostly black as if in mourning. Dark hair was perfectly in place. There were traces of blue ringed beneath his eyes, markings like those caused by certain drugs. His gaze was infinite.

"Son of Laure, you have kept me waiting." His speech was accented—with no kind of accent Daniel had ever heard—sounding exotic, elegant, and very clear.

Daniel shrugged uneasily. "I got lost. My compass is pointing south." And becoming more nervous under the steady gaze, Daniel continued, compelled to explain so as not to seem completely ignorant. "There must be some magnetic rocks around here."

39

"Quite the star traveler you are." The tone had not changed, the face had not changed. Perhaps it was only in the words but Daniel sensed mockery—and no effort expended in expressing it.

"Don't be like that. Just tell me what I'm doing wrong," Daniel said shortly.

"You are assuming that all planets are like Earth."

Finding that less than informative, Daniel became even more annoyed. "And what is that supposed to mean to me?"

"What you call magnetic north lies very close to the geographical south pole of Kistraal."

Daniel stared at his southward-pointing compass. *The poles are reversed.* He had never thought he would be wealthy enough to travel to other planets, and so had never paid attention to such things.

Then he became aware that the man had called the planet Kistraal. Not Aeolis.

"The Earthlings," the man continued, "made the mistake of referring to the magnetic north as south and the south as north."

Mistake? "So what makes your way right and Earth's way wrong?" said Daniel.

"I was here first."

Daniel was once again aware of *age,* a sense of great age that silenced any further thought of challenge. The man's face was like some pictures of angels, youthful yet ancient, fluid yet immobile, lineless, serene. Daniel marveled at how much expression there could be in a face without creasing it.

Still waters. "Who are you?" said Daniel.

"Who do you think."

"There are no humanoid Kistraalians left."

"And you do not exist either."

Daniel nodded, conceding the point. Evidently Earth's information on Kistraal was even more incomplete than Daniel first knew.

The man moved, a simple motion so clean, focused, and controlled that it mesmerized. He turned his head and pointed to the side of the glen where there was a shovel jabbed into the earth. "You are to dig," he said.

"Are all Kistraalians like you?" said Daniel.

"No one is like me," said the man with mild offense.

"Good," said Daniel and walked over to the shovel. He turned back to the Kistraalian. "They have robots programmed for this sort of thing, you know."

"It must be hand-dug."

40

Daniel took off his sweater and tossed it aside. He gripped the handle of the shovel. "Here?"

The Kistraalian nodded. "A lateral shaft into the hillside."

Eyeing the dark-curtained carriage and the man's black clothing, Daniel made a good guess as to what size hole he was to dig. No one had to tell him he was burying a wind who had wanted to die and so had reverted to a humanoid form far too aged to hold a life.

As Daniel began to dig, the Kistraalian said, "You are to learn a proper language."

"Which is that?" Daniel grunted, heaving a load of black dirt aside.

"Ours."

Daniel felt a stirring inside at being so simply and matter-of-factly claimed in a single word. Not *mine,* but *ours,* the Kistraalian had said, and it came home to Daniel for the first time: *I am a Kistraalian.* He was not sure how he felt about that. *I am an alien.*

And the Kistraalian began to outline for him, rapid-fire, the structure of the ancient language.

The sun rose higher, burning away the mist. Daniel took off his shirt and wiped his face with it. His muscles ached and his brown skin was ashine with sweat.

At last his shovel thumped against something solid. "I've hit rock," said Daniel.

"No you haven't," said the Kistraalian and went on with his lecture.

The rock turned out to be a metal door. When Daniel cleared the earth away, he opened it to reveal a clean metal shaft-vault, barely large enough for a small casket. It was then that the Kistraalian stopped speaking, an action as precise and marked as his starting, and Daniel immediately missed the sound. He moved back and sat on the hillside, pushed away his sweaty red-streaked bangs, and waited.

The Kistraalian, who had been leaning at the carriage door, rose to stand fully straight. He brought forth a glove from his breast pocket and drew it onto his left hand, then walked to the front of the carriage—with a limp.

Till now so smooth and controlled, he was suddenly at the mercy of an ankle that would not support his weight, and there was nothing he could do to disguise it. The pain in his dark eyes was shame more than physical hurt, as if in a moment he had become human and vulnerable and was appalled by it.

He took the horses' reins beneath their muzzles in his

41

gloved hand, and stroked their noses with his other hand, another gesture so human that suddenly there was a terribly young man, hardly older than Daniel, where a sphinx used to be. He gave the horses a command and a push, and they slowly backed the carriage to the vault.

Then the Kistraalian turned, sphinx once more, and ordered with a glance, not needing to speak.

Daniel got to his feet and lowered the rear hatch of the carriage. There was a small casket inside. Daniel struggled it into the vault.

The Kistraalian had not spoken a word to Daniel since the opening of the vault, and he did not speak again until the vault was closed and all the dirt replaced.

When at last Daniel turned with the shovel, the Kistraalian was standing midway between two pine trees and pointing to the ground at his feet. "Here."

Son of a bitch! "There are two sets of hands in this graveyard," said Daniel, but the astonished, then thunderous expression that crossed the sphinx eyes made Daniel guess that that was a bad idea after all.

Daniel dug a hole.

It was not very wide nor very deep when the Kistraalian bid him stop, brought forth a very small pine tree from the carriage, and held it out to Daniel.

As Daniel took the tree, he touched the ungloved hand, almost surprised to feel it warm and human, and he looked at the Kistraalian's face to see his eyelids flicker involuntarily in not quite pain, not quite revulsion, but some deep and unbearable feeling that Daniel could not understand.

Daniel pretended not to notice; he took the tree and set it in the hole. He saw something gleaming metallic in the little tree's roots, started to reach for it, but a soft voice that sounded as if it were right beside him said, "Touch it and I will kill you."

Taboo. A bad one.

Daniel filled in the soil around the little tree's roots.

The Kistraalian limped to the grave, crossed his arms, fists on his shoulders, and bowed his head a moment. Then he moved to the tree and spat at its roots, all with the feeling of ritual, and he murmured two words that Daniel would learn meant *Never stir*.

Then it was done. The Kistraalian said a few more words to Daniel concerning the Kistraalian language, then asked, "Do you have all that?"

"You can't be serious," said Daniel.

"You are wasting my time," said the Kistraalian; it was like the cold accusation of a capital crime. He turned to climb into his carriage.

"Wait," said Daniel. "I have a message from my mother."

"In Kistraalian," the man commanded without turning.

"I can't," said Daniel.

"Then let your mother bear the message," said the Kistraalian and started to go.

"Then you'll be waiting till pine trees talk!" Daniel yelled at his back.

The Kistraalian turned sharply, shock and realization on his face. "I regret," he said softly. "Our last child."

"Are there no others?" said Daniel. The Earth Service authorities did not know about this man and they did not know about Daniel; perhaps there were others.

But the Kistraalian shook his head. "In human form, just you and I. Unless you have a sister? A brother?"

"No," said Daniel.

The Kistraalian looked sad. "What is your message, son of Laure?"

Daniel told him of the device that killed inorganic life, and what Laure feared it might be for.

The Kistraalian cocked his head, expression intent and thoughtful. At last he said, "They have our world. What more do they want that they need a weapon?"

Daniel guessed, "What you have and they can't have."

Dark eyes shifted, then became enigmatic and guarded once more. The son of a bitch was beautiful, Daniel could not help but think so. Imperceptibly his lips moved into a rueful almost-smile. "Immortality."

"We can't have it. I guess they figure you shouldn't either."

Daniel's use of *we* and *you* did not escape the Kistraalian. "Do you consider yourself one of them or one of us?"

Daniel hadn't time to think. "I don't know," he said.

"Decide," said the Kistraalian and turned again to go.

"What is your name?" Daniel asked quickly.

The Kistraalian stiffened in affront. Another taboo over-stepped. "Never ask that of anyone. Call me whatever you please, but never ask who one is."

"Like the Navaho," Daniel murmured and was surprised to get an answer.

"Yes, something like."

The carriage door closed. The dark curtains parted briefly for a last word. "It *is* permitted to tell your grandfather your name."

My grandfather. Daniel thought first of Old East. Then he pictured a wind, tried to, and it all seemed incredible.

The carriage moved away down a narrow lane. Daniel could not see what was directing the horses.

He tied his shirt around his waist and sat down to compose a letter.

Dear Father,
I met a madman today . . .

VI.

"It was not an idle question that I asked you before," said Admiral Czals. He had come to the scientist once again, seeing all the fears he had only sensed before now materializing out of the air like a Kistraalian wind creature.

"Which question was that, Admiral?" said the scientist.

"If a child has been born of an Earthwoman by a Kistraalian sire."

"I wouldn't know where to begin to look for the answer to that," said the scientist. "Perhaps you could give me a direction. You seem to have someone in mind?"

"I do. Laure LaFayette-Remington East."

"Possible."

Not what the admiral wanted to hear. "Why do you say so?" he asked.

"Because, sir, I've discovered how the Kistraalians in their wind form communicated with Kistraalians in their human form. It's not telepathy, and it's not high-frequency sound. It's *low*-frequency—below twenty cycles per second, which is below an Earthling's normal hearing range. It seems the Kistraalians in their human form had a slightly lower range than ours. Now if the lady Laure could hear the winds speak, as she was reported to have done, how did she come by that extraordinary range? And why did the winds talk to her, when they are perfectly content to ignore us?"

"Yes, damn them, they do ignore us," the admiral muttered, nodding gravely. Almost as much as for their immortality, Czals hated the winds for their complete and total lack of interest in diplomatic relations with anyone else. The winds had little in common with corporeal, single-lived, mortal creatures, and chose not to associate with them. Their behavior smacked of elitism, and Admiral Czals, being an elitist himself, hated being looked down upon.

"But, on the other hand," said the scientist, "since the lady Laure was a well-bred aristocrat, surely it is known who her father was."

45

Admiral Czals smiled bitterly. "No. It's a skeleton in the LaFayette family closet that Jean-Marcus LaFayette cannot have been Laure's father."

The scientist raised scant eyebrows. "For certain?"

If one had access to the classified records of the Universal Bank Computer, one could discover just about anything. Admiral Czals had such access. "Jean-Marcus LaFayette, upon marrying his first cousin Lorelyn LaFayette, had himself permanently sterilized," said Czals. "Yet the lady Lorelyn bore Laure nonetheless. And whoever the father was, Lorelyn died without telling."

The scientist nodded. "Then Laure LaFayette could be the Earthling/Kistraalian you were inquiring after."

"Except," said the admiral, hoping to lay this matter to rest with a fatal stroke, "Laure was fertile. Wouldn't such a cross between species be infertile? After all, the Kistraalians couldn't even produce fertile children by crossbreeding between castes of their own kind."

But the admiral's hopes fell when he saw the scientist shaking his head.

"The reason cross castes produce infertile children," said the scientist, "is that the different animal forms in each of the twenty castes makes each caste a distinct species, and crossbreeding between them is like crossing horses and jackasses—you get mules for offspring. But when it comes to crossing a Kistraalian with an Earthling, in order for a child to be conceived at all, there must be none of those animal genes present."

"You mean that one in a million purely human gamete you were talking about," said the admiral.

"Yes. Without that you won't get a mule; you will get no child at all—like crossing horses and tigers. So if a child were to be born, it would not be a hybird; gene-wise it would be *Homo sapiens* from both parents, and its chance's of being fertile would be very good. So if Laure LaFayette were actually the child of a Kistraalian, I would not find her fertility alarming."

"Not alarming? It's utterly unthinkable," said the admiral. "I won't have it." *Earthlings cannot mate with its!*

"I only said it was possible," said the scientist. "What I told you is just theory. The evidence for Laure's actually being the child of such a union is not at all certain."

"The evidence is damning," said the admiral, handsome face flushed with outrage. "We have been tracking Laure's husband, East, ever since her death. The UBC is set to alert

46

us should East try to enter Aeolis." In the modern galaxy, tracking a man from planet to planet without ever leaving the room oneself was an easy matter, for little action was possible these days without coming in contact with a computer—and that meant a record in the omniscient UBC. "Now after we have tracked the man halfway across the galaxy, he has finally settled safely in Arizona," Czals continued. "I almost lifted the priority code on the case. Then *this* was intercepted today."

Czals handed the scientist a computer transcript. It was of a letter addressed to East:

> *Dear Father,*
> *I met a madman today . . .*

"*East* is in Arizona," said Czals. "The damned *son* is on Aeolis!" Who had been paying attention to a fifteen-year-old kid? "Read that: 'I did what I came for.' *Madman* indeed! There is every reason to believe that the boy is of Kistraalian descent, *knows* it, and has made contact with a Kistraalian—a *humanoid* Kistraalian."

Twenty years earlier there had been twenty-two humanoid Kistraalians left—so Czals had been led to believe by the Kistraalian go-between called Speaker—and Czals had counted them as they died, twenty-two, with Speaker the last one to go. Now it seemed there was one more—at *least* one more. They had deceived him! How did they dare? Deceit was the province of men who knew how to use it properly.

The scientist frowned. "If the boy has made contact, then the Kistraalians most likely will know about our weapon. We'll never get a volunteer to test the device now that they know it is supposed to kill them." The weapon had never been given its final test—to kill a Kistraalian wind. "Shall I dispose of the boy?"

"No," said the admiral. Though Czals would have happily strangled Daniel with his own hands, there was no purpose to it now, and the admiral was not trigger-happy. Extreme measures were for extreme cases. Laure LaFayette-Remington East had been a proven troublemaker of inestimable power and unlimited potential to do damage to the Service's plans. The boy Daniel had done all the harm he could actively do. Yet still there remained the problem of his Kistraalian descent to be neutralized. Extermination was not the answer, however. "I want you to manufacture proof that Laure LaFayette had a human father. We have to assume the boy knows what he is. *No one else is to know*. If he starts broadcasting I want him to appear to be just the son of a bastard girl with delusions of importance. Dredge up a likely lover for Lorelyn LaFayette. Make him a real person—someone who is dead and so can't deny it—but don't kill anyone. Then feed a suitable geneprint into the Universal Bank Computer for him to be Laure's father."

"Might be difficult," said the scientist. "Aristocrats are bred like racehorses. Most of them have very detailed geneprints already logged in the UBC. Erasing one could be impossible."

"Then don't make Laure's father an aristocrat. Make him a servant."

"Lady Lorelyn and a servant? Would that be credible?"

"It would be ideal. After all, look what the daughter married. Yes, that will do nicely. Like mother, like daughter."

And that should have taken care of the boy Daniel.

But how a fifteen-year-old boy could cause so much trouble, Czals would never understand.

It was in the Remington house on Daniel's second estate that a little hologram caught Daniel's eye—the miniature images of two dancers poised on the coffee table. One figure was a pretty ballerina, a fragile-looking wraith with luminous brown eyes. The other figure Daniel had met that morning in a graveyard.

Lord LaFayette noticed Daniel staring at the hologram. "Niki Thea and Mercedes Stokolska," he said.

Niki Thea. So that was what he called himself.

"Miss Stokolska was the finest ballerina of this century," the lord continued.

"What about him?" said Daniel.

"Niki Thea?" Lord LaFayette said in surprise—as if everyone should know the answer. "He was very simply the greatest dancer of all time."

"Oh."

"Last time he danced was twenty years ago or more. That's when that was recorded." Lord LaFayette nodded at the hologram. "It's priceless now."

"What happened to him?"

"Disappeared. Died maybe. He was thoroughly mad. Some say he was one of *them.*" By *them* he meant the Kistraalians, the winds.

Some say. "Can I turn it on?"

"Of course. It's yours."

"I keep forgetting," Daniel mumbled to himself and activated the recording.

48

The walls of the room melted away, replaced by a boundless space that was nowhere at all, filled with music, filled with light; and in the center the two figures—full-sized now—came to life. And all the power locked in a sphinx's ancient eyes suddenly was *there* in awesome totality, from the turn of a hand to a leap that seemed to be flight itself, to when he looked at her, to when he touched her and in that moment suns exploded and there seemed nothing left but dying. He was life; she was love. She was a dream, a fairy queen, light as gossamer with a gossamer's hidden strength, yet just a mortal barely twenty years old. They needed only to breathe and Daniel was in love with them both, she an ephemeral youth, he an immortal power.

And suddenly it was over. A lingering exchange of gazes and the magical place disappeared, the walls returned, and Daniel was standing in the drawing room, shaking, naked of spirit, soul spilled out and painted across the floor. He was close to tears, not really knowing why.

He heard a sigh of a wind that had paused to watch, and he needed to speak. But he knew no words.

At his mother's estate with no one else around to think him insane, Daniel tried to sort out the sounds he heard on the air. But incomprehensibility like a closed window left him outside like an unclaimed street child with his nose pressed against the pane looking in. He tried to remember what Niki Thea had told him, but Daniel had not been listening in the first place, and it was like retrieving water spilled in the sand. More lonely than he had ever been in his life, belonging nowhere, and frustrated to the breaking point, the language was a barrier against which he could throw himself until he died. And he did want to die, until a Kistraalian came to him, forced him up from the floor where he had lain face down for two days, and made him understand something— that this was Laure's father.

Daniel opened his hands, and the wind being rushed through his fingers. All Daniel could do was say "Hi" in a croaking voice and grin idiotically, opening his hands to the wind. *This is my grandfather.* "Hi." And his grandfather helped him learn to hear and to talk.

Soon other winds came to him. The first thing each would say was a title by which it might be called in place of a name, and its caste. Daniel would reply that he could be called Daniel and that his caste was *laitine*. Though he could not and never had been able to turn into the animal, the

49

great beautiful white bird *laitis,* he had been claimed by the caste through his grandfather's blood; and Daniel loved the caste because he was *in* it.

He counted nineteen different castes among the Kistraalians he met. There were supposed to be twenty.

"What caste is Niki Thea?" he asked.

"No caste. There is one Niki."

"What is his animal?"

"He does not have one. He is himself" was the answer.

Daniel's grandfather explained, half in Kistraalian, half in mutilated French, "Niki was one of the first of our kind. Before the makers tried to give animal forms to humans, first they made a human who could turn into an identical human, just to see if it could be done. Niki turns into Niki."

"One of the first?" Daniel echoed in disbelief, not sure he was interpreting the words correctly. How could one of the first possibly still be alive? "How old does that make him?"

The winds conferred, then answered, "Older than the rest of us."

"Like . . . ten thousand years?"

"More."

Daniel remembered: *I was here first.* Then he considered that in a society such as this where age was equated with veneration, Niki must be up with the gods. But since the Kistraalians had no gods, that left just Niki.

Daniel winced to remember some of the things he had said to Niki, and wished he hadn't. Just once a pagan god descended from the sky and talked to him, and Daniel was certain that was the last time. He would have to be content talking with the others.

Till one morning no one came, and Daniel wondered where they were. He sprawled on his unmade bed, playing his harmonica, waiting for something to happen. It came with a movement caught at the corner of his eye and the soft plop of something dropped on the bed beside him.

It was a piece of white jade the size of a big man's fist, carved into the figure of a cat. The rock flowed in long snowy fur over the powerful muscles of a fierce and beautiful creature, its eyes of green jade fiery and alive. Daniel picked it up, half expecting to feel soft pelt give under his hand instead of hard cold gemstone.

"The missing caste," said a voice on the wind. *"Volaia."*

So he hadn't miscounted. Along with the other castes, the birds, the snakes, the wolves, and the sea creatures, there were at one time these great snowy cats. There were none

50

now. At least there were none coming to Daniel. "What happened to them?" Daniel asked.

The wind wove him a story in a voice different from all the others, clear and sharp as if a human being with lips and teeth and tongue were speaking. Daniel felt his heartbeat pick up and he became strangely nervous as he realized who had come to him. It had to be Niki. Daniel listened, humbled this time, and breathed very softly to hear every word of the very old story.

Ten thousand years ago when the world Kistraal died and there was nothing left of civilization and life but carbon ash and the winds, it was for the winds to decide whether to live or die, for this was to be life, with no change—ever. The winds either accepted it or died, except for one caste, the *volaia*, who looked toward the stars. The *volaia* left in one mass exodus with no idea that there was anyone else out there or even anywhere to go. They simply set their sights on a star that seemed like their own, without reason to hope, and they left. Curtains of fire waved in the sky on their leaving.

"Auroras," said Daniel.

"Several were lost in the magnetosphere," said Niki. "They died or were trapped—I am not sure what happens in the end. There are perils to the careless, even as wind. It tore them apart. The world sang—like nothing you have ever heard. A scream almost. I still hear it."

Those that passed the magnetosphere discovered that they could exist in the vacuum of space, but they were no longer wind, only entity. Once in space they could move at or near light speed, and they went toward the closest of those stars that were yellow and single like Kistraal's sun.

"But there's nothing there," said Daniel. "Just a few dead planetoids."

"I know."

Niki had gone to that system in an Earth ship 250 years ago to tell the *volaia* to come home. He searched, dead world to dead world, listening to methane winds on frozen seas. "They are gone."

Daniel felt more for Niki than he ever thought he could. Something touched him—besides the dance—a loyalty to his own. There was a quiet horror in his simple recounting of his tale. Niki had a long memory. After ten thousand years he had gone to call his friends home, but they were not there.

"Did you look anywhere else?" asked Daniel.

A windy snort of futility sounded. "Where?"

Where.

Daniel looked out the window, toward the sky, holding the white jade cat in his hands. Someone else was out there—if they had not given up and died of despair—creeping no faster than light in the vast ocean of space. Lost. So lost. It chilled him, and he knew it was time to go home again.

VII.

Daniel sat with his clique of friends, whom he was now two school units behind. His father was out somewhere in space with the guerrilla fighter on a job by contract. East never said where he was going or on what kind of job, and Daniel did not want to ask. He suspected part of East was trying to get himself killed.

Daniel was staring at the sky, remembering a jumble of things. He was barely aware of his friends around him discussing one of their usual topics—who knew which girl wore what color underwear and how he happened to gain that information.

A younger boy gradually dropped out of the conversation on noticing Daniel was keeping apart. Anything Daniel did was right as far as he was concerned.

"What are you thinking about?" the boy ventured.

"Nothing," said Daniel, whispering. "The stars."

When East did come home, the silences were long and tense. Silence had never been tense in this house. Now there pervaded an almost tangible sense of things off balance, of upheaval, an electricity in the air so that all movement brought sparks. Daniel and his father had become cogs of wheels that did not fit, and sometimes the silence was violent. At best it was restless, as if something were trying to seek a level.

Came the night Daniel brought Mira-Jo home after a dance very late, not intending to return her to her own home till morning. Mother had always been the one who outlawed such things; Father was in no position to object, for East could make no claims to purity when he had been young. On that basis Daniel was prepared to destroy all possible opposition. But none came. The evening seemed to go well, with no questions, no objections, and East was even helpful. Daniel and Mira-Jo had put on some music and were trying to figure out an old dance that had become new again, but they were having trouble, so they asked East, who had known the dance when it was new in the first place.

East consented to show them, and he took Mira-Jo in his arms. The girl learned quickly, but once she caught on to the steps, East did not give her up and she showed no sign of wanting to be given up. There was no mistaking that look; her smile sparkled. She was carrying herself differently, trying and half succeeding at a semblance of adult sophistication. East knew how to hold a woman and make her feel beautiful. She fit easily into his arms and moved with his lead.

Daniel stood completely and utterly ignored.

After an awkward, stupidly gawking minute, Daniel retreated to the back porch, shamed and breathing out hatred.

Damn him!

Against his father's experience and primitive magnetism, Daniel could not begin to compete. All the higher ground was on East's end of the battlefield. East was a man; Daniel a boy. While East's voice was a low seductive rumble, Daniel's was a frog's with a squeak. East was taller; East was surer; and in a test of physical strength, East could probably still show himself the victor.

Threat of tears fought down and locked inside him, Daniel went back into the house. East and Mira-Jo were much closer. An excited glow shone on the girl's cheeks. East's smile, his eyes, were intensely sensual, yet cold. Daniel was repelled.

One hand low on the small of Mira-Jo's back, East pressed her firmly against his body, and she moved against him as she'd seen actresses do in shows, her lips parted, gazing at his mouth.

The only word that would form in Daniel's brain was *Stop!* But he could see no graceful way out. All that was left was to play the fool—since he already looked about as stupid and childish as they could make him look. He shut off the music, seized Mira-Jo by the wrist, tore her away from his father, and growled in his newly dropped voice, "You're going home!" And he dragged her out the door.

He returned from Mira-Jo's home, fuming and rehearsing acid tirades to hurl at his father.

Damn him!

Daniel knew he had been wronged. The right was on his side. He would show no mercy. The truth could destroy, and Daniel wanted East totally destroyed. He knew where East was vulnerable.

Damn him!

He imagined different reactions—from a fight to abject apology—and Daniel would crush them all, step on East's face and grind it with his heel. There was no defense that could withstand him. "I am stronger than he is," Daniel told himself aloud. He had convinced himself of that. "And I am right."

Damn him!

He was ready.

He stalked in the front door and faced East, who was seated in a chair, drunk. Daniel opened his mouth to speak. Blue eyes looked up and froze him in mid-word.

The eyes held a challenge, a bit of mockery, no penitence, but maybe a hint of regret. Daniel could only stare, paralyzed by his father's eyes.

"You were going to say something, Daniel," said East.

All the righteous, angry words deserted Daniel, and what voice came out was no better than a bleat. *"Why?"* He found tears on his face, wiped them away fast.

With a tone that was curious, as if he would like to know himself, more than sorry—in fact *not* sorry—East said, "I don't know."

Daniel was speechless, helpless, shaking. Like a cub batted head over heels with a single sweep of a bear's paw, so effortlessly had Daniel been dealt with by East. East had not moved, hadn't even set down his drink.

Now he moved. He rose, and any thought of questioning his dominance died as he looked down on Daniel. He spoke, a low command, a threat. "Don't bring another woman into this house."

"Yes, sir," Daniel whispered.

"Daniel."

"Yes, sir?"

"If you do, I warn you, you *won't* take her home."

Nothing was supposed to be right about it; it just was.

Daniel breathed in a voice a wind might speak. "Yes, sir."

Late in the night a silhouette paused in the doorway of Daniel's dark bedroom. "Dan, are you awake?" East said softly.

"Don't turn on the light." The tremolo in Daniel's voice would tell him why.

East came in and sat on the edge of the bed, his back to Daniel. He was not going to apologize. That was never a possibility. East was not sorry. But that did not mean he could see Daniel suffer without stinging himself.

55

After a while he spoke again. "Have you ever thought about killing yourself?" East was not so naive as to think Daniel's time of life was all carefree and innocent.

"Yeah, I've thought about it," said Daniel. He bunched his wet pillow behind his head and tried to sniff, but his nose was stuffed.

"I mean actually held the pills in your hand, or leaned over the bridge rail, or looked up the barrel—"

"Barrel to the head," said Daniel. "Your 946."

"You do it with my gun and I'll feed pigeons with you, Danny," East growled. "You want to kill yourself, you get your own gun."

"Yes, sir." Daniel could tell East was speaking partly a nonsensical joke and partly deadly serious. East could not survive Daniel's death—and certainly not if he provided the means.

"I've inspected the barrel of that gun myself a lot in the past months," said East, not emotional, though there was emotion there. "I never looked up a gun barrel before."

"You've had guns pointed at you," Daniel said.

"Don't look at the gun, Danny. Always look at the man holding the gun," East warned, turning to look at Daniel. He could not see much in the dark. He turned away again and rested his elbows on his knees, big gnarled hands clasped. "You are probably the only thing keeping me alive," he said quietly. "But if you think that will let you get away with anything you please, you can forget it. Step on my toes, I'll kick your teeth in. Got it?"

"Yes, sir," Daniel almost smiled, something resolved. All the jagged pieces fell into place.

East left the room. Daniel rolled over and went to sleep.

"Dan, you're flunking out." It was simple statement, without reproach, almost a question. Any friction between East and Daniel had been spent the night Mira-Jo had come.

"I know."

East paused to consider this. "What do you want to do?"

Daniel hung his head, lifted it hopefully, then thought better of what he was going to say and bowed his head again. "I just . . . I want there to be others. I want so badly for the *volaia* to have made it."

"The what?"

"Big snowy cats. The other Kistraalians. I told you," said Daniel. "I can't stop thinking about them. They come to me in dreams."

"And?"

"I've been thinking. Since they can't travel faster than light, and they left Aeolis ten thousand years ago, if they're still alive, they're within a ten-thousand-light-year radius of Aeolis. I—" He swallowed. "I want to look for them."

"Danny, do you know how many stars are within a ten-thousand-light-year radius of Aeolis?"

"Millions."

"It's a needle in a haystack."

"No it's not." Daniel went to his dresser and pulled out a drawer full of star charts, maps, reference works, hologramic projections, and chaotically organized notes of star temperatures, distances, planets inhabited and not, and hand-scribbled diagrams. "I know the first place they went when they left Aeolis and why those chose it—it was the closest normal G-type star to Aeolis' sun that wasn't part of a multiple system. It's fifty light-years from Aeolis. There's planets there but no life. Since the *volaia* aren't there, and they didn't turn back and go home, they must've gone somewhere else."

"You think you know where they went?"

"The closest single normal G-type star to where they were," Daniel answered. "Just like the first try."

"How could they tell which star that was without instruments?"

"The winds pick up a lot more than we can with five senses. Just about anything an instrument can pick up they can too—radio waves, X-rays, ultraviolet light. I think they can tell which star is what."

"All right, so you've got your snow cats to the next-closest G-type star. What do they find?"

"Another dead system."

"After that?"

"Another one."

"Then?"

"Same thing. But from there, their path divides. I can't decide whether they would've gone to this star"—he pointed into the hologramic map—"which is the closest G-type star. Or this one, which is slightly farther but almost identical to Aeolis' sun. The closer one is so bright it's almost an F-type, and I'm not sure where the *volaia* would draw the line on a star's being too bright."

"So what did you decide?"

"I didn't. I followed both paths. Call them A and B. If they took route A, they would've gone through fifteen more dead systems and then ended up in the Haverin system. Haverin III is inhabited, and the *volaia* would've stopped there."

"You think they're on Haverin III?"

"They might be."

"There are no cats on Haverin III."

"And for two hundred and twenty-five years they said there were no natives on Aeolis," Daniel countered.

"That's a point," said East. Kistraalians could be elusive when they wished; and they often wished. "When would your snow cats have arrived, assuming they went to Haverin?"

"It would've taken them at least a thousand years to get there, so nine thousand years ago at the earliest."

"That's assuming they didn't give up and die after the first failure."

"Yeah, I did sort of make that assumption."

"Where does path B go?"

"Path B sort of divides and subdivides a couple times."

"Giving you how many possible ends?"

"Six. Seven including Haverin. They all end before the *volaia* would've clocked ten thousand years. So if they were systematic about it, they should be on one of these worlds by now."

"But since Kistraalians like to hide—at least no planet has ever reported having snow cats arrive from outer space—how would you search these seven planets?"

"I have bioscans for the four modern ones," said Daniel and brought out the computer reports he had gained from the UBC outlet at the library. "I've been looking through the unaccounted recordings in the bioscans but I haven't found anything that looks as if it could be the *volaia*. I've also been collecting records of spectacular auroras and stories and legends of ghosts and monsters from all the planets dating back to the earliest possible arrival date of the *volaia*—like the monster stories on Aeolis that no one paid attention to until the Service proved they were true."

"That wasn't the Service, buddy, that was *me*," East growled. *I slew a dragon for a princess.*

"Well, maybe finding Kistraalians runs in the family. I have all these leads; I just have to follow them. What do you think?" Daniel asked.

East glanced over all the charts, the diagrams, the notes. "You've done a lot of work." Daniel had not been lazy. He had been busy—just not with schoolwork.

"Yes, sir."

"You also made a whole lot of assumptions."

58

"Yes." Daniel nearly choked on his own whisper. *He's going to talk me out of it.* Suddenly all his notes seemed a heap of worthless ash, all his hours of work a waste. He should have known better. He'd been a fool; he'd been obsessed. Why couldn't he just think about sex as his friends did—as he used to? Why couldn't he just be an Earthling and forget it? Daniel was afraid he was going to cry—as if he hadn't done enough of that of late.

"Still, seven planets doesn't seem like too many if you know what you're after."

Daniel's brown eyes flew very wide. "You mean . . . ?"

"They're your people. Do what you think you have to."

Dusk was deepening. Ships streaked up the ramps or rose off their pads periodically. Daniel was surrounded by people going somewhere. He was starkly aware that he was alone—even though his father waited with him, this journey was his. Once the clearance came, Daniel was on his own, a step into the void.

He waited in the main compound at the spaceport. He had a brand-new ship. He could see her out on the ramp, awaiting the go-ahead. She was beautiful. Ships were to Daniel either he, she, or it, depending on their make. His was a she—a LaFayette 0600 one-man speedcraft. She was christened *Laure*. East had outfitted her for the voyage—including a mine-sweep and one illegal gun.

Daniel dried his palms on his pantlegs, felt for his harmonica in his shirt pocket, scratched his nose, then tried to look calm. He had gotten his hair cut and no longer had long bangs to hide behind. He felt exposed—just when he felt most in need of hiding.

Dusk grew into night and still the ships rose, their lights quickly swallowed in the infinite night so vast it could consume the Earth itself, reduce the sun to a point of light, the galaxy to a spinning disk of bright dust.

On the verge of realizing a dream that now looked like a nightmare, Daniel wanted to go home—to a little ten-foot-wide house amid hundreds of others just like it in a little Texas town. He wanted to sleep in his own bed and wake up with everything all right, as it used to be.

"LaFayette 0600 *Laure*, fueled and cleared to board."

That was it. Daniel cleared his throat and said a stiff, husky-voiced goodbye. East grunted, wished him luck, started to say something else but only shrugged. Daniel started away to the ramp.

59

As he walked he remembered his last parting with his mother, remembered he hadn't looked at her.

He looked back at his father.

East was as ever, silver-maned, lean, and tough, but isolated, lost-looking. East and Daniel stood the same when they were uncomfortable—shoulders tense and forward, fists in pockets, meeting no one's eyes directly. So East was standing.

Daniel ran back, hugged his father tight in the middle of the compound, planted a kiss on his battered cheek. "I love you, Dad." And ran to his ship before he could change his mind.

PART TWO: A Ship Called Laure

I.

Laure had owned a string of mining towns on Haverin III. When asked, Daniel said he had come to check out the property.

Now why did I say that?

He told no one his real motive for coming—as if he had something to hide. As if he were being watched.

He shook the idea but not the feeling.

His search on this world turned up nothing. There were simply no traces of anything that might indicate the presence of Kistraalians, and Daniel was quick to move on. Even though many Haveriners spoke Earth languages, it did not take Daniel long to miss human company, and he was glad to be going to the next world, long shot as it was, an Earth colony called Hell.

Hell offered little hope. Even if the Kistraalian *volaia* had come here, Daniel doubted they would have stayed. Barely this side of habitable, Hell was a hard world of volcanic activity and mud rains, where little grew and the air was poisonous in areas. The Earthlings' settlements were covered by vast domes, which would not have been built at the time when the *volaia* would have come.

The residents of Hell were mostly Earthlings, hardworking laborers without refinement or pretense. Unlike on Haverin, Daniel did not come to them as the young heir LaFayette-Remington. Here he was Daniel East—and these were his kind of people. He had lived as an East a lot longer than he had as a LaFayette-Remington. The first place he went was a tavern in the dome Main Station, looking for someone to talk to.

It was the wrong tavern. Half of the clientele were alien and the other half were Earthlings who did not speak English or Americanese. Even the bartender was a big, snout-nosed Ctaulenute.

The place was crowded, dim, and smoky. At least that much was right.

Daniel sighed, elbowed his way to the bar, shoved a stinking drunk German twice his size off a barstool onto the floor, and took his place, hoping the man was too drunk to fight and had no friends here to do it for him.

The Ctaulenute lumbered over in his own good time, crossed his gray arms, and asked what Daniel was drinking. Rather Daniel assumed that was what he asked. Daniel did not know Ctaulenute.

"Whiskey," said Daniel.

The alien pretended not to understand.

Daniel cursed under his breath, turned briefly to shove the rising German back down to the floor, then made an attempt at the Ctaulenute word for whiskey. *"Alin,"* he said.

Guffaws and chuckles rippled down the bar, and the bartender snorted.

"Now what?" Daniel said tiredly.

The stinking drunk Turk to Daniel's right suddenly toppled off his stool onto the floor in a heap with the German, and the small coppery-gold pixie of a Tyi who had pushed him hopped onto the stool in his stead, snapped red-gold fingers at the bartender, pointed at the counter before Daniel, and said something in nativelike Ctaulenute.

A shot glass of whiskey appeared on the bar before Daniel.

Daniel turned to the Tyi who had rescued him. "Thanks. Don't know why he wouldn't give it to me when *I* ordered it."

"You forgot the alif, spaceboy," said the Tyi.

Daniel always ignored alifs. They were not native to American speakers and they sounded like stuttering to Daniel's ears. Instead of *ali'in,* he had said *alin.* He shrugged. "So?"

The Tyi rolled coppery eyes. "Just drink your woman."

"Do what?"

"That's what you ordered. *Alin.* Woman."

"Wouldn't mind one of those either," Daniel admitted.

"Can't help you there." The alien winked.

The Tyi were hermaphrodites. Among the most attractive humanoid species, they were small and lithe—all of them—

62

with reddish skin and features like pretty Earthling adolescents, smooth-faced, and flat-chested or nearly so. Their body hair was fine as a child's, downy and blond; the hair on their heads grew in two lengths, like an animal's coat or a bird's feathers, a short bright gold mane with a shorter chestnut-red undercoat like down underneath. Tyi eyes were the color of tarnished copper with bright-gold flecks within. Small hands had short agile tapering fingers with paper-thin nails that had almost evolved away.

Daniel considered which pronoun to attach to the Tyi beside him, and at last settled on he, the creature being too sassy for a she and too human for an it. His name was Tavi.

Tavi nodded at Daniel's drink. "Buy me one?"

Daniel was puzzled. The alien seemed affluent enough to buy his own drinks. He was dressed Earth-style in reddish corduroy battlejacket and slacks of real cotton—anyone who could wear natural fibers was not destitute—and Daniel wondered if Tavi had some other reason for not wanting to use his own ID. Regardless, Daniel supposed he had earned a drink. "Sure."

Tavi smiled brightly, his teeth very white, and yelled at the bartender in Americanese, "Hey. Give me a beer, you big pig."

The bartender did so.

"He understands American," Daniel said, confused.

"Sure he does," said Tavi.

"Well damn."

"Damn it to Hell," said Tavi; he touched his glass to Daniel's and drank.

After a few more shots and the aliens did not look any better—the Earthlings in fact started to look alien—Daniel asked Tavi if there was a bar where Earthlings went and spoke English or Americanese.

"Aha. Mother language and bastard. I know a place. The Corfu. All the Americans, Texans, Canadians, Australians, New Zealanders, Scots, South Africans, and whatever go there. Come on."

Daniel and Tavi slid off their barstools, stepped over the German and the Turk, who were snoring on the floor, and pushed their way out of the tavern.

Daniel braced himself for when the fresh air hit him, but none hit. They were under a dome. There was no such thing as fresh air.

As the two of them weaved through the narrow alleyways

of Main Station, they encountered an unsteady group of Earthlings of uncertain nationality coming the other way. The men hissed and whistled at Tavi as if he were a woman, not half male. "Desperate. Really desperate," said Tavi to Daniel, and tried to get past the group, but they barred his way, and one pinched him.

The little alien sprang into the air and wheeled with a kick that caught the man on the chin, and Daniel saw that he had a brawl on his hands. The only thing to do was punch the nearest man in the kidney before he could turn around. Daniel knew a few things about fighting men bigger than he—at his age that was the only kind of man there was—and Tavi was glorious in a brawl. He also knew when to run. In the thick of it a small red-gold hand grabbed Daniel's wrist with surprising strength and yanked him out of the fray, and the two of them fled down the alley.

Tavi's heels clattered on the pavement through the endless twists and turns of countless alleys like the ringing trot of pony hoofs that seemed to be striking Daniel's temples. Daniel's breath rattled and a stitch caught in his side before they finally stopped. His nose was bleeding. He wiped it on his sleeve, and the pain made his eyes water.

Daniel sank to the ground and leaned his head on a dirty wall. Tavi crouched next to him. "That was fun," said Tavi.

Daniel jerked his head up in surprise, then said slowly, "Yeah. It was." He realized he had felt like hitting someone for a long time. He did not admit that it was because he was afraid. "I think my nose is broken."

"C'mon," said Tavi, hauling him to his feet. For a girlish little creature that only came up to Daniel's eyes, Tavi was amazingly tough—like some little girls Daniel knew. "We'll get you fixed up at the Corfu."

"A nose-fixer in a bar?" said Daniel.

"Can you think of a better place for one? This is Hell, friend."

And the residents were not called Hellions for nothing.

The owner of the Corfu was a tall blond husky American named Rivers. He knew Daniel's father. Evidently they had been friends, because Rivers repaired Daniel's nose, gave him a soberant, then got him drunk again on better liquor than he'd gotten at the other tavern and sat him down at a good poker game.

The Corfu was as dim and smoky and crowded as the other place, but Daniel could understand what all the loud voices were saying. It made him oddly homesick, and he wondered what had possessed him to embark on this quest—he, the boy who did not know north from south, or woman from whiskey. He needed allies.

But he did not trust Tavi. Daniel would spend his days alone searching Hell for signs of the snow cats, then retreat evenings to the Corfu to drink, talk, and lose at poker. Tavi was always there, never using his own ID, and it became apparent to Daniel that Tavi was doing his best to keep his name off the Universal Bank Computer records. Someone was after him.

So, though Daniel was longing for someone to confide in, when Tavi asked him what the hell he was doing on Hell besides losing poker games, Daniel snapped, "None of your business."

It was at the poker tables that Daniel heard Hell's secrets—the things the UBC could not or would not tell him. It was here he heard of the demon in the abandoned dome.

The Dome. Quiet. Eerie quiet. All Daniel could hear was his own breath whispering through his face mask that filtered out the natural gas but not its artificial smell. Extensive gas pockets lay beneath the settlement, the last rupture never capped, and Daniel had been warned to make a frictionless landing. He had left his ship, *Laure,* by the gang doors at the very edge of the dome.

He took a few steps, and his footfalls rang very loud in the hollow stillness. The dome was a cavernous museum where time had stopped a hundred years before. Everything lay just where it had been dropped on its final day. There was no sign of a gradual move, no forethought. The leaving had been panicked flight.

Windows of the deserted buildings stared like hollow eyes. The wide streets of the ghost town should have been wind-swept, but there was no wind, not even a breeze.

Daniel toed a gold vase that someone had dropped in the street and had not paused the split-second it would have taken to pick it up. Apprehension crept over him like a chill in the air. His heart was galloping; he felt it pulsing in his chest, in his hands.

And he became aware that there was something here. He started to speak in Kistraalian, but the sound died in his throat. Something was wrong, very wrong.

Something there. Unseen. A presence. Definitely there.

65

But there was no wind. Nothing stirred. This was not a Kistraalian.

God help me, what have I found?

He had been prepared to find Kistraalians, to find nothing, but he never considered that the demon in the dome might be something *else*.

Fear.

This was a monster.

Daniel ran down the street, echoes of his footsteps clapping close behind like something in pursuit, and he dove in through the ship's hatch, which he'd left open in case of the need for a quick exit.

But open hatches were open to other things as well.

II.

The *Laure* bolted out and aloft at a speed that might have ignited the gas in the dome and sent it up in an inferno, but Daniel was thinking of nothing but escape and did not care.

Once in the air, he laid his head down on the console, feeling weak, and listened to his pounding heart. He groaned, and his breath began to come easier.

Then it crept over him again, the feeling of something *there*.

He lifted his head, clutched the edge of the console and sat perfectly still.

He was not alone.

It's in here.

Fear. Unreasoning fear that consumed thought and blotted out all but itself. Daniel grabbed at the manual controls and the ship screamed into a burning dive. Daniel lost any sense of logic, abandoned the controls, and tried to open the hatch to jump out from a thousand kilometers up. Then he saw through the viewport the ground rushing up fast, and, salvaging a shred of reason, he hit the emergency brake.

The ship set down hard, almost a crash; the hatch flew open as Daniel slammed to the deck and rolled out.

Creeping. A mud flat. Hot. Sun. Wavy, heated air bending the pale-blue sky without cloud. Bones were broken; it was difficult to breathe. Daniel reached out a hand; fingers dug into mud, and he pulled himself forward another inch, then quit. It was too hard. He did not want to die, but there seemed to be no choice.

Must have passed out, for when he opened his eyes again he was not where he had been. There was a hard pallet beneath him, artificial lights above, and Tavi was there, placing a cool wet cloth across Daniel's forehead with a light touch.

"You're crazy, Dan-iel," said Tavi. The only hint of his native accent that ever surfaced was in the peculiar way he spoke Daniel's name. "Pulling ghost tails. What were you trying to do?"

"None of your business," Daniel mumbled with a split lip; he tried to rise, but the pain shot through him from his ribs to his eyes.

"Stay quiet," said another voice. That was Rivers. "We'll have the medics at you as soon as we get back to Main Station."

Daniel glanced around him. He was surrounded by liquor crates. He felt as if everything was rolling. This must be Rivers' ground transport. He closed his eyes, moaned. "What *was* it?"

"Who the Hell knows," Rivers muttered. "The Service says it's nothing, but the whole population of an entire dome doesn't stampede out inside of ten minutes for nothing. No matter what the officials say, there's something in there. Everyone on Hell knows it, and so do they. Some say it's Satan himself." He looked straight at Daniel, and the color rose in his face. "And you, you *idiot*, I don't know what got into you to make you think you had any business going in there!"

Daniel would have to reveal too much to defend himself, so he said nothing at all. The motion of the transport—or the bump on his head—was making him sleepy.

Rivers returned to the controls. Tavi stayed with Daniel. He asked softly, "What was it like, Dan-iel?"

Daniel tried to think. He could remember vividly, but he did not know what to say. "It's . . ." he opened his eyes. "It's *fear*." And that was the best he could answer.

After the medics at Main Station repaired Daniel, he rented a ship and flew back to the mud flat to recover *Laure* despite the warnings that his ship now belonged to Hell; the creature, the demon, whatever it was, once it claimed something, never let go. But Daniel had to go back. He had to retrieve his harmonica if nothing else.

Optimistically he dragged Tavi along, because he would need someone to pilot the rental ship back to Main Station when he flew back in the *Laure*.

He sighted her down below. She was spattered with mud and sunk one full meter into it. Her landing legs were twisted, one of them completely sheared off.

Tavi gazed at her through the viewport. "Oh, Daniel, it's a LaFayette," he said wistfully. "How could you do that to such a ship? No wonder you want it back so badly."

Daniel landed the rented ship a hundred meters away.

68

"Stay here," he told Tavi and gave him the controls. "Keep it running, but keep the hatch shut."

Daniel jumped out. He heard the hatch snap closed behind him.

There she was. The mud flat was very wide, desolate, and forbidding, nothing but red-yellow clay and bubbling sink-holes under a thin sky, and *Laure* looked like a ghost ship sitting there, wrecked, her hatch hanging open to the foul hot wind. He couldn't leave her there.

He swallowed down dread and walked toward her. He could not recall a longer, slower walk in his life.

He was not far from the ship when cold terror seized him at the sight of a trail of red claw marks leading from the ship's gaping hatch.

Then terror left him, but the cold remained as he realized that he had made the tracks. The claws were his own hands that had gouged the clay, trying to pull himself away from the monster in the ship. A chill ran up his back even under the sweltering sun.

He inhaled, squared his shoulders, and walked briskly to the ship.

Hot air like a wall made him stop in the hatchway. She was like an oven inside, heat so intense it made his eyes water.

He ventured inside—first to the atmospheric control—then he tiptoed through all the compartments.

He returned to the controls, shut the hatch, and touched the radio. "Tavi?"

"Dan-iel!" Tavi cried, relieved to hear his voice.

"Everything's OK." The ship was his again.

"But Dan-iel, what about *it*?"

"It's gone." *And it's time I was too.*

What Daniel sought was not here. He had found something on this planet, all right, but it was not a Kistraalian, so he was not going to stay and find out what it was. That was for someone else to discover. Daniel had his own quest, and this did not concern him.

So to Hell with it.

"Where are you going, Dan-iel?" Tavi asked, ghosting Daniel as he restocked his gleaming, newly repaired ship.

"Bhaccaa," said Daniel.

"That's where I was going," said Tavi.

Sure you were.

Tavi was not going anywhere. He had no destination. He was just running and hiding.

"Want to dock ships?" Tavi asked.

Surely the Tyi did not believe he was deceiving anyone. His motive was obvious. If they left port together they would be registered as "LaFayette 0600 *Laure* and rider." Tavi's craft would not be specifically on record and no one could trace him. He hadn't even used his own ship to rescue Daniel from the mud flat—and it *had* been Tavi's idea to search for Daniel, though Tavi had used Rivers' transport to do it. Computer-wise, Tavi was keeping a very low profile. Daniel certainly did not need a fugitive attached to him.

But, on the other hand, Tavi could be useful as an interpreter for someone like Daniel who did not have a language nodule. And Daniel did owe him his life.

"All right," said Daniel.

Tavi's was a small Polybios ship. "My pride and joy," said Tavi, ushering Daniel into the hangar. "Like it?"

"It's great," said Daniel, ducking in through the hatch. "It's built like a missle."

It was a versatile machine, capable of operating in space, in atmosphere, or under water. Its hull was burned as from an extreme amount of friction. "You scorched her hide," said Daniel. "How did you manage that?"

"Real quick entry," said Tavi.

Exit is more likely, Daniel guessed, feeling worse and worse about this alliance, afraid he was taking aboard another monster, one that would not leave of its own accord.

He shrugged aside his misgivings for the time being and arranged for the docking of the two ships.

Once Tavi was sure the monster was really gone from *Laure*, he made himself at home. He was sitting on one of the cabinets, swinging his feet like a child. He had become intrigued with Daniel's ice-maker—he had never seen one on a spaceship—and he was amusing himself making cubes and juggling them to oblivion.

Tavi had better be a good translator, that was all Daniel could think. He could see no language nodule under all that hair, though Tavi had already demonstrated fluency in two nonnative languages.

Daniel grabbed Tavi by the hair and pulled his head down to take a look for a nodule that must surely be there. He was immediately surprised at how soft was something that looked like a snarl of red and gold straw. Tangles in Tavi's hair undid with a pass of the fingers.

"Is there something in it?" Tavi asked, perplexed. The ice,

70

which he had stopped juggling when Daniel grabbed him, was melting in his hands.

"Nothing," said Daniel. "That's the point." Daniel could not see a language nodule because Tavi did not have one. Daniel let go of him. "How many languages do you know?"

"All of 'em," said Tavi proudly, shaking back his hair. "Well, most of 'em."

"Without a nodule?" said Daniel, black eyebrows disappearing into brown bangs.

"Are you kidding?" Tavi smiled, with his very white teeth. "I *make* them." He began juggling again, sitting cocky, looking out of the corner of his coppery eyes to see if Daniel was impressed.

Daniel was.

"What do *you* do for a living?" Tavi asked.

"Me?" said Daniel. "I'm idle rich."

"Should have guessed from this ship," said Tavi. "Not just anybody flies a LaFayette."

Daniel knew he shouldn't, but he wanted to see Tavi drop his ice cubes. "*I*," said Daniel, "am a LaFayette."

Tavi missed a beat and lunged to catch his cubes, some of which escaped and went shooting across the deck. He stared at Daniel. "Um. *How* LaFayette are you?"

"Extremely," said Daniel.

"Second cousin . . . or . . . ?"

Daniel was shaking his head.

"You don't talk like one," said Tavi.

Daniel nodded in agreement.

"Heir incognito?" said Tavi.

Daniel nodded.

"Um." Tavi gingerly removed himself from the cabinet. "Anything I can do for you, milord? Dust your ice cubes? Feed the computer?"

Daniel smiled briefly and became suddenly serious again; a sense of urgency that was seldom far from mind pushed itself to the fore. Daniel had a mission. "Let's just get on our way," he said.

Tavi seconded the idea, and Daniel turned to the radio to request clearance for exit procedures.

Once off and away, Daniel faced the little alien. Now was the time for confrontations. "All right, who's chasing you?"

Tavi's pixie face assumed his best wide-eyed innocent look. His longer blond hair sticking out past the red even gave him a light halo. "No one."

Daniel crossed his arms, unconvinced, and he countered

71

with one of his father's best *you're a liar, son* expressions. "I played your game this far," said Daniel. "Who should I expect to see over my shoulder?"

"Dan-iel, I—" Tavi started to protest.

"You want to walk the dog?"

"You don't have a dog."

"That's real fortunate, seeing's as how it's a long hike to the nearest tree, friend. Talk."

"I'm not being chased. I'm really not," Tavi said earnestly. He'd dropped his usual bantering tone and sounded curiously close to tears. "Someone *is* trying to keep track of me," he admitted. It hurt him to say so. His eyes were wet, and he was blinking quickly. Small hands were fidgeting and rearranging things—his jacket, his hair—like creatures with an independent mind, for Tavi was not really aware of what they were doing. "He knows where I am constantly. He's not following me. He just keeps track of everything I do. It's oppressive. I just don't want him to know," said Tavi. He turned his pixie face and wet eyes endearingly to Daniel. "Don't make me walk the dog, Dan-iel."

Damn! Daniel did not know why he believed him, but he did. Sort of. "All right, you can stay," Daniel said in defeat, and Tavi smiled brightly. *But if you get me into trouble, you little son/daughter of a bitch . . .*

But Tavi was not the only one being monitored, and Tavi was not the one who was dangerous to be with.

Admiral Czals looked over the computer records of all the transactions of Daniel East which the tracker had presented to him. It was an odd agglomeration of information ranging from bar tabs (beer and whiskey together? Anyone who drank boilermakers was a barbarian in Czals' catalog) to the purchase and registration of a ship, LaFayette 0600 *Laure.*

Laure. He called the ship *Laure.* Czals did not like that at all.

Most disturbing, however, was the great number of strange requests for information from the UBC in the past months: stellar maps; survey reports; bioscans for seven worlds, only four of which had such scans; and all manner of disconnected data regarding those seven worlds. Then suddenly Daniel had been reported to *be* on one of those seven worlds, then on another. Today he had left Hell, where he'd requested information on the abandoned dome—which, of course, was unavailable to him, for it was classified.

Czals perused the report on the dome which Daniel had

been unable to obtain, the salient feature of which was the acknowledgment of the existence of a code black, class zero, hazardous and hostile alien form—the so-called demon of the abandoned dome.

Also from Hell came bills for extensive repairs to the ship *Laure* and to Daniel himself. It was possible that Daniel had actually gone to the abandoned dome and met the monster. But to what end? In a situation where most people would be screaming for an explanation, Daniel had packed up and left without further question. And it was not at all obvious how anything on Hell connected with the other six worlds Daniel was interested in. The data, at best, was difficult to interpret. Did it, Czals worried, have anything to do with Aeolis?

What is he up to?

"What do you think it means?" asked the tracker.

Czals shook his head. "I'm afraid to guess."

Tavi was a nuisance. Older than he looked or acted, he would break into fits of giggles when Daniel's voice squealed in mid-word, and he would cover his ears and howl when Daniel played his harmonica. Out of the blue he told Daniel, "You're good-looking." It threw Daniel off balance to hear another male say so—he kept forgetting what Tavi was—and it made him a little nervous to be appreciated. He thought Tavi was good-looking too, but he'd be damned if he'd say so.

But, pest that Tavi was, Daniel did not mind having his company to fill the silence. Besides, he liked him.

He made the mistake of telling Tavi his mission, that he was looking for a lost caste of Kistraalians. He did not add that he himself was part Kistraalian or that he thought the Service was trying to destroy the Kistraalian winds.

On route to Bhaccaa, Daniel was awakened in the middle of his sleep cycle by Tavi shaking him and pulling his arm. "Dan-iel! I think I found them! Your winds!"

Daniel let himself be dragged out of his compartment, not quite awake, to the control room, where the radio was picking up a strong standard signal, not a long-distance phase jumper, though the sensor registered no other ships in the vicinity. It sounded like people talking, but it was no language Tavi knew or had ever heard of.

Daniel groaned. "That's thousands of years old, particle-brain."

He focused sleep-blurred eyes through the viewport at the field of stars. Somewhere among them was a world known as

Planet K, which had been destroyed in an internal war two thousand years ago. Nothing remained of its civilization or its inhabitants. Only its ancient signals persisted. The natives had never developed a phase jumper and they had, instead, relied on these slow, speed-of-light transmissions for communications, transmissions of a type that remained astoundingly undiffused after thousands of light-years. Even at this time and distance the message was but slightly garbled from the original one sent out from a transmitter that had since gone silent.

"Oh," said Tavi and sheepishly retreated into his own ship.

Daniel sat down at the console, zombielike, the radio noise flowing through him like an ocean wave through something hollow. He switched on the filter/integrator, and the voices became instantly more distinct, but still untranslated, untranslatable. He listened a while, but could distinguish nothing; the language was not even vaguely Kistraalian.

He was dully awake now, settled into a numb peacefulness alone with the stars—the starlight shed years upon years ago—and the lonely signal from a people long dead.

He wondered where people, or at least their souls, went when they died. Mother had believed in ghosts. Father didn't believe in anything anymore. Old East had once said, "When I die, I'm not going anywhere. I'm staying right *here,* dammit!"

But where could he go when the Earth was gone? Only space was always the same—eternal nothing.

Daniel stared at his own youthful hands clasped on the console and felt suddenly mortal.

He heard the dead voices, didn't know what they were saying. They sounded so human.

A breath of age. A strong sense of *déjà vu* crept over him, and it was as if he were back in the Kistraalian cemetery with Niki.

It was an old part of the galaxy, this. He wondered how many planets here had already spawned life and civilizations that had become great and had died.

Or had destroyed themselves, like Kistraal.

On Bhaccaa, Daniel enlisted the aid of a native research scientist. He told her the project was "sort of secret," and she was more than happy to keep this wonderful puzzle all to herself and gleefully set out to solve it. She was amazing to watch, her spindly fingers and prehensile toes flying across the keyboards of four different computer terminals, while she gave voice commands to a fifth.

Daniel was not exactly sure why he felt the need for secrecy. If he did find the missing winds, they would be settled somewhere, ten thousand years removed from Aeolis/Kistraal, and not likely to be willing to return, so it was not as if Daniel were threatening Earth's ownership of Aeolis by this search for the planet's natives. Yet someone might think so—if someone knew.

And something told Daniel that someone did know.

I'm getting paranoid, he thought. *Tavi's rubbing off on me.*

Tavi, in the meantime, was instituting a search of his own and found the only young, pretty, human female on all of Bhaccaa. They promptly seduced each other, and Tavi quit complaining about "this boring planet" and making remarks about Daniel's "skinny, bald girlfriend."

"I think she's beautiful," said Daniel in defense of his research scientist.

But at last the Bhaccaan scientist ran up her last dead end. She rotated her whiteless eyes to Daniel and rasped a Bhaccaan sigh. "I am afraid, Mr. East, your Kistraalians are not here."

What sealed the matter was that the Bhaccaans possessed the same low hearing range as the Kistraalians, and someone surely would have noticed by now if the winds of Bhaccaa had been talking.

Nevertheless the research scientist gave Daniel a gift in appreciation of his giving her such an interesting problem. It was a low-frequency transmitter with a recorded message for him to take to the other planets of his search. The message said in Kistraalian, "Are you *volaia?* I am called Daniel. My caste is *laitine.* Come talk to me."

Daniel kissed the Bhaccaan's hairless head—she really *was* beautiful, in a wrinkled bony alien way—and bid her good-bye.

Dragging Tavi away from his new playmate was not too difficult, since the girl was irritated at Tavi for never spending a whole night with her.

Once in space, the creeping paranoia returned to Daniel, the feeling of someone looking over his shoulder. He actually turned around to look. Of course he was alone.

"Tavi?" he called.

"Yo!" Tavi called from way over in his own ship.

"Never mind," said Daniel.

He started to compose a letter to his father, but ended up wording it in generalities—as if he were not talking to his father but to someone else.

Admiral Czals sifted through all the records he had on Daniel East one more time, including the boy's latest letter to his father. It said nothing, and that in itself was disturbing.

Czals' cigarette holder snapped between his fingers. He hadn't realized how much he had let this business affect him. His unconscious knew something he did not.

He had less information than he might have had, since Daniel's request for information on Bhaccaa were predominantly not in Daniel's name. Still, Czals was a shrewd man and did not require many tracks to see a trail.

His flesh crawled, chilled. "Others," he said.

"Sir?" said the tracker.

Czals thundered, "Dammit, he's looking for others!"

Something had made Daniel East think that there were other Kistraalians out there. Czals could not see the method in the search just yet, but he would figure it out. He gave all the information over to the loathed scientist who had arranged Laure's death, and let *him* figure it out.

The scientist considered the material, nodded his birdlike head at Czals' assessment of the boy's activities, and asked, "Shall we kill him?"

Is that the only answer these toads and fools can come up with?

Czals prided himself on not being of the mercenary mentality that shoots at anything that moves. Surely there were other options open. Czals was not backed into a corner yet, not by a boy.

"We are officers of the United Earth Service," said Czals coolly. "Not underworld racketeers. I want you to watch Daniel's actions closely. I want to know what makes him think there are other Kistraalians; I want to know how he is choosing his worlds to search; I want our own search begun, and *I want us to find those Kistraalians first!*"

"If they exist," the scientist amended.

Czals nodded. Now *there* was a comforting doubt. But it would not do to be optimistic at this point. "If they exist," said Czals, "I want them found *before* Daniel East can make contact."

Steel eyes glanced left, right. The admiral straightened his shoulders stiffly, cleared his throat, sucked in his dignity, and moved to the door. *"Then* kill him."

76

III.

From Bhaccaa, Daniel had originally planned to go to the fourth and last planet for which he had a bioscan, Crucis One. But nothing in the Crucis bioscan indicated the possible presence of Kistraalians, and Daniel felt confident enough now to take on a primitive world, so he set course instead for Stranthm.

During the journey Tavi made a monster on shipboard.

"Oh my God, Tavi, what's that?"

"Don't ask me; I found it in your storeroom. It was supposed to be instant peachbread. I think I did something wrong."

Daniel walked over to it and broke off a piece—or tried to. "I don't know, Tavi. You've invented a new glue."

"An alien life form, I think," Tavi suggested. "Kistraalian, maybe?"

"Hm. No, it's not hairy enough to be a snow cat. *Almost,* but no."

Inevitably Tavi asked, "Why is it so important to you to find those Kistraalians?"

Daniel had prepared numerous dodges for that question, but to his own surprise, instead of dodging, he answered it. He told Tavi much more than he'd ever intended to tell anyone; and Tavi's coppery eyes grew rounder and rounder.

"Oh, did I ever pick one hell of a shadow to hide in," Tavi said to himself, then to Daniel, "Did you ever consider maybe your mother was murdered?"

"Of course not. She was bitten by a snake," said Daniel.

"Sure it wasn't a Serviceman crawling on his belly? I hear they do that."

"Get off it, Tavi. Nobody murdered my mother."

Tavi jumped to his feet, commandeered *Laure*'s controls, and altered course slightly.

"Hey! What are you doing?" said Daniel.

"There's someone you have to meet," said Tavi. "It's right on our way."

77

"Who? Where?"

"You'll see."

The place Tavi piloted them to was a small private space station. There were no other ships around. Tavi asked no permission or clearance, and, without even announcing himself, he attached *Laure* to a station lock, opened the hatch, and admitted himself.

"C'mon." He beckoned Daniel and trotted down the corridor.

"Boy, you don't believe in knocking, do you?" said Daniel and followed uncertainly.

The place was a mess. In fact, it was a literal zoo, with animals wandering amid all kinds of clutter, haphazardly placed antique furniture, and gadgets. Robot caretakers kept it livable, but not ordered. It looked like a giant pack rat's nest. "Ain't it great?" Tavi winked.

He led the way at a trot down a narrow staircase.

Stairs? Daniel followed.

"Noah!" Tavi called.

"Earthling?" said Daniel at his shoulder.

"Yeah," said Tavi. "Noah! It's Tavi!"

A gruff voice from below said, "I know who you are."

Daniel was taken aback, but Tavi smiled and ran down the remaining stairs into a wide chamber, startling a flock of birds that took flight and squawked and chittered at him from atop stacks of old chests of drawers and grandfather clocks.

Daniel caught up with Tavi, who was trying to get around a herd of goats, when he saw the man seated in an overstuffed chair on the far side of the chamber.

Wearing a frayed black coat, with a chipmunk in the pocket, gripping a wooden cane, he was old, with grizzled beard, fuzzy white hair, and white eyes.

Cataracts. He was blind.

Daniel whispered to Tavi, "Why doesn't he have them removed?"

"He doesn't like what there is to see," Tavi whispered back and kicked a goat out of his way.

The man spoke crossly. "Clip-clop down my stairs and you have to tell me it's Tavi. I know it's Tavi."

The little Tyi jumped over the last goat, ran to the old man, and threw his arms around his neck. "Noah!"

The old man patted Tavi's head and pulled his hair, touched his face and sniffed him. "Tavi." His cracked face

78

approximated a smile. Then he pulled Tavi back by his shoulders and said in surprise, "Tavi, you married without telling me."

"I'm not married, Noah," said Tavi.

Noah sniffed him. "You've been a bad girl, Tavi."

"Yes, I have."

Noah rapped the deck with his cane and raised his voice, "Go home and marry now. Or there'll be trouble for you."

Tavi pouted petulantly. "I don't want to talk about it."

"Who is the white boy?" said Noah.

Tavi turned and winked at Daniel, who was staring in amazement, jaw dropped open. "Just someone I picked up in Hell. His name is Dan-iel East."

Noah scowled at Daniel, brows meeting over sightless eyes. "What is your nationality?" he demanded.

"I'm a tri-national," said Daniel from across the chamber.

"Well?" said Noah impatiently.

"Oh. Um." Daniel shifted self-consciously, fists buried in the pockets of his navy pea jacket. "I was born Texas; my dad's American, and my ma was a Tunisian citizen."

"Hrumph. Smelled like a mixed breed," Noah muttered.

Daniel came closer, glancing around him at the menagerie. A cow walked by in slow pursuit of an automaton that carried grain and was not about to give her any. "Is this supposed to be an Ark?"

"Yeah," said Tavi. "He's got two of just about everything—except people."

Daniel spoke to Noah. "Why don't you just take Tavi and save space?"

"Don't want no people. Too many people," said Noah and nodded to himself.

Daniel's eyes wandered.

"The girl aardvark died," Noah said and Daniel suddenly realized that what he was staring at was a long furry nose poking out from under Noah's overstuffed chair. Daniel leaned over and came face to nose with the boy aardvark, which looked up at him with lovelorn eyes, or so Daniel fancied.

"Does he bite?" said Daniel.

"No, but he might tongue you to death," said Tavi.

Daniel gave up trying to make sense, and he let the two crazies talk to each other. Himself, he drifted away to roam the chamber, looking at all the clocks—none of them running—the ancient cottonpicker, the coffee grinder, and the electric can opener. He said hello to the myna bird. The bird told Daniel in gruff tones not to do anything on its shoulder. Daniel jerked his head back in startlement, then sauntered on.

He had made a complete circuit of the chamber when suddenly in the middle of the calm, the old man Noah grabbed him as he passed close by, held his wrist hard enough to hurt, and rubbed the skin with his thumb as if he would rub it off. "White, white," he muttered.

"Yeah, it's white. Leave it on!" Daniel snapped.

But the old man seized Daniel's hair and inspected that too, ungently. Then he bellowed in horror, "Tavi, *what have you brought me!*" Daniel was scared.

Tavi smiled at Daniel. "He can tell, Dan-iel. So it's true. I didn't believe it."

"A stranger," Noah was saying. "What kind of stranger?"

"He's what you think he is, Noah."

The old man released Daniel abruptly, trembling hands poised on either side of him as if he might hold him but was afraid to touch, his attitude reverent, almost adoring. "Oh my lord, my lord."

"Huh?"

"You have no idea, do you Dan-iel?" said Tavi. "You can't see."

"See *what?*" his voice broke and shot up to a squeal.

"Let me ask you this: What are the chances of a randomly evolved species being so exactly the same as another independently evolved species that they can crossbreed?"

"I don't know."

"They're practically nil, spaceboy. Zero. You're a walking miracle, Dan-iel. You still don't see. This—*you*—simply can't happen. Unless, of course, species don't evolve randomly and someone planned all this."

"You mean God."

"Yeah, and that idea is not so popular just everywhere," said Tavi. "Still sure about your mother?"

Daniel covered his ears. "Stop it! Nobody killed my mother! Nobody knew what she was but me!" He didn't know why he was screaming.

Tavi stayed calm and skeptical. "Don't be so sure. Some secrets don't rest easy."

After breaking another cigarette holder, Admiral Czals returned to the scientist, goaded by where his thoughts were leading.

If there were more Kistraalians in existence besides the im-

80

potent winds on Aeolis, and if those Kistraalians came into contact with Earthlings before Czals could prevent it, then there would always be the danger of crossbreeding. If he could find those Kistraalians and liquidate them and Daniel before contact, there would be no problem. But there were too many variables, too many chances for things to go wrong. He needed a backup plan—in case.

"I want proof of a connection between the origin of Earthlings and the origin of Kistraalians," said Czals.

"Proof?" said the scientist in surprise. "Are you sure it exists?"

"It must," Czals said, grim. "Left to chance, the odds against the two disconnected species interbreeding are astronomical."

"That is true, Admiral. But there is no other evidence even to suggest such a connection—besides the odds."

"Isn't that evidence enough?" Czals demanded.

"If it is enough, Admiral, why are you asking me for more?" said the scientist.

I am talking to a tunnel-visioned nitwit. Let me spell this out for you. "When something that seemingly cannot happen happens, the stupid masses will always say that a miracle has happened. And understand this: There will be no miracles in my jurisdiction."

"And if the connection you seek does not exist?" said the scientist.

"Then make one."

Skimming over the water very low, *Laure* and her rider ship flew for leagues and leagues across a seemingly endless sea that was the planet Stranthm. To steer by there was the sun, the stars, and the magnetic field. Below was only blue water broken here and there by dolphin wakes and, at one point, a column of hissing black smoke that belched up from an undersea volcano and rose through a ring of boiling white seafoam to tower into the heavens and cast a pall of starless twilight and thrashing rains over *Laure*'s path.

When it seemed the ship would be lost forever in cloudcast dark, abruptly she was free again under a sky that was half blue, half still black, a moon shining bright overhead at the schism between day and volcanic night, the sun close to the western horizon, and a rainbow arched at the edge of the storm. It looked like some kind of portent, a promise exchanged between the chthonic deities and those of the sky, if Daniel could only figure out what it meant.

81

And, as if commanded by a greater power, the storm did not follow him to the west, its fury turned aside by a Coriolus wind.

Or some kind of wind.

Daniel felt heartened, and, a short way farther into daylight, *Laure*'s scanner lit up in specks.

"What's that?" said Tavi.

"Birds," said Daniel. They were near land.

Daniel cut speed and climbed high, watching for the birds.

At last, far below, he sighted a ring of islands green and thick with a dense mossy growth upon the mountains, and jungles of alien tropical trees like giant ferns in the valleys, so that the entire atoll stood out against the eternal blue of the ocean like an emerald necklace.

As the ship circled in lower and lower, Daniel could see catamarans upon the water and people in them, pointing up at him. High on the gentle hills near the islands' shores stood their fragile huts, looking very vulnerable to the elements— but then little shelter was needed when Nature was always kind.

Daniel had already fallen in love with the place as he brought *Laure* to rest on a wide beach of white sand on the largest of the islands, whose name meant Vigilance. He had a feeling something was *right*.

He opened the hatch to a balmy, shifting breeze that brought to him fresh green smells from the jungle, tang of salt from the sea, and cries of birds riding the surf as the breakers rolled in from the windward side of the island. The birds were the ones that had lit up Daniel's scanner, those points of light now incarnated to brilliant-hued creatures the color of sea and sky, the tips of their wings dashed white like the crests of the waves they rode and chased.

Daniel jumped out the ship's hatch and immediately got sand in his shoes. He took them off, rolled up his pantlegs, and took a short walk to take his bearings. He listened, said hello to a wind, but it was only an insentient westerly.

He quickly became too warm. He took off his shirt and tied the sleeves around his neck. He stretched, his skin tingling in the bright sunlight. He inhaled deeply. The air was thin, and he felt very light. He turned and tossed his shoes back into the ship. Tavi yelped from inside; the shoes had carried a little farther than he'd expected.

"Sorry," Daniel called.

He walked a short way up the beach along the tidemark on wet fine-grained sand as the edge of the ocean rushed up to touch his feet, then retreated to gather up and try again. He had landed his ship well apart from the huts and loose-clustered settlements on the leeward side of the island facing the lagoon. He had a sense that it would have been like riding a horse into a house were he to have dropped out of the sky and landed square in their midst. He did not know what the natives thought, but he felt it was wiser to go to them on foot.

He could see them still watching him from their catamarans and peering from the jungle beyond the sea strand—curious, not alarmed, not menacing. They were tall, delicate-looking humanoids. Their hair was light in color and thin, no more than a diaphanous veil on their heads. The women were golden—the men too, but Daniel was not so struck by those. None of them, male or female, was overly awed by Daniel. They knew where he came from—"Out There," they called it—and the alien boy did not frighten them. But still they kept their distance, for Daniel had not been approved yet.

All paradises had their guardians, and the islands of Stranthm were watched over by the High Priestess of Vigilance. It was for her to say whether an outsider were welcome or not. If she put a religious taboo on one, he remained at his peril. The climate of her moods was known across the galaxy.

Few ships came to Stranthm.

Daniel was growing apprehensive, wondering how he would approach the woman. She had to let him stay. Didn't she? But he did not know where to find her.

"Dan-iel, look."

Tavi had climbed atop his ship, which rode piggyback on *Laure*, and he was pointing down the beach. Daniel turned to look.

Out of the rush and draw of the sea sounds he could distinguish the distant beat of a tambourine. Then it came into view—a procession of islanders in bright array filing up the beach, all barefoot but one borne along by the others in a sedan chair curtained with grass and canopied with green boughs, dropping blossoms and leaves with which they were laden. An important person and entourage. The priestess. She was coming to Daniel.

Daniel was terrified. It was like watching his own demise march toward him. He desperately wanted to stay on Stranthm. This woman must not cut him off before his search here had even begun. And she had the power.

83

"Tavi, get down here!" He was going to need a translator.

Tavi climbed down from the ship, unhurried and not terribly concerned. He was not afraid, not even for Daniel's sake. What did it matter to Tavi if the priestess said stay or go? Tavi could not care. Tavi could not know. Daniel felt his whole life tying itself into knots in his gut as he watched the priestess come.

He could hear the tambourine clearly now, an intricate skillful beat, primitive and sophisticated at once. Though the natives looked like savages and though they hadn't any technology beyond the building of a catamaran, these were not naive children. The music told him so.

They came closer, fantastic and outlandish as a troupe of mummers, adorned with flowers and shells and feathers of birds of paradise. They were looking straight at Daniel. He could no longer pretend they might not be coming to him, and he thought perhaps he should take a few steps to go out to meet them, but he could not move, paralyzed. Then he remembered what he looked like and felt self-conscious and ridiculous waiting to meet a priestess with his pantlegs rolled up, but it was too late to kick them down. He could only hope she wouldn't know that Earthlings did not meet important personages with their pantlegs rolled up or that shirt sleeves were for arms, not for tying around one's neck.

The tall golden natives brought the greenwood chair before him and set it down, strings of sea shells clattering and jingling as they moved. The grass curtain was swept aside, and Daniel beheld the priestess, astonished.

The priestess could have been a child, could have been an old woman for her beautiful ageless face and knowing agate eyes. Her hair was like a waterfall, white and shimmering with a glistening ornament in it that Daniel realized was a live creature like a glass-bodied moth. So too her necklaces of red beads crept and adjusted themselves, and a slender serpent stayed coiled around her wrist, asleep. What looked like a skirt was a layer of woven living ivy, still rooted, trailing up from a bed of soil set in the base of the chair.

Daniel had rehearsed a salutation, but he could no more speak than he could move.

The priestess inclined her head toward him in a slight bow. Daniel returned the gesture on impulse—something popped into his head and bid him *bow!*

When he looked up at her again, the priestess said, "My lord."

Daniel was thunderstruck. She'd spoken in English. And

84

what she had said. *Is it written on my face?* How did she know? She read him as if he were as transparent as the moth in her hair. Or she had been told. Foretold?

Not given to mysticism, Daniel nevertheless sensed a feeling of purpose. He was meant to come here. He'd had a sign from the skies.

Conscious of the living things she wore, the priestess turned her head ever so slowly to Tavi and spoke in an alien tongue which Daniel guessed was Tyi. Then she looked to Daniel again. "You have a mission, young lord. Abide with us in peace." Her voice was smooth and rolling as a wave. "A blessing on your quest. Only stay out of the caves. Angry gods dwell there."

Daniel's eyes slid aside to Tavi and exchanged glances with him, their minds on the same track, making the same connections:

Angry gods?

IV.

So Daniel went down to the caves in search of gods. Beings that changed shape and lived forever could be taken as gods, and Daniel hoped that the *volaia* had been.

The path to the caves led through a jungle that was deep and lush and painted all the colors of paradise. Hummingbirds like jewels in flight hovered over huge blooms grown so thick they weighed down the vines and stalks on which they grew. The forest was fragrant with life, rich soil, and rotting logs that were covered with wet moss and fire-red fungus.

Tavi picked a creamy white blossom from one of the boughs overhead and put it in his hair.

"Don't do that," said Daniel.

"Why?" said Tavi.

" 'Cause you're a guy," said Daniel without thinking.

"The hell you say," said the Tyi.

Flustered, Daniel growled something to the effect of "Skip it," and stalked on down the path to the jungle's end.

The forest quit abruptly at a treeless limestone plateau, a wasteland of thick spongy moss, nothing else. There was little soil on the rock, if any, and no streams, no pools of water to support anything larger than the moss. It looked like a likely place to find a cave.

The path continued across the plateau, a narrow trail of bare rock where the moss was worn away by pilgrims' tread. It stopped at an altar. The altar stood at the mouth of a cave.

Between the flower-decked altar and the cave's maw the moss grew thick, undisturbed by pathmakers. No one ever dared beyond that point.

Daniel exchanged glances again with Tavi, then activated his Bhaccaan transmitter, switched on a lamp, and ventured ahead, into the cave. Tavi trailed close behind, carrying another lamp and a panic box full of just-in-case equipment that would have been a burden except that nothing felt very heavy on Stranthm.

The cave was dank and grew colder, the stone walls progressing gradually from furry to slimy as Daniel and Tavi went deeper. A green patina on the rocks could have been minerals, could have been mold.

The passage narrowed, and Daniel and Tavi had to squeeze between rock walls, then climb over a boulder and jump down a short drop.

"We're stupid, Dan-iel," said Tavi, crawling through a tunnel on his hands and knees, his words garbled because he was holding the lamp handle between his teeth. "We don't know nothing about caving. We could get killed."

But he followed.

The passage enlarged again and divided in two. Daniel shone his lamp to the right, Tavi to the left. Tavi wandered down his branch a few yards and disappeared round a corner.

Daniel heard the Tyi's voice echoing as if in a large space. "Dan-iel, look at this—" Then there was a splash.

"Tavi?" Daniel's voice cracked and squealed up in alarm.

There was a splashing and sputtering, then a barrage of words revealing Tavi's shocking fluency in Americanese, a huge vocabulary in amazing combinations.

Daniel followed the curses around the corner. "Tavi, are you OK—?"

And was silenced in wonderment.

A magnificent chamber of stalactites and columns turned gold and rose and emerald and ghostly white in the flood of his lamplight. And there was a lake, a vast lake filling the chamber, its surface a mirror so perfect Tavi had stepped right in, and Daniel would have done so too had Tavi not set it rippling.

An intensely cold and indignant Tyi, outraged as a wet cat, pulled himself out of the water. He could not be badly hurt to swear like that, and Daniel turned his attention to the cave itself. He directed his light toward the roof, igniting into color wavy sheaths and curtains of calcite and argonite, row upon row of them like ranks of flown teasers in a theater. Along the walls were tiered columns of palmate forms within forms.

Daniel brought his light down and held it on the most astonishing thing in the immense cavern. He nudged his wet companion and spoke low with barely controlled emotion. "Tavi." He pointed.

It was a boat. An ancient wooden rowboat set on a rock at the edge of the water.

Someone was not afraid of angry gods.

The boat looked heavier than it actually was, and Daniel and Tavi were able to heave it off the rock and let it slap down into the water with little effort. They climbed in and pinned the petrified oars into rusted oarlocks, then looked for leaks, but the old craft was still watertight, the wood preserved with black resin.

Daniel manned the oars, pointed the bow toward the far side of the chamber where there looked to be a passage, and set off at an even, quiet, fisherman's stroke. Tavi crossed his arms and shivered, crouched in the stern—where there would have been athwart had it been an Earthmade boat—his white teeth chattering.

The lake was enormous, seeming bigger with every dip of the oars. They took turns rowing, neither speaking much, gazing at the display of spires, icicles, and jaws. The curtains overhead gave way to straws thick as meadow grass, perfectly straight, none really long, the mass of them fringed with delicate, contorted helictites, their reflections below cut with ripples fanning out from the spearhead wake of the boat.

Daniel leaned over the gunwale to see his own face upon the water, older than he remembered it. He stared at it a long time. What had the priestess seen? What had sightless Noah seen?

This is the face of a miracle.

The idea was ludicrous.

"Tavi?"

"Yeah?"

"You knew the priestess would let us stay, didn't you?" He remembered Tavi's lack of concern on the priestess' approach.

"Sort of."

"You could have told me."

"Well, I didn't know she would like *you*," said Tavi, pulling at both oars. "I knew she'd like *me*. As she said, 'The Tyi are always welcome here.' "

So that was what she'd said to Tavi. "The Tyi are? Why the Tyi?"

"We're known as a gentle people," said Tavi.

"*You?*" Daniel cried, and Tavi smacked both oars on the water, splashing Daniel with an icy spray.

"Like *that*! See?" Daniel pointed as if Tavi had just confirmed his doubts.

But despite that, and for all Tavi's insults and love of a good brawl, Daniel had to admit that at the core, as much of it as he was allowed to see, Tavi was a gentle creature.

Which still left Daniel puzzled over what the priestess had seen in him. She had called him lord. She had known he was on a quest. How? Who else knew?

He thought he heard something; he turned off his transmitter and made Tavi stop rowing for a moment. All was still but for an occasional echoing musical *drip drop* of water somewhere in the cavern. And Tavi's chattering teeth.

Tavi started rowing again. Daniel sighed and turned the transmitter back on. It whispered at the lower edge of his range: *I am called Daniel of the laitine. Is anyone there?*

The boat came to the far end of the cavern and met with a sheer white calcite dam rising a meter above the waterline, blocking its passage to what appeared to be a corridor beyond. Daniel stood carefully in the boat and looked over the dam.

"There's a passageway, all right. The ground is about five feet down on the other side of this wall."

With that, Tavi produced a length of wire-thin cable from his panic box, tied one end to an oarlock, lacking a bow-eye, and threw the coil over the dam.

Daniel scrambled out of the boat and over the dam after it, pulled the line up taut, and looked for something to tie it to. He opted for a fat column and fastened the line with an unnautical but secure knot.

"OK, Tavi," he said, and Tavi stowed the oars, passed Daniel his transmitter, and followed him over the dam.

The passageway sloped downward from the lake level, but there was little water—a few shallow standing pools with nests of white cave pearls in them. The rest was dry and the going was easy. All around them stalagmites grew, some fallen like pillars of an ancient temple, and the flowstone floor was littered with broken straw stalactites as if the place had been ravaged by some vandal who did not fear angry gods.

Or by the angry gods themselves.

Tavi stopped. "Hear that?"

Daniel turned off his transmitter and listened. "No."

This was a switch; before, it had always been Daniel who heard things and Tavi who told him he was crazy because his own range was too high.

"What do you think you hear?" said Daniel.

Tavi snapped, "I don't *think* I hear—there!" He stopped, and Daniel strained to listen. He shook his head. "I don't hear anything." He continued down the passage.

The way turned up ahead, and from around the corner

shone the faintest glow of light. Daniel turned off his lamp to be certain. Still came the glow, here deep underground. Daniel's pulse quickened.

He rounded the corner, Tavi at his heels, and came into a chamber full of glowing white bats. Hundreds of thousands.

And woke them up.

Tavi screamed. "I hate bats! I hate bats! Oh, I hate bats!"

The bats flapped and squeaked on every side, diving and swooping on the intruders. Tavi shrieked in mortal terror, waving his arms wildly.

Daniel grabbed him and ran.

The two charged up the flowstone incline, through the swarm of bats, to the calcite dam. Daniel vaulted up, straddled the wall, hauled the thrashing screaming Tavi up bodily, threw him into the lake, and jumped in after him, the outraged bats wheeling and fluttering overhead by the hundreds.

Daniel found a submerged ledge he could stand on and keep just his nose above the surface like a honeybear hiding from a hiveful of enraged bees. He held onto Tavi as much for warmth in the frigid water as to keep the Tyi from thrashing. Tavi's eyes had turned from copper to black in terror, and his red hands turned white holding fast to Daniel, his legs wrapped tight around Daniel as if Daniel were a tree and Tavi would fall not float if he let go.

Daniel guessed Tavi really hated bats.

It had rained while they were down in the caves, but now the sky was clear again and the mossy plateau was steaming with rising mist.

Out in the sunlight Tavi still looked pale. He had lost his lamp and panic box, and had made Daniel drop his transmitter. He peeled off his wet battlejacket and wrung it out with unsteady hands. "You know, Dan-iel, I should have noticed something."

"What's that."

"Besides the fact that your wind friends wouldn't need a boat to get across the water, did you notice which side of the lake we found it on?"

"Damn," said Daniel. Whoever had taken the boat down there was not down there now.

It had probably been the person who'd discovered the angry gods.

A roaring from the sky drew their gazes upward.

"A Service ship," said Tavi in mild surprise.

90

Daniel uttered a small grunt of passing curiosity. "Wonder what they're doing on Stranthm."

Daniel turned sixteen on Stranthm. He was still upset about his voice, which did not squeal so much anymore, but when it had dropped it had been a long way down, and the new voice sounded froggish to his own ears. He hadn't yet the stature that should accompany a voice that deep, so he still tended to whisper. Or let Tavi talk. And talk.

Daniel tried to grow a beard to make himself look older and more fitting of the voice, but Tavi said, "Why don't you take that fuzz off your face? It looks stupid." And that put an end to that idea.

Every day Daniel and his clean-shaven face and froggy voice journeyed island to island looking for snow cats.

He stood out on the beach of the smallest island, arms akimbo, naked, and brown head to toe, squinting across the gleaming water of the lagoon to the other islands of the atoll. "Tavi, I think they're here."

"What makes you say that? We haven't found anything," said Tavi, skipping seashells on the water.

"The wind . . . I could've sworn." He stopped and spoke in Kistraalian. "Is anyone there?"

Tavi waited. His eyes slid from side to side, then up, then back to Daniel. "I think you hope too much, Dan-iel. This wind seems pretty dumb to me."

But Daniel did not give up. There was always the possibility—Tavi had suggested it—that after ten thousand years away from Kistraal, the *volaia* language had changed so much that they would not understand Daniel even if they were there to hear him. And Daniel felt that they *were* here. All he needed was a trace, a track, a whisper.

Stranthm was a big world, bigger than Earth, but its land area was only the barest fraction of Earth's and could literally be searched on foot. Daniel intended to do just that, first scouring the islands in the atoll, then taking *Laure* out to the uninhabited places on Stranthm—strings of volcano-born islands and places where submerged continents in collision heaved up mountains, the summits of which broke the surface of the world's Ocean.

Tavi stayed behind on the atoll and chased women. Only women.

"Why not men?" Daniel asked between forays.

"What do you think I am?" Tavi cried.

91

"Weird, that's what," Daniel said and left again. He had heard of double standards, but this was absurd.

Then at last Daniel ran out of places to go. He had searched the whole world. He returned to the atoll in defeat.

Tavi met him, jumping up and down like a puppy and eager to tell him news. "Guess what the priestess said!"

Daniel could not guess and was in no mood to try. "What did she say? And this better be good." How dare Tavi smile at a time like this?

Tavi told him.

The High Priestess had spoken a prophecy from the highest mountaintop announcing the return of the old gods and that They would reveal Themselves to all.

"When?" Daniel demanded. "Did she say?"

" 'Soon,' she said."

"That could mean anything."

"No, that's another word. This 'soon' means *soon*."

"What does she mean, *old gods*? We're not chasing bats again, are we?"

"I don't know, Dan-iel. Once upon a time, there was an island out there." Tavi pointed to the middle of the lagoon. "And this atoll was just that island's barrier reef. There was a temple on that island, and it's still down there. The whole thing sank a long time ago, and the old gods sank with it—or drowned; they're the same word. Those gods are the ones that are coming back. That's all I can tell you."

Daniel stared at the water. "Looks as though I'm going to have to take a look at that temple."

Daniel had brought diving equipment for only one, but Tavi would not swim anyway, especially after the last escapade, so it made no difference—drowned gods, angry gods, Tavi wanted nothing to do with them. He would wait on the beach. He enlisted native coral divers to show Daniel the way. They giggled and puzzled at Daniel's face mask and filter.

"What are they saying?" Daniel asked, lifting an earguard.

"They say you look funny," said Tavi. "You do."

Daniel made a face at him through the mask.

"Take a harpoon, Dan-iel. There might be jellyfish down there."

"Don't tell me you hate jellyfish."

"There's nothing in Creation I hate as much as bats, Daniel."

Daniel replaced his earguard and nodded toward his guides. "Tell them let's go."

Tavi said something and the natives filled their lungs with great breaths and dove into the lagoon, Daniel after them.

The water was warm, then pleasantly cool as they descended, calmer than the surrounding sea, a quiet oasis in the Ocean, its color a deep, brilliant indigo.

Daniel felt his face mask fit tighter, the earguards adjust to the pressure as he went down, but not so deep that there was not light.

The reef abounded with life and color, fish singly and in schools that looked to be millions, pearlsides and glassfish and iridescent blueheads. He could see eels lurking in a coral grotto, sponges clinging to a rocky ledge, a nautilus spotted like a leopard burying itself in the sand. Otherworld crustaceans scooted for cover in the spines of poison anemones. And there was the coral—ferns, fans, leaves, antlers, webs of it, banded, branching, and in fields of waving grass. There was a cactus coral, flower coral, stars, tubes, and ever-present Stranthm moss coral and coralline algae. They were vivid red, green, gold and amber, fire orange, black, white, fragile pink, and sandy. There were purple urchins and lavender seabells. Daniel wanted to stop and stare, but his guides waved him on toward the dark imposing shape of the sunken island, Stranthm's Atlantis.

He saw the temple first as a silhouette in indigo, and a shiver ran up his spine with a deep feeling of awe. He saw columns, a row of them like a Greek temple's, tall, stately, and commanding reverence.

Closer, he could see the pillars were made of limestone or marble, barnacled and encrusted with coral and mineral nodules. It was completely intact and so unlike the grass huts, so atypical, it left one conclusion. He ran a hand over a waterpocked stone column as if to confirm its reality.

Suddenly the natives were gesturing at him and tugging at him, pointing upward, signaling something imperative.

He shot up to the surface with them and swam ashore where Tavi waited.

The natives babbled at Tavi, and Daniel asked him, "What do they want?" He was afraid he had inadvertently committed sacrilege and was about to be bounced from Stranthm.

"They thought you were going to drown," said Tavi. "They didn't know why you wouldn't come up for air."

Daniel snorted. "Tell them I'm all right. I'm going back down."

"Did you see it?" Tavi asked before Daniel could replace his earguard.

"Yeah."

"What do you think?"

"Tavi, it's totally different from anything on this planet."

"You think the *volaia* built it?"

"Maybe."

"And *volaia* will return?"

"I hope so."

He dove back into the indigo water and returned to the temple, alone this time. He swam in between the salt-damaged columns, startling creatures that hid in the dark. He paused inside, pensive, filled with wonder. How much would it take for beings that knew no gods to become another people's gods?

A sound came to him; he felt it, then heard it, a deep grinding growl of stone on stone, and he darted out of the temple.

Now *that* had been stupid, he chided himself, going in there at all much less alone—like going into the rotten wreck of a sunken ship; the whole thing could have come down on his head and no one would have known until he was past help.

As he swam back up to shore, he realized he'd been breaking all the rules throughout his search. Someone must be looking out for him considering all the mistakes he had made. He felt someone was watching him.

He came out of the water, took off his mask, and dropped down in the sand, naked as a native, next to Tavi, who was dressed to the neck as always. Tavi did have his shoes off, and was lying half-asleep in the hot sand. The heat never bothered him, and of course a Tyi would not tan. Daniel, however, was getting to be Tavi's color, and his hair was streaked almost as red.

Tavi had the prettiest skin and the strangest hair. The longer blond ones—Daniel supposed they would be called guard hairs if Tavi were a mink—were shining in the sun. Daniel brushed a few wisps out of Tavi's face with the back of his hand. "Well, are they back yet?"

Copper eyes opened to slits. "Is who back?"

"The old gods."

Copper eyes rolled.

"Well, how soon is *soon*?" Daniel pestered.

Tavi started to sneer, then his gaze focused beyond Daniel and he sat up. "Will you look at that," he said appreciatively.

Daniel turned. It was not an old god; it was a native girl. Daniel had been too preoccupied to notice much how truly beautiful the women were. He half smiled to himself wryly, thinking his friends back home would not recognize him without his neck craned around to view some girl or other.

He wondered about Tavi. As a male, Tavi was as promiscuous as Daniel used to be; as a female he—she—was as guarded as a nun. And a whole race of hermaphrodites seemed to be an awfully inefficient way to operate reproduction. But on the other hand, they would not have to worry about a population imbalance such as the Kistraalians had at the end—too many females to no males—because any two Tyi made a pair.

"Tavi?"

"Yeah?"

"Have you ever made love as a female?"

"Well," Tavi began doubtfully, "I've done it as a female but I wouldn't call it lovemaking, and I didn't exactly have much to say about it."

That shut Daniel up for a few minutes. He'd never met a girl that *that* had happened to. He didn't understand *that*. He wondered if that was why Tavi was running and hiding. "A Tyi?" he asked at last.

"Yes."

"Did he hate you?"

"No. Yes. We were close. We weren't friends, though. He just wanted to control me. I should hammer out your ears for hearing that. Tell, and I'll rip your tongue."

"Tell what?"

Tavi nodded. They understood each other.

The sun set quickly, but the air stayed warm. It was one of those nights when nothing moved. Daniel fell asleep out on the beach.

He woke to native cries: *"Sophi cathalay!"*

He sat up, disoriented. He looked at Tavi beside him, shook him awake. "What's a *sophi cathalay?*"

Tavi looked as if he'd seen a bat and jumped to his feet. "It's a big *big* earthquake."

The ground began to tremble and groan. The little alien pulled at Daniel, stumbling and dragging him up the shifting sinking sand toward solid ground as the beach was being sucked down into the ocean.

They made it to a hill and huddled there, away from the trees, off the sand, grass huts collapsing around them, the ground heaving like a wave.

And the gods came back.

95

V.

With the slow rise of the early rockets and with as much thunder, out of the bubbling frothing brine of the lagoon, the whole island rose, water gushing down its sides as it left the sea; Atlantis returned, a dark Aphrodite borne out of sea foam. And at the peak of the massive shivering hulk, like a battered crown, stood the temple, its columns intact, gleaming wet as any newborn—reborn—triumphant survivor of its undersea captivity, returned to light by powers of earth. There it stood and there it stayed when the tumult subsided, battleweary citadel dripping with clinging dark seaweed, crusted with coral, little creatures scurrying out of its sanctuary, bewildered in the open air and light of early dawn.

When all was still again, besides the new island set in the lagoon, the islands on one side of the atoll itself had risen five meters higher than they had been before. A great wave had come in from the surrounding Ocean, but the atoll's new height had preserved its inhabitants.

People lined the shores of all the islands, hands outstretched toward the temple in worship. Their primordial gods had revealed their enormous power.

The ground shuddered once more gently, a groan after great effort.

Daniel lifted his head and brushed away dirt and sand that had clotted on the tracks of his tears; he hadn't realized he had been crying. He'd been too terrified.

He looked to the flimsy huts of the natives, all collapsed. He could see people picking their way out from under the reedy ruins, unhurt. He knew now that he'd been deceived by the fragility of the shelters. He had taken it as a sign of Nature's mildness. But the huts were not flimsy because Nature was kind, but rather because she was not. The natives bowed to powers too great to be resisted, rather than stand unyielding against the Fury and be destroyed utterly.

He looked to the stone temple. That had been another mistake in interpretation. The temple was not different because it was alien-made. It was different because it was a temple. Stone was for eternal gods; grass was for transitory mortals.

Daniel shook his head. How could he have been so thoroughly wrong? The old gods were not snow cats; they were Stranthm itself.

Tavi was round-eyed. He murmured, "Dan-iel, their gods are *gods!*"

"Either that or their priestess is a damn good seismologist," said Daniel, discouraged and bitter. "Let's go."

Then he remembered. "Oh, no. *Laure!*" And he took off through the jungle at a run. He had left his ship sitting on the beach on the outer side of the island—where the wave would have hit hardest.

Still running, he reached the plateau, his lungs aching from effort to get enough oxygen out of the thin air, and he ran into a Service ship at the edge of a huge sinkhole. He halted, surprised and needing a rest.

Nearby, a spaceman and lowly ensign were frantically begging aid from natives, who shunned the outworlders as unclean, unholy, and blasphemous.

What was going on here? Daniel wondered. Where were the officers? He could not understand the words, for they were all in other tongues.

Then all at once it was too clear. It occurred to Daniel exactly where he was and what should have been there but was not. The cave. It had collapsed in the quake and left this gaping sinkhole—under which the officers were, buried alive.

Daniel shuddered. *It could have been us.* He now saw the face of the vandal that had broken the stalagmites. *Angry gods.* They weren't bats after all.

Tavi came running up the path after Daniel. He saw what had happened and uttered an oath.

Then a native came to Daniel and pulled at his arm, talking urgently and beckoning to Tavi.

"What's she saying?" Daniel demanded from Tavi.

"She says, 'Come away from them. They are evil.' "

Daniel let the girl lead him away from the "evil" Servicemen. He guessed they were branded blasphemers because their officers had been caught down in the caves. He wondered what they'd been doing down there.

More than before, he prayed his own ship was all right. He didn't want to be forced to leave Stranthm by hitching a ride aboard a Service ship with a half-dead crew.

But his fears were unfounded. *Laure* and her rider were safe and unscratched, if not quite where he'd left them. They were no longer on the beach, but up on a rise at the jungle's edge.

Now how did she get up there?

She hadn't *walked*, had she? Daniel supposed the ships could have washed up on a wave. Unlikely, but there was no other explanation he could think of.

He and Tavi climbed aboard and secured for takeoff—it seemed odd not to have to ask for clearance—and they left the water world Stranthm behind.

Daniel was beginning to feel a little depressed and a little scared. He was over halfway through his search; only three planets remained. His hopes had been so high for this one. Surely the *volaia* would not just happen to be on the last planet he chose to search. Or worse, what if the *volaia* were on none of them? He shook off that idea, refusing to consider it until there was no other choice.

He wanted something to eat. He was not hungry; he just wanted something. He opened the frig. "Oh my God. Oh Tavi. Oh no."

"What is it?" Tavi climbed down from his own ship into Daniel's.

"Tavi, what did you do with the peachbread?" Daniel asked, pseudo-casually.

"I put it in your frig. Why?"

"Because it ate everything else in there, that's why!"

Tavi looked over Daniel's shoulder. The peachbread was not only hairy now, it was ferocious. "Oh dear. What should we do?"

"You are going to heave it out the chute."

"What if we're responsible for a terrible accident? You just can't leave that thing floating out there."

"Tavi."

"All right. All right." He started to reach for the peachbread, pulled back, and eyed it dubiously. "You wouldn't happen to have a whip and a chair, would you?"

Daniel glared at him, growled, searched for something dry-preserved he could eat, then decided he was not hungry anyway. He sat and sulked.

"The boy has left Stranthm, sir," the young lieutenant reported uneasily to the admiral. "The information comes from a sight report by the ensign of the search ship on Stranthm."

Czals scowled. He did not like sight reports, and not by ensigns who were supposed to be looking for Kistraalians, not tracking Daniel East. If a Serviceman was close enough to see Daniel, then Daniel was close enough to look back. "Who is the incompetent captain of that search ship?" Czals muttered, mostly to himself, looking through his records. He found the culprit's name. "Ah. Morley."

"Uh . . . there's been a slight mishap on Stranthm, sir," said the lieutenant.

Czals seemed to grow with his anger. He glared at the lieutenant with hard steel eyes. His voice began very soft, words clipped. "How *slight* a *mishap?*"

"Captain Morley, three officers, and two crewmen of the search ship were killed in a landfall. Ensign Khu has assumed command."

Czals relaxed. "Very well," he said. As long as the mission was not in jeopardy that matter had been correctly titled a mishap. He was glad that the lieutenant was not an alarmist who placed undue stock in the "value of human life." Only certain human lives had value in Czals' book—like this young officer perhaps. Czals liked his attitude. He looked at the lieutenant for the first time with any real attention. Young, black-haired, clean-faced, solid jaw. Not a crook. A career man. *Good boy.*

"What's your name, mister?" said Czals.

"Martin, sir."

Czals nodded and turned his attention back to the Kistraalian affair, irritated at his own miscalculation regarding Stranthm. That world had been a five-star nuisance from the beginning, and the boy was well away from it. The High Priestess had been thoroughly uncooperative. She had been warned that a boy would come from the sky claiming lordship and seeking to work evil among her people, and she must put the taboo on him. The Priestess had turned right around and put her taboo on the Servicemen who'd brought her the warning, and welcomed Daniel East with a reception rare on Stranthm.

Czals had not counted on the woman's deep suspicion of the Service. He could not afford any more mistakes like that. Mistakes made Czals very nervous, especially his own.

"Did the search ship find any evidence of Kistraalians on Stranthm?" said Czals.

"No, sir."

"I trust Daniel East fared no better?"

"By all indications, sir. Our people assure us there are no Kistraalians on Stranthm."

"Where is the boy now?"

99

The lieutenant paled slightly. "In transit, it is believed, either to Crucis One, Jarsheno, or Warhi."

Czals nodded grimly. At this point blank spaces were to be expected. The computer was set to notify them as soon as Daniel's ship appeared in any port. But Czals was well aware that on backwater places like Jarsheno and Warhi there were few modern ports, and Daniel could slip by computer notice.

"I assume there has been nothing found on Jarsheno, Warhi, or Crucis One to indicate the presence of Kistraalians." said Czals.

"No, sir. Not yet."

And let's hope not ever. Gods, I hate this waiting.

"Intensify all efforts to locate Daniel East and to find those Kistraalians if they exist. Notify me as soon as something breaks. You may go, Lieutenant Martin."

Tavi screamed.

"Dan-iel, there's a monster stuck to my viewport!"

Daniel covered his eyes and spoke slowly. "Tavi, which ejector chute did you throw the peachbread out of?"

He had told Tavi a dozen times that anything going out chute number one would bull's-eye his own rider ship.

"Oh." Tavi grinned sheepishly, backstepping from the cabin. "Um, how do I get it off?"

Daniel shook his head, distracted. "Don't worry about it. We'll burn it off when we enter atmosphere."

"Of which planet?"

"Jarsheno."

They entered the Jarsheno system, pausing first at an orbiting Earth station to collect some local currency from a Universal Bank Computer outlet.

And on Earth an admiral smiled, feeling in control again.

The search on Jarsheno began slowly and discouragingly. The land was vast, splintered into different nations, and Tavi did not have perfect command of any of the languages. It was not that Tavi was unfamiliar with them. He knew the words, but concepts and fine shades of connotations escaped him. All the languages in the world were of one family, one stock; they were all structured alike, so one key would unlock all, but it eluded him. It was the entire way of thinking that he could not grasp. To know a language was to know its people—how they thought. Tavi could never catch hold of Jarsheno's. Something was not fitting in. They defied logic.

So before long Tavi and Daniel came to a tavern to get drunk—again—Tavi on beer, Daniel on whiskey. Daniel was drunk first. Tavi kept getting up to relieve himself. Daniel wondered how hermaphrodites managed that process. He looked to see if Tavi was going to the men's room or the women's room, but there were none, not that Daniel could have read the signs anyway. Everyone just went out and did it in the street. Jarsheno was not an advanced world.

Tavi came back the fifth time with a native man in tow.

"Tell him what you told me," said Tavi to the native.

The man began to speak an unintelligible tongue.

"Hear that?" said Tavi to Daniel excitedly.

Daniel rubbed his watery drunken eyes. "Are you nuts? What did he say?"

"He said it's the solstice. The White Nights have begun up at Port Lyco. You might find your cats there. They say anything can happen during the White Nights."

"Sounds like our kind of place. Buy him a drink."

Tavi took out some coins and bought the man something awful-colored, while Daniel produced a map. "Where is this Port Lyco?"

There was an alien exchange, then Tavi said, "It's not on the map. Some things just aren't written."

Daniel slammed the map down on the counter. "Wonderful."

The man reached a pale Caucasian-ish arm across Tavi and pointed a hairy finger on the map at the northernmost tip of the bigger of the two northern continents. He grunted.

"Right there," said Tavi.

"Yeah, I guess," said Daniel. "Tavi, am I drunk or does that man have a tail?"

Tavi looked. "Yeah, that's a tail all right."

"Buy him another drink; maybe it'll go away."

Tavi did. The tail stayed right where it was.

"So what kinds of things happen at these White Nights?" Daniel asked.

Tavi relayed the question and the answer: "Some things just aren't said."

Daniel scowled drunkenly. "Are you sure you got that right, Tavi?"

"No, I'm not sure!" said Tavi.

Daniel got up. "Then let's go see for ourselves."

Port Lyco was glittering mosaic streets; it was white marble buildings with rose marble columns in spacious porticoes; it was painted minarets, exotic music, perfume scents, a midnight sun, azure sky and crystal waters.

Today is yesterday is tomorrow.

Anything can happen.

There was dancing in the streets, food, drink, bright costumes. "It's Mardi Gras," said Daniel.

The natives here were a different race than in the south. Their skin was white—truly white—their eyes violet with thick white brows and thick white lashes. There was a purple cast to their lips, the color some Earthwomen tinted theirs. Their ears were tipped with tufts of white fur. Their hair was actually more like fur, and it trailed from the head down the back like a horse's mane and ended in a little faun tail at the base of the spine. And for today (which was yesterday, which was tomorrow) none of them had a care in the world.

And Daniel decided to join them. He found a hangar in which to store *Laure*—Lyco was a busy port for not being on the map—and rented the best room in the city. It was high and airy, all glazed tiles and hand-polished, hand-carved wood, copper inlays and gold leaf. He stood out on the belvedere and watched far out on the sea the ships with pointed bows and painted sails. The waters were cold but clear, almost colorless, the palest blue.

It would have been night. The sky turned lapis on the southern horizon, but the sun still hung in the north at its nadir, dipping only so low, ready to rise again.

The whole city glistened below him, clean, polished, newly painted, from the minarets to the great shining plazas of checkered tile, to the railings on the balconies, to the many-colored streets themselves, as if the whole year had been spent in preparation for this festival.

Tavi strode into the room laughing. "Is this a room or a spaceship hangar?" He waved his arms at its sheer size.

Daniel turned and smiled, his teeth white against his face dark-tanned from Stranthm. "It's fantastic."

Tavi came to his side. He was carrying a white lilylike blossom.

"What have you got there?" Daniel asked.

"An eternity flower. They live forever, or until you pollinate them. The Itiri give them to their wives. They're very rare."

"Can I have it?"

"Sure, but I won't marry you."

Daniel took it. He had a sudden impulse to send something

102

home to Two Braids. He hoped she would like it and maybe forgive him for being an ass.

He refreshed himself, washing his face in a silver basin and taking a sleep pill instead of actually sleeping, and then skipped down the winding marble stairs with Tavi to join the party.

The port was teeming with merry humans and humanoids. There was a constant flux of people coming in and people going out. The ones leaving sent a chill through Daniel. "Did you see their eyes? Who are all those people leaving in such a big hurry?"

Tavi assailed a passing native for the answer. "Prisoners," he translated for Daniel. "They free the prisoners during the White Nights."

Daniel nodded, satisfied with the answer. "I'll just have to be careful in case there are any murderers running around loose." He remembered East had told him on his departure, "Take nothing for granted among aliens. They don't think like we do."

"Yeah," said Tavi. "Anything can happen."

As if proving the point, a native girl scented with spice and clad in a sheer tunic threw a lavender veil jingling with copper bangles around Daniel's neck and led him to a plaza to dance with her—rather, he stood and let her dance. She writhed and rubbed against him till he couldn't see straight, his cheeks aflame. In an effort to cool down he drank himself silly—on what, he didn't know; it wasn't whiskey. He staggered away from the plaza, leaning on the girl like a bacchant and maenad, weaving through someone's garden of exquisite flowers and fruit trees, where the breeze was cool and fresh-smelling. "Oh lord, carry me home." He dropped in a bed of green leafy vines and passed out.

He woke alone. He heard a woman just beyond the garden, screaming with outrage.

The noise stopped by the time Daniel had struggled up to rest on his elbows. Then Tavi was trotting through the garden and dropped to his knees at Daniel's side. "Did you know there are no laws during the White Nights? They were abusing that woman, and there's no law against it."

"That's awful," said Daniel.

"Well, there wasn't any law against punching out the guys that were doing it either."

Tavi's knuckles were bruised blue, skin unbroken but bloodied.

103

It was a relief in a way to know there was no law; Daniel had been afraid of breaking one inadvertently and becoming one of those wild-eyed prisoners.

He tried to shake his head clear. "What day is it?"

"This one. Yesterday is today is tomorrow."

"Oh yeah," Daniel remembered. He fell back in the ivy. "Drop me off at the tree, boys." His bladder was making demands, but Daniel could not get up.

"Don't pass out on me now," said Tavi. "There's a party starting in the North Square that I'm told is *the* party in Lyco."

"Tavi, I gotta sleep."

"Well, sleep fast."

Daniel envied his father's ability to go without sleep indefinitely, ever wakeful like a wind being. East had sometimes managed to fall asleep with Laure, but had been completely unable since Laure died.

Daniel sat up with a groan, brushing flower petals off his navy peajacket. "All right, help me up."

On the North Square, Daniel met a girl who spoke a little English, and he felt the need to do something he realized he hadn't done in a while. He looked at her and ached. He really wanted to lose himself with someone. Anyone.

"Love me?" he said.

"Tomorrow," she said.

Today is tomorrow is yesterday. Daniel guessed that was a yes.

It was.

Lyco was intoxicating. Days literally blended into one another. A person could forget what he was doing, and Daniel's mission was left suspended for a time. The festival, after all, was only a couple weeks. He supposed he could have set his transmitter working somewhere if he hadn't lost it on Stranthm, but he realized what a long shot that would have been—like setting down on Earth somewhere at random and speaking Maori or Basque and hoping there would be someone nearby who could understand. So Daniel did not concern himself with it, for today.

During the festival, the steady exodus of prisoners continued. Many of them were aliens; some were southerners. None looked like natives of Lyco.

Then Tavi made a discovery. "Dan-iel, there aren't any prisons in Lyco."

"So?"

"So, the prisoners that are leaving—what were they prisoners of?"

"Tavi, you're making me nervous."

"I'm making *me* nervous."

"Go lay someone," said Daniel.

"Can't," said Tavi.

"*You? Can't?*"

"It's those furry ears. I can't get past those furry ears. Besides, I don't know what the native women see in us anyway. The native men have such big . . . propagators."

Daniel smirked. Was that the best word a professional translator could come up with?

"I mean they're *this* big," Tavi indicated an unlikely size.

"Yeah, right."

"And you should see when they get it up!"

"Tavi, go propagate yourself!"

Daniel could not figure out what was wrong with him. But Daniel was asking himself the wrong question. It was what was wrong with *her*.

"Tavi," Daniel called after the Tyi as he was walking away. Tavi turned. "When exactly does the sun go down?"

"I don't know. A week or two after the solstice at this latitude." The sun had been circling lower and lower. They both looked at it, a huge red orb just above the northern horizon. "Pretty soon, I guess."

Czals knew his aide came bearing bad news when the slim blond youth stood stiffly and silently in the doorway rather than coming in and spilling his information all at once.

The tracker had lost Daniel East again.

The last record on Daniel dated from a week ago; it was a tab for whiskey and beer. He was still drinking those ghastly boilermakers. The boy would kill himself at that pace. That would solve a lot of problems. But it appeared that Daniel had his father's ungodly capacity for alcohol.

A bar tab. This is what I have to operate with.

Czals rubbed his temples with his fingertips. He was tired.

Primitive planets always presented gaping holes in the data flow. Jarsheno was a shadowy world with few computers, only slightly more advanced than Stranthm, and in some ways more barbaric.

Czals had sent a civilian-appearing chase ship to Daniel's last known position on Jarsheno in an attempt to locate Daniel while the tracker back on Earth was computer-blind, but his aide reported failure. Daniel could be anywhere on the

105

world, and attempts to question the natives met with the perennial Jarshen blackout: Some things just aren't said.

The boy could disappear forever on that half-charted rock and never be heard of again.

Dragonflies. Slight breeze through alien willow fronds. Alive?

Daniel hovered between waking and sleep. His eyes closed. Opened.

Dragonfly. A hunter on wings of gossamer hung above the reeds at the water's edge, then darted. Some living things looked the same everywhere one went.

Gurgle of a spring. Hum of insects. Trellised bridge over a pond of lilies. Tall soft grass.

Daniel shut his eyes and slept.

The dream began with a strange voice and strange sung music. Then the figures coalesced out of the gray void, all in shades of gray, black, and white—Niki and Mercedes, the dancers. She paused on toe, shimmered and trembled, fragile as a dragonfly wing. Niki danced as he had in the hologram recording.

Then it was Mercedes' ankle that was bad. She fell and died. Daniel wanted to cry out but had no strength.

Niki knelt by the fallen ballerina, head bowed. When he looked up again he had Laure's face, clear as life, more precise than Daniel had ever pictured her since her death, her wide teasing mouth, dark teasing eyes, high cheeks, firm feminine chinline, a straight and perfect nose, slender curved neck, white skin against dark hair unbound. She spoke with Niki's voice. She told him it was time to go.

He called to her. "Mother."

And he woke. He heard at the edge of his consciousness the final instant of his own voice as it ceased, and realized he had actually called aloud.

He got up, smelled crushed grass where he'd lain, parted the willow fronds that dangled in his face, and went to look for Tavi.

He found him nearby, asleep beneath the drooping branches of the water lilacs. "Tavi. Tavi." He shook the Tyi awake.

Tavi groaned, covered his eyes with his red hands. "What day is it?"

"Still the same one it was a week ago," said Daniel.

Tavi groaned, uncovered his eyes, and blinked them clear. "Tavi, let's go."

"The party's not over."

"I know. I don't want to be here when it is. I bet this place is horrible when the sun goes down."

Tavi looked about. It was dusk/dawn. This was the darkest part of the day, darker than it had been the day before, which had been darker than the day before that. It felt eerie, and he was aware of a sudden chill in the air. "I think you're right."

He reached for Daniel's hand and stood up.

They started to walk toward the hangar, then, inexplicably, broke into a run. Something felt very wrong.

"Where are our ships?" Daniel cried into the empty hangar.

An ancient balding native hobbled into the hangar from a rear door and looked surprised. He croaked in English, "You are too late."

A younger native appeared behind the first one. She spoke, and Tavi told Daniel what she had said: "The sun is still up. Give them their ships, old man."

The old Jarshen narrowed his eyes angrily at her, his tail switching like a cat's, then he snarled at Daniel, "I already put them away. You will have to wait."

"Wait until when?" said Daniel, but the old man did not have to answer. Daniel knew.

Until tomorrow. And, except during the White Nights when today is yesterday is tomorrow, tomorrow never came. Until tomorrow they were prisoners.

Of Lyco.

VI.

"This makes no sense!"

Take nothing for granted among aliens. They don't think like we do.

No one had warned him. Because some things just aren't said. Not even the freed prisoners had warned him. Because some things were impossible to be said. Didn't they have tongues? Didn't they have minds? Perhaps not. Daniel shivered in growing awareness. To balance the White Nights, there must be Black Days a half year from now at the winter solstice when the sun never rose. How black, Daniel had no intention of ever seeing.

He seized the old Jarshen with a savagery he did not know he possessed and roared in a new and powerful voice, *"Where is my ship?"*

The old man would not speak. The younger woman pointed through a door and down a long sloping ramp that led to underground chambers where could be heard sounds of machinery. *"Ta-o,"* she said.

"That way!" Tavi said, took a skipping step into a run, and bolted down the ramp, block heels clattering and echoing in the cavernous space.

Daniel threw the old man out of his way and raced after Tavi.

Down the ramp into the bowels of Port Lyco the sounds of machinery and screaming torn metal grew louder, till Daniel reached the lower level and crashed into Tavi, who had stopped dead before a moving conveyer belt loaded with ships and vehicles of every kind, all bound for a crusher. *Laure*—with Tavi's Polybios ship still riding—was on it.

Daniel ran past Tavi and alongside the moving belt to overtake *Laure*.

"Dan-iel, what are you doing!" Tavi cried and ran after him.

Daniel vaulted onto the conveyer belt, clear of the moving

parts below that could seize and tear him, and jumped inside his ship.

Tavi leaped after him, lost his balance on the conveyer belt, and grabbed tight to the edge of *Laure*'s hatchway to keep from falling. He steadied himself, heart racing, and glanced down at the big-toothed gears he had narrowly avoided, then to the crusher he was headed for now. He blanched and climbed aboard *Laure*.

"Dan-iel, you can't stay here, you'll be killed!"

The crusher flattened an aluminum airship as if it were paper. The jaws parted, passed the ruin through, and admitted the ship directly in front of *Laure*.

"I'm not staying here," said Daniel, starting the engines. The hatch snapped shut. Tavi was trapped inside with a mad Earthman, staring through the viewport at death. The massive jaws closed on the ship ahead of them. Tavi could hear the metal tear and scrape shrilly over the whine of *Laure*'s quickening primary engines. "We're taking off," said Daniel.

The crusher's jaws opened. The belt was starting to move again.

Tavi pounded on the sealed hatch. "Dan-iel, give it up. You can't fly a ship inside a building!"

"Who said?" Daniel was the son of a woman who had been known to fly a spaceship through a hangar roof.

And they were off.

Tavi dropped to the deck and covered his eyes as the ship lifted, heeled at an impossible angle, straightened, and rose. He could hear metal on metal, didn't know if it was their ships being torn apart, and he glanced up to see they were hurtling up the ramp, the ceiling very low, Jarshens leaping out to the sides, out of their path; then suddenly they were in sunlight—alive—even the rider ship still miraculously attached. The engines whined and the secondary system took over as *Laure* lurched into a steep climb that flattened Tavi to the deck, unable to get up had he wanted to. The angle steepened and *Laure*, barely clearing the tops of the minarets of Lyco, shot up like a rocket into the sky. "Hoo ha!"

Hoo ha? "Dan-iel, you're a wild man."

"Remember the Alamo."

"I should've listened to my mother," Tavi said weakly, clawing himself off the deck.

"What did she say?"

" 'I never met a Texan I liked.' "

Tavi peered over the console and out the viewport to the ground below. He shrieked and ducked back under the

109

console as Daniel drove the ship into a barrel roll—rider and all—on sighting the antiaircraft gun emplaced on the mountain rise just beyond Lyco.

"God help me, this planet is insane," Daniel muttered through clenched teeth, breaking out in a cold sweat as *Laure* lost stability in the roll—it was the rider's fault—regained it again, pulled out, and climbed.

His scanner registered a missile behind him. *What now?* He climbed.

No wonder Tavi hadn't been able to learn the language. These people did not think rationally.

Daniel looked back at the missile. *Culture shock in the extreme.* But he was outpacing it, the gap between them widening fast.

"*Aliens,*" Daniel said bitterly like a curse.

Tavi glared sourly at him from under the console and said in the same tone. "*Yeah.*"

The atmosphere thinned with increased altitude, and the missile fell off its trajectory.

Having exceeded escape velocity, *Laure* switched over to her space system. The fourth system would be hyperdrive, but Daniel was not leaving Jarshen space—not that he did not want to—so he left the ship in space mode. He relaxed his hands on the controls; his fingernails left crescent imprints in his palms.

He instructed the computer to doublecheck *Laure*'s adjustment system; he had become a bit tunnel-visioned for a moment or two during ascent, and Tavi had been plastered to the deck like a squashed bug. Still, for what he had put the ship through, it was a wonder she responded at all.

Tavi climbed into the seat beside him. "You've got a real talent for getting into trouble, Dan-iel."

East had always said that about Laure. "Yeah, I take after my mother," said Daniel.

"Her name wasn't Laure, was it?" said Tavi.

"Sure was."

Tavi was calming down, the sight of the stars through the viewport comforting. He could not believe he was still in one piece. "Do you believe a power inhabits a name?" Tavi asked.

Daniel glanced aside at him. "I'm beginning to," he said.

Daniel remained in orbit around the planet Jarsheno, his search there hardly begun. But it was difficult to know how to proceed when the answer to every question was "Some things just aren't said."

"Must be a religious stricture," said Tavi. "I've found as a general rule when people have practices that don't make sense, God is usually behind it."

"Huh?" said Daniel.

"Well, He gets the blame anyway," Tavi explained. "A lot of weird things are done in the name of religion."

Daniel nodded absently. He was staring through the viewport to the planet below. "Wish I had a bioscan," he muttered.

"Have one done," said Tavi.

Daniel turned to the Tyi, annoyed. "Are you nuts, Tavi? Do you know how much that *costs?*"

"Dan-iel, do you have any idea how much you are *worth?*"

Daniel's expression went slack, taken off guard. He was a LaFayette-Remington. He'd forgotten. It occurred to him that he didn't know exactly how much he was worth.

"Tavi, if you didn't have balls I'd kiss you," said Daniel, then changed his mind and kissed him anyway.

He broke orbit and went to the Earth station that revolved around Jarsheno's sun. He rang up a list of his assets on a UBC screen. The list went on forever. All the while Daniel kept repeating, "Oh my God. Oh my God," and finally shut the thing off. He never did see the end of it.

Compared to the list he had just seen, the exorbitant cost of a bioscan for a world seemed a paltry sum, so Daniel had no reservations about ordering a scan of Jarsheno—and of Stranthm and Warhi while he was at it.

Having done so, he sat back with a shot of whiskey and waited to see what turned up.

"Sir, we've picked up the track of Daniel East again," said the pale young aide.

Admiral Czals answered without looking at him, "Good. Still on Jarsheno?"

"Well, sir . . ." The aide hesitated. "He's at an Earth station in the Jarshen system. He's—he's just ordered a bioscan of the planet."

Czals was on his feet. "He *what?*"

"Yes, sir. And Stranthm and Warhi." The aide gave him the tracker's report.

Czals sank back into his seat. His envy knew no bounds. Even he, the Officer in Charge of Aeolian Affairs, hadn't access to those kinds of funds. The boy had virtually limitless

111

resources at his fingertips. He had rung up a list that was appalling. A *partial* list at that. The boy had begun to realize his own power.

Not good.

Czals wondered offhand if there was a way to confiscate Daniel's title and fortune. Czals had always thought of himself as an aristocrat who, by a caprice of Fate, had been born without a title. He really ought to have one—and LaFayette-Remington would do nicely. He certainly was more worthy of it than a boy who was only one quarter blueblood, half barbarian, and one quarter *creature*.

But enough of what ought to be. He chased the musings away for now. He had to make sure his chief scientist received copies of those bioscans. He would have a team of scientists pick the information apart while Czals waited, ready to act on the least evidence of Kistraalians before the boy could sift it out of the avalanche of data.

And now that Czals considered it, Daniel had just done the Service a great favor.

"Well damn!"

Tavi ducked and a harmonica went whizzing over his head. When Daniel was sad, he played his harmonica; when he was angry, he threw it.

Tavi guessed that after the interminable wait—several weeks it had been—the bioscans had not turned up any Kistraalians.

But Tavi was in no mood to care, too preoccupied with his own problems. "I'm so frustrated I could do it with an eggplant."

"Why not?" Daniel grumbled, stalking after his harmonica. "You've done it with everything else." He retrieved the harmonica and put it in his pocket.

"You don't understand," said Tavi, blushing. "Doing it as a male doesn't help the female part."

"So do it with a man," said Daniel. Any idiot could figure out that solution. But Tavi's cheeks turned so bright red that Daniel guessed that hadn't been such a good suggestion after all. "What exactly is your problem, anyway, Tavi?"

"It's the way we're put together," said Tavi, arms crossed, embarrassed and defensive. "You do it once as a female and the female part of you wakes up and wants to get pregnant. As females we're very guarded—you wait till you're married and have a secure situation for children, because if you do it once, your hormones don't let up and you're going to have to

112

keep doing it till you're pregnant and have a kid, then you settle down again. Noah warned me I should go home and get married. I don't want to be a female. It scares me. I mean I want to, but I don't dare." His eyes glistened. "I think I'm going to die."

"I can't help you," said Daniel, distracted.

"So who asked you, prick!" Tavi yelled savagely.

And Daniel suddenly realized that he *had* been asked—and had turned Tavi down. Tavi had retreated up to his own ship. Daniel threw his harmonica.

Well damn!

The scientist for once had good news. He was overflowing with it, and what he said almost made his syrupy singing-like voice bearable. "There is nothing in any of the bioscans to indicate the existence of Kistraalians beyond Kistraal/Aeolis."

Czals was reluctant to believe anything good. "Are you sure?"

"Yes, and our findings have been reinforced by a Bhaccaan analysis."

"Bhaccaan! Who involved the Bhaccaans in this?" *This was top-secret, dammit!*

"Daniel East," said the scientist. "Evidently he has a friend there, because he shipped the reports to her. The Bhaccaans as analysts are without peer."

"And?"

"And her answer is the same: No Kistraalians."

Good. Czals nodded, reassured. "Good."

"There is something else, sir."

Bad. "What is it?"

"I've been going over the boy's pattern of inquiry. He seems to be very interested in auroras." The scientist beamed.

"Which is supposed to tell me what?" Czals asked, feeling ignorant and furious at being made to feel ignorant.

"He's looking for wind. *Solar* wind. If auroras are manifestations of Kistraalians, then Kistraalians are made up of charged particles. Our weapon is based on the premise that the Kistraalians are matter, not energy. It's supposed to tell you that our weapon should work."

Should. Czals did not like *should.* "*Should* work, not *will* work?" he asked.

The scientist grinned. "You should have been a scientist, sir," he sang.

Don't make me gag.

The scientist continued. "I say *should* because the weapon has not been tested on a Kistraalian."

Czals frowned in thought. "You say you know what they are made of."

"Yes, sir. I believe we do now."

"Then build me an instrument that can detect them. Scan Aeolis with it to see if it works, then scan those seven planets Daniel East is interested in. Oh, and if the scanner does work, I want them left in place over Aeolis also." *I want to be able to see what we'll be shooting at.*

There were only two planets to go. Warhi was a primitive world; Crucis One was a modern Earth colony. Evidence on bioscans for both was negative, and Daniel's hopes were becoming very low. He chose Warhi to try next.

"This is where I get off," said Tavi, securing his ship to go his own way.

Daniel was startled. He had gotten used to Tavi. Like an extra arm, Tavi had been a pain in the side at first, then had become something very natural to have around till Daniel never thought of *not* having him around. "Why?" he said.

"Warhi," said Tavi. "It's not under treaty. They deal in my people like yours do in thoroughbred horses."

"They buy and sell you?" Daniel said, incredulous.

Tavi nodded.

"Who would pay good money for *you?*"

"We make pretty slaves and bedfellows."

"If you're strange, I suppose," said Daniel, not enthusiastic about the idea of hermaphrodism, no matter how attractive the Tyi were.

"Some things need not be permanent, Dan-iel," said Tavi.

"What do you mean?"

"Unwanted features can be removed; we provide the choices. It all depends on the gender, orientation, and mercy of one's owner. And with the Warhin level of medical technology, it wouldn't be fun."

"I think I'm going to throw up," said Daniel.

"I think I leave now," said Tavi.

Daniel stared at Tavi for a moment in silence, then spoke. "Dammit, Tavi."

"What?"

"I'll miss you."

Tavi shrugged. "Yeah, I guess you've been better than nothing—even with the harmonica."

Upon arriving on Warhi, Daniel hired a native translator, then approached the local ruler of the district in which he had landed to ask permission to move freely. The ruler was delighted to receive the alien lord and insisted Daniel stay under his roof. For all the tapestries, the guest chamber was still a cold cinderblock cubicle heated poorly with a sooty wood-burning contraption tended to by a pretty Tyi slave.

That evening, the ruler threw an unappetizing banquet of local delicacies at which to show off his new guest/status symbol Daniel. Daniel smiled weakly through it and spent the rest of the night burping, passing gas, and shivering.

The next day Daniel visited a wise man, showed him his carved jade snow cat, and asked the mahatma, through his translator, if he knew of one.

"Oh yes, yes, yes," the man said and nodded, smiling.

Daniel was stunned. *Yes?* He turned to his translator. "Are you sure he said yes?"

"Yes," said the translator.

"Where?" said Daniel, heart galloping despite the mind's efforts to restrain hope. "Can I see it?"

"Yes, yes, yes," said the mahatma and reached for the jade cat. Daniel handed it to him. The wise man turned it over and over. "Three day," he said. "Come back in three day."

Daniel nodded, smiling despite himself. "Three day."

In three days the mahatma produced the snow cat—a small jade creature identical to Daniel's in every way. It was a marvel in itself. Daniel was bitterly disappointed.

"Yes?" said the mahatma.

Daniel nodded, gave the man gifts—the translator warned that money would be unwise—and left with two jade snow cats.

He asked his host if he knew of any white cats.

The man nodded. "Oh yes, yes, yes. What is a cat?"

Daniel pressed his lips together into a straight line. *I think I see a pattern here.*

And he became more pessimistic with every yes, yes, yes.

Finally he asked his translator, "Is there any word for *no* here?"

"Yes," said the translator.

"What is it?"

The man smiled confusedly.

Out of the corner of his eye, Daniel caught the Tyi slave stoking the furnace, suppressing a grin. Daniel dismissed his translator, turned to the Tyi, and asked, "Do you speak American?"

"I can speak English," she (Daniel had decided this one was a she) said. She was a lot like Tavi—Daniel supposed all Tyi were—but she was taller, more feminine, and she had a breakable quality Tavi lacked.

"Do these people know how to say *no*?"

The Tyi smiled and chuckled compassionately. "You're just now finding that out, are you? No, there's no such thing as *no* here." Her smile turned bitter. "You can scream *no* bloody murder and it makes not a bloody bit of difference."

Daniel wondered what had given this Tyi reason to scream bloody murder.

He soon learned there were other things he could say besides no: "I would rather *this*," or "How about *that*?" Or he could change the subject completely: "What do you think of the gold standard?" And whenever he could, he avoided the Warhins' company. He did not like them. They were primitive and *barbaric*. He ate his meals alone, then didn't feel like eating at all. He wanted to get drunk but was afraid he was becoming—or already was—an alcoholic. Besides, he couldn't get the local brew past his nose. He wanted someone in bed with him, but he couldn't get the local women past his nose either. All Warhins were a bit gamy. His host offered him the Tyi slave, but that conjured up visions of Tavi hacked to pieces. He said he would rather sleep alone.

He woke disoriented one night, thought he heard humming, and became excited. "Tavi?" Then he remembered where he was. He looked up at the crudely painted ceiling.

Hello, God? This is your miracle here. Help me.

Tears welled in his eyes but did not fall.

Why have you abandoned me? Give me some hope, *dammit!*

He felt a breeze at his cheek. "Mom?"

The wind did not answer.

"Help me?"

Mornings were bitter cold. Daniel shivered under a scratchy blanket as the tall and limber Tyi slave squatted to tend the furance. She stood up, soot on her hands and smudged on her nose. She was pretty. "Is there anything else I can do for you?"

"Not unless you can tell me how low the Warhins' hearing range goes, no," Daniel said flatly.

"About sixteen hertz," said the slave.

116

Daniel reacted with a start. That was not the kind of information he would expect someone to have immediately on hand. His question had been facetious. "Are you serious?"

The Tyi smiled. "Perfectly. It is in the interest of a slave to know exactly what its master can and cannot hear."

Tyi had high ranges. Daniel imagined the supposedly silent night air was actually crammed with high-frequency messages between unhappy Tyi.

Sixteen hertz. That settled that; just as on Bhaccaa, had the winds been talking, someone would have noticed by now. Daniel was wasting his time here.

The speed of his departure rivaled even his exit from Port Lyco.

Out in space again he was still hounded by a feeling he could not pinpoint, a vague discomfort he thought he had left behind on Warhi. Not fear, he thought. But what?

"I'm OK. I'm a phase jump away from help if I need it. My ship is good. I'm well stocked . . . and I am talking to a harmonica."

He was aware of the limitless void around him, a lone boy in a lone ship in an infinity of space where light-years were reduced to insignificance like drops of rain in an ocean.

Tears tapped at his eyes once again. *Lonely. God, I am lonely.*

He went to sleep to blot out the lonely.

He woke late by ship's time, still lonely. He did not want to get out of the bed. He could not even bring himself to play his harmonica.

At last he dragged himself to his feet, sat himself at the computer console, and was staring forlornly out the viewport when—

Glob!

It looked strangely like peachbread.

The radio crackled. "Banzai, spaceboy!"

"Tavi!"

He was not registering on Daniel's scanner. Daniel leaned forward and looked up through the viewport—around the glob—and there was Tavi's Polybios craft right on top of him, inside his asteroid screen and close enough to sit on him. The Tyi had been waiting for him, drawing endless loops around the forbidden world.

"I thought you didn't like my harmonica," said Daniel.

"Yeah, well, I'm getting used to it. Let me dock."

Daniel was overjoyed to have him back aboard. But it did

117

not take long to see that all was not well with Tavi. At first Daniel thought he was sick. But no, that was not it.

Tavi was afraid to go home and hot as a bitch in heat. The little Tyi was totally wretched and ashamed.

Daniel was becoming uncomfortable and bothered—because he was reacting. Tavi seemed a girl beside him—small, slender, and soft-skinned.

That frame of mind lasted briefly. Daniel had called Tavi *he* too long. Daniel's father and grandfather would be aghast that he was even considering it. But if aliens did not mate with Earthlings, Daniel would not exist. Daniel knew why Mother had never told Father what she was. It would have been something that stuck in the mind; and if Daniel was having trouble now, East would have found it impossible.

However, it was not Tavi's difference that was jarring. It was his sameness. *Dammit, he's male.*

But in the end he decided what the hell. He had caught himself more than once wishing Tavi were female—*really* female. He liked Tavi. A lot.

Tavi had fallen immediately to sleep. Daniel was lying in Tavi's bed beside him, tired, absently running his hand over the Tyi's smooth skin, when Tavi awoke.

The Tyi opened his eyes, disturbed. Why did Daniel still have his hands on him? Tavi wanted to cover himself and go back to sleep. Why was Daniel still here? "Take your hands off me."

Daniel pulled back, surprised and affronted, then hurt.

Tavi wrapped himself up in the sheet like a mummy up to his nose and closed his eyes to sleep.

By now Daniel was angry. "What's wrong with you?"

Tavi opened his eyes. "What's wrong with *you?*"

Here was a difference they hadn't anticipated. Daniel couldn't even see the problem—only knew that it was Tavi's and not his own. He got up to go, then turned, deciding he was too angry and wanted to fight. He got it into his head that he had done Tavi a favor and was owed at least a warm body at his side the rest of the night. "I guess this is what happens when you give yourself to outerspace *creatures.*" He should have been like his father; there was a reason for prejudices.

Tavi's eyes above the sheet were wide and hurt. Daniel reached and tore the sheet away from him. Tavi shrank and skittered like a bug whose rock had just been lifted. "Daniel, are you crazy?" He wanted cover; he wanted to be alone and not to be touched.

"Are *you*? I've seen it already!"

Tavi blushed deep dark red. "Dan-iel, I don't understand you." He grabbed the sheet back and disappeared under it up to his wide coppery eyes. Daniel was pacing from side to side of the cabin in fury. He stopped. They stared at each other, and Daniel spoke in a thick voice with slight tremolo, pushing down hurt and anger, and making a resolution between friends, "We don't do this again. Ever."

Round eyes stared back over the sheet. Tavi nodded.

Daniel picked up his clothes, climbed naked and chilled back down to his own ship, to his own cabin, and hugged a cold pillow.

It was never brought up between them, as if it had never happened, except for a strangeness between them at first. Tavi blushed all the time when Daniel looked at him, and there was a lasting sense of bruised vulnerability about him as if Daniel had something of his that he wanted back.

Daniel for his part let it go quickly and turned his hopes and attention to the one planet left to be searched. Crucis One.

The *volaia* had to be there.

VII.

They were not.

Daniel almost expected it by now, his hopes drained slowly with the growing realization that there were many many variables he had not considered and that what his father had said was so true, "You've made a lot of assumptions." But none of that was enough to buffer the disappointment. He had been ignoring the most obvious possibility all along: If he felt this badly after nearly a year of search and failure, how would the *volaia* have felt after traveling fifty years to the closest yellow star only to find a dead world? Then another after more years? Then another? They could have died of despair.

Daniel had ignored that probability for no good reason—only because he wanted to. He wanted not to be the last one left. He and Niki.

He had wanted to return to Aeolis, summon the almost-god Niki, and say to him, "I have found your people."

He could not believe he had failed. Maybe he had skipped over Jarsheno too fast. Maybe he ought to go back to Haverin. Maybe, maybe, maybe, but no.

He gripped the sides of Tavi's jacket, his hands white, and just stood there, rigid, ready to cry. But he was too old to cry. He'd grown old looking for the *volaia*. He blinked rapidly, leaning forehead to forehead with Tavi, so close that Tavi had three eyes. He was breathing hard, trying not to think, because all he could think of was how disappointed and how alone he was.

"Tavi, I wanted to find them so bad."

This was it, the painful end to a long journey.

"What now?" said Tavi.

Daniel lifted his head. "I go home. I go back to school." He dropped his hands, took a shaky breath. "What do you do?"

"I go home and get married," Tavi said simply.

"Just like that?" said Daniel. "To who?"

"It's an arranged marriage. I left him at the altar, so to speak."

"Will he take you back after that?"

"Yeah. He's an idiot—he's in love with me."

Daniel was skeptical. "Are you sure this is going to work?"

"If I ever grow up and quit running away from him, it might."

Daniel had a forbidding thought. "This isn't the one who . . . ?" He couldn't say it.

"No, that was the one I ran away *with.*"

"Oh, Tavi."

"I know. I'm not too bright sometimes."

Daniel pushed his fists into the pockets of his peajacket. He shrugged. "I guess I'll see you home."

"Just take me back to Hell where you found me. I think I'm going to sell my ship there first."

Daniel shrugged. He set course for Hell and beamed a letter home to East.

> *Dear Father,*
> *I failed . . .*

> *. . . and I am coming home.*
> *Love, Daniel*

"How touching. 'Love, Daniel.' " Czals read the intercepted letter, gloating. "You, my boy, have just signed your own reprieve from the death sentence." The admiral was enormously pleased. Like Daniel, the Service had found no evidence of Kistraalians anywhere else than Kistraal/Aeolis. A nagging fear had been laid to rest with complete finality.

"There, you see what we've gained by not killing him?" he said to the scientist—he of the cyborg snakes.

Then Czals spoke at the letter. "Daniel, you've been a good little boy; now go home and let's see what we can do with all you've taught us."

There was a great benefit to be gleaned from what at first had seemed like disaster. The main thing the Service had learned from Daniel's expedition was that the Kistraalians were particulate—that the new weapon should be effective in eliminating those that remained. Also the scientist had men at work constructing a scanner that should detect the wind beings. That work could continue, but Czals halted construction of the weapon itself for now. He wanted the prototype tested first. He did not want to incur the expense of large-scale construction around Aeolis until he knew for cer-

121

tain it was going to work. There was no hurry now. The only Kistraalians that existed were on Aeolis; and those were not going anywhere.

The only other problem was the possible presence of a male humanoid Kistraalian still on Aeolis—the "madman" Daniel had mentioned in a letter to his father. Daniel had been so good as to inform Czals of that problem as well—albeit unwittingly.

But the remaining delays and problems shrank to minor dimensions in light of Daniel's defeated return home. Czals took the priority rating off the case. He would sleep well tonight.

Approaching Hell, Tavi was sitting at *Laure*'s computer console, monitoring the radio. "There's that signal again," he murmured. He meant the transmission from Planet K, intact after thousands of years.

Daniel stopped in midstride, turned, his eyes widening. He began to speak softly and ended in a crescendo. "How could I have been so *stupid!*"

"I don't know, Dan-iel. Exactly how stupid have you been?" said Tavi, turning in his seat, head cocked, one elbow on the console.

Daniel was excited. He could hardly speak coherently. "If you were a Kistraalian, where would you have diverted from your original plan of going from closest yellow star to closest yellow star?"

Tavi shrugged.

"Radio signals," said Daniel, ecstatic. "They would've followed the radio signals."

"I thought they heard low," said Tavi.

"As *people* they hear low. As winds they detect just about anything."

"All right, but would these radio signals have been here ten thousand years ago?" said Tavi.

"Yes!" Daniel cried joyfully. "Planet K is ancient. They were transmitting for millennia." He gazed out at the starfield in jubilation. Then his face changed and he blanched.

Planet K. A world that had destroyed itself thousands of years ago. Like Kistraal.

Oh my God, no. All joy drained from him—he physically felt it slip away—and was replaced by dull horror. "They're dead. They did it again!"

"Dan-iel—" Tavi reached for his arm, but Daniel backed away stiffly. *Oh God, no.*

"Dan-*iel*," Tavi called to him, insistent, as if he were far away, retreated deep inside himself.

Daniel was staring, zombie-like, slowly shaking his head to deny the abomination he saw as truth.

"Dan-iel, will you listen to me for a minute?" Tavi yelled at him.

Daniel would not. He was in shock. Tavi talked anyway. "How far is Planet K from Aeolis?"

Daniel wagged his head from side to side, hopelessly. He gave a weak, futile laugh and checked the computer record. "Eighty-five hundred light-years."

"And when did Planet K kamikaze?" said Tavi.

Daniel thought, blinked, started to laugh hysterically. He kissed Tavi on the mouth.

The Kistraalians, had they traveled as fast as they could, could not have arrived on Planet K before the world died. They would have arrived and found the planet already dead for at least five hundred years.

Daniel was smiling, laughing in relief. He looked at Tavi. "Kamikaze. Why did you pick that word?"

"Why not?"

"It means 'divine wind,' doesn't it?"

"You have the makings of a linguist," said Tavi.

"No, I don't," said Daniel. He turned hopeful brown eyes to the starfield. "So they came to a dead world. *Then* what did they do?"

Tavi grinned. "What makes me think we're not going to Hell?"

Daniel smiled at him. "You didn't want to get married anyway," he said and told the computer to set course for Planet K.

There was an Earth station orbiting Planet K. Earthlings had discovered the planet three hundred years ago, by following the same signal the Kistraalians would have followed. The space station was basically a hive of scientists who studied the dead world, tried to piece together the remnants of the old civilization and find out what had gone wrong. Daniel wanted to go down to the planet surface to see what the winds would have seen. If the winds had found evidence of life—even ruins of destroyed life—it would have given them hope to keep searching. Then Daniel would have to find what yellow star was closest to the K system.

But a station attendant talked him out of going down to the planet. "They nuked themselves. You don't want to go

123

near that place," said the attendant. Daniel could talk with this man without going through a translator because the man was a Yankee—though he objected to being called one. "I am *not* a Yankee!" he said indignantly.

Southerner, Daniel guessed. All Americans were Yankees to non-Americans like the Texan Daniel, but the southern Americans didn't like it. It had something to do with a war before the turn of the millennium, but Daniel hadn't gotten to that period of history in school yet.

"What's left down there?" Daniel asked the American. Along with Tavi, they both were leaning on a rail at an observation platform watching the planet below. Daniel fancied it was glowing.

"Nothing much." The man shrugged. "Nothing but some really big cockroaches."

"You should see 'em at home," Daniel said.

"Big ones, huh?"

"Are you kidding? In Texas we've got roaches big as Tavi's mouth," said Daniel, and his ribs discovered that Tyi had sharp elbows.

"Seriously, you want to know what's down there?" the southerner said. "Look in the library. They've got pictures of every inch of the planet. Or ask a bookend." He meant a scientist. "That's all they do here is look at that planet backwards and forwards."

"OK. Thanks," said Daniel and started away.

"Oh, yeah, and Tex?" The man detained him a moment. "If you haven't been warned, keep a man in your ship at all times—especially night cycle. Unmanned ships have a way of taking a walk."

"Hijack?" said Daniel.

"All the time."

"Poor security," Daniel muttered.

The southerner bristled. He had often heard that ignorant comment before. "Don't blame the security. You wait and see, Tex. This space has always been pirate-plagued, and they're the damnedest craftiest pirates you ever did see—or *didn't* see. They'll get past any guard—or if they don't, they *have* been known to leave good men and women dead behind them."

"All right, I've been warned," Daniel backed down.

But he stayed irritated at the incompetent security that made him assume their responsibility. Tavi was even more annoyed at being confined at night to his little Polybios rider ship.

Daniel law awake in *Laure*, fretting. Eventually he dozed off.

A voice in a dream spoke to him in ancient speech. It was a Kistraalian wind. It bid him *come*.

He woke with a start.

Daniel Lawrence East, you are an ass!

It came to him all at once. It was impossible for the *volaia* to have arrived at the K system earlier than fifteen hundred years ago, but there was nothing to say they could not have arrived *later* than that—say twelve hundred years later than that—and found not just a dead world but a space station in orbit.

Pirates!

What other kind of pirate could get past even the tightest security?

He was going to get out of bed when a sound made him freeze. The hair on his arms and up his back pricked up and his skin roughened with chill bumps.

He had not been dreaming. The voices were real and they were aboard his ship.

He caught the slurred words—in Kistraalian—"See you anyone?" spoken as a question.

He rose stealthily, hid beneath his cot, and tried not to breathe.

Tavi woke to his ship's collision alarm.

It had to be a malfunction. Collision was impossible—he was docked to Daniel's ship, which was securely docked to the space station.

Wasn't he?

He got up and saw the station looming large and close through his viewport. He'd been cast adrift.

He cut in the stabilizers, took manual control of his Polybois craft, and docked it to the station.

He disembarked, shaking, and cursing in every language he knew. *"Dan-iel!"*

A group of station workers and security people looked at the Tyi, puzzled.

"Where's Dan-iel? Where's *Laure*—the LaFayette ship?" Tavi demanded.

The puzzled stares dissolved into grim, tired understanding. They had seen such scenes before. "Not again," one woman said.

"What? What are you saying?" said Tavi, growing wary. "Where's Dan-iel?" He looked over the frustrated and sick-

125

hearted expression of the Earthlings. "You mean . . . ? Oh, no."

The ship *Laure* with Daniel aboard was gone.

Czals woke, disoriented. He was in bed, head propped up on a satin pillow. His reading light was on. It was night.

He had fallen asleep rereading the Melian Dialogue from the leatherbound copy of Thucydides' *Ton Polemon Ton Peloponnesion kai Athenaion* which he kept under his pillow. It lay open, face down, on his chest.

It was three in the morning. The phone was ringing.

He looked aside to where his wife would have lain if she hadn't divorced him.

He carefully closed his book, replaced it beneath his pillow, and answered the phone.

The hologram of the scientist materialized in Czals' bedroom. This was uncalled for. The man was distasteful enough to have present at work; he had no right to stand here between the Van Gogh and the Manet.

"What the hell!" said Czals in a graveled voice. This had damn well better be important.

"Perhaps reinstating the priority on young East is in order, sir," the scientist said silkily.

"What do you mean?" Czals got up, threw on a dressing gown, and smoothed his tousled hair.

"Daniel has disappeared."

Czals was already irritated and was becoming impatient. "What do you mean, 'disappeared'?" Daniel was on his way home. He would turn up in a few days. *He's in transit, for God's sake.*

"His name just showed up on the interstellar police's list of missing persons."

Czals was speechless. *Dammit, he was on his way home!*

"What are your orders, sir?"

Orders? "Find him, Goddammit!"

Daniel held his breath and listened to sounds of whispering, then sounds of bare feet running through his ship, of things dropping out of the air, of hatches closing, of engines starting, then of voices—human voices, not wind voices—calling to each other. He could not tell how many there were. Several.

From his hiding place he glimpsed one of them, one of his hijackers, as she ran past his cabin door. She was naked and she held a weapon—that was what he'd heard dropping. She

126

spoke a few words to a comrade, some of which Daniel recognized as Kistraalian.

I found them! He sensed danger from them. The girl he'd seen carried a weapon. They were pirates. They could kill him. They *had* killed.

This was not a boy's game anymore. It never had been. What had he gotten himself into?

He could feel the blood in his veins racing very fast. He was becoming intensely uncomfortable remaining motionless under the bed, neck cricked from holding his head off the deck. He had to show himself sometime.

But he could not talk to them. His slight knowledge of Kistraalian was no help at all, because these people were not speaking it as Daniel had learned it. After ten thousand years it was amazing that the language retained anything at all of its original form.

Daniel hoped they still called themselves *volaia*, because that was how he was going to address them.

He crawled out from under the cot and stepped into the corridor.

A naked little boy screamed, a woman shouted, and a man raised a beam weapon before Daniel could say a word and opened fire.

PART THREE: Kistraal Ab Seeba

I.

Daniel threw his arms up in front of his face on reflex as if to block a punch—for all the good that would do. He knew he was dead.

So why was he still breathing? He heard the beam weapon firing—still firing—and he lowered his hands from his eyes to see the frantic Kistraalian locking the trigger down with his fingers, his teeth gritted in disbelieving terror and sweating effort as the energy beam streamed out toward Daniel but did not reach him as if a force field had come between the gun and him.

Something had come between them. Something powerful.

The Kistraalian man stopped shooting, and all the others backed away from Daniel a few steps, frightened. Daniel just stared at them; they stared at Daniel. The man with the gun fired again till the air between them glowed white hot and took shape as a swirling, molten cloud.

A young girl pushed her way to the fore of the dumbfounded Kistraalians, put her hand on the shoulder of the man with the gun, and made him stop shooting. She looked at Daniel hard, then at the glowing space between that quickly faded as the heat dissipated into the surrounding air. She looked back to Daniel and demanded, "Who is that with you?"

Who is that with you?

Daniel stood mute a baffled moment, then he knew who was with him—had *been* with him from the beginning. A voice out of the heated air, a voice Daniel knew, bristling with anger, spoke in clear Kistraalian even Daniel had no trouble understanding. "Speak to *me* and answer you to *me.*"

And there materialized between Daniel and the Kistraalians the shape of a man, naked, sleek, and taller than the rest, as a god among mortals, still as a statue of a young athlete and as idealized, with eyes like a sphinx.

The Kistraalians knew him at once for their elder, and they began to shake.

Niki stood before them, angry and magnificent, with the physical power and sexuality of a stallion, the purity of an angel, the innocence of a boy, and knowledge of ten thousand years. He barked at the Kistralians, his voice like a whip cracking, "Lead us to your home and your Leader, *volaia.*"

They gaped at him as if beholding a burning bush, then made haste to comply, setting *Laure* on course to space uncharted by Earthlings.

Daniel stayed close to Niki, feeling alien and odd, conspicuous in all his clothing—a navy peajacket, denim shirt, blue-gray trousers, and low boots—while his ship was in the hands of naked strangers, of whose speech he understood one word in five.

Niki had taken a seat at the computer console in the control room. Daniel came and crouched beside his chair. He sat back on his heels, elbows on his knees, hands clasped, hiding his face behind long, red-streaked bangs. He asked in a shy whisper, "Where are we going?"

Niki lifted his beautiful head to gaze out the viewport, his lips parted, eyes far away. "Kistraal Ab Seeba," he said, slightly perplexed himself. "The World Within the Ships."

The Polybios craft came crashing out of a jump within Earth's horizon guard and blazed into the atmosphere high over Texas, leaving a rent in the sky that closed behind it with a thunderclap. The ship landed on the lawn of a little house that looked like so many other little houses on the Texas plain. While neighbors ran for cover and peered out their windows, a lean silver-haired man stood on the back porch of the house, beer in hand, wondering what this spaceship was doing in his backyard. Eyes in his hard, lined face were slits of startling blue, glittering with the hard brilliance of blue diamonds. He watched the ship's hatch open.

A copper-skinned, pixie-face alien came running out of the

130

ship and up to the porch, grabbed the man by his jacket, and cried, "Mr. East! I lost him!"

Some kind of nut. Had to be a friend of his. East took the little Tyi's shoulders between his big, gnarled hands and spoke deep, low, and calm, "Who? Who did you lose?"

The Tyi was tugging on East's sleeves and panting like a puppydog come running home for help for its master. "Daniel! I lost him!" Tavi cried.

"Dead?" said East.

"*Lost!*" Tavi wailed.

And moments later, before the police could arrive to investigate, a guerilla ship rose from its underground hangar and burned its way out of the atmosphere in an illegal exit, a Polybios rider on its back.

By the time Czals dressed, took a sleep pill, and reached his office, his aide had a report of a new development in the Daniel East case. "East, the boy's father, just made a panic exit from Earth and appears to be headed toward Daniel's last known location."

Can't be. No messages had been sent from Daniel to his father since Daniel's coming-home message. How could they have been in communication? *I don't like this.* Czals looked at his men gathered around him: his pale-blond aide, the tracker; handsome, calm, and competent Lieutenant Martin; and the abhorred scientist. "What was Daniel's last known location?"

"A space station, sir," said the tracker.

A station. What was he doing there? He was supposed to be on his way home! "Which?"

"K Station, sir."

"*That* one," Czals muttered. "Damned pirate-infested hole. We've lost more ships there than at any other five com—" Czals stopped mid-word and smacked his forehead with his palm heel. "That's it. He's made contact."

Lieutenant Martin spoke hesitantly. "Sir, doesn't it look like pirates took care of him for us?"

"Pirates my eye!" Czals thundered. " 'Pirates' have been stealing ships from K for the past three hundred years, and no one could ever figure out how they did it. They're *invisible,* that's how!"

The scientist was nodding. Czals hated nodders.

"And now they have Daniel East," said Czals. He rounded on the tracker. "Find him. Take all the men you need. Find him."

"And what of the elder East?" said the scientist expectantly. "He is on his way to K Station—hotfoot, as it were."

"Stop him," said Czals. He saw the scientist's eyes light up, thinking the order was directed to him. *No, not you, you turkey vulture.* Czals turned to Lieutenant Martin. "You."

Lieutenant Martin snapped to attention.

"See to it. Personally," said Czals. These things were best left to a military man.

"Kill him?" Martin asked uncertainly.

"That's what I said." Czals had wanted to kill *that* one a long time ago—for aesthetic reasons if nothing else. East inspired a personal revulsion in Czals. The man was an animal. Czals wondered what the highborn Laure LaFayette had ever seen in him.

"How, sir?" said Martin.

"I don't care, as long as it is not traceable to us," said Czals and dismissed him—then called in afterthought, "And no more cyborg snakes!"

II.

Tavi returned to K Station with East in search of Daniel, not sure what he expected East to be able to accomplish that the police could not. But Daniel had always spoken highly of his father and made it seem that East could do anything.

But East came up blank, and the two of them ended up getting blazingly drunk, destroying a bar, and passing out in a storage bin somewhere in the station.

Tavi woke up feeling dirty, his mouth tasting like glue. He was cold except on one side—that was the side next to East. At least East was who he'd passed out with. On a second thought Tavi opened his eyes to make sure it was in fact East.

It was. East's was a homely, aging face, but Tavi could feel a taut hard body against him through the rumpled clothes which smelled of tobacco. His breath smelled of whiskey. A scar cleft one black eyebrow, and above that was a fresh bruise from last night. His skin was paper-dry and warm, almost hot. He had one whipcord-muscled arm thrown across Tavi as if the Tyi were a dog or a pet. Tavi considered biting his leg to wake him up.

But East was not asleep. He had been awake for some time and was lying there, thinking. Feeling Tavi stir, he spoke without opening his eyes. "I just don't know where to look."

Tavi rubbed his throbbing temples, trying to concentrate. "Where would you go if you were a pirate?" he said.

"I *am* a pirate and I'm right here," said East.

"Are you really?" said Tavi.

"I've been called one," said East.

Tavi squirmed closer for warmth; it was cold in the storage bin. "Doesn't the UBC have any information on these particular pirates?" said Tavi.

The Earthman's eyes opened, blue fire. "It might," said East. "But everything on the K Station pirates has been restricted—very recently." The Service was suddenly extremely interested in an old problem—a development which looked

133

curious enough for East to suspect the answer to his questions might lie down that path. He tried to think if he knew anyone in the Service of sufficient rank to obtain restricted data.

"Got one possibility, kid," said East. "Someone I knew. She owes me a favor from way back." He unwound his arm from around Tavi and stood up in the storage bin. Tavi's side was cold.

"Meet me back at the ship," East said, climbed over the side of the bin, dropped down, landed lightly on his feet, agile as a big cat, and strode down the corridor.

Tavi sat up and shook his red and blond hair like a wet dog, then immediately regretted the action, his head ringing. Tavi was hungover. East had just gotten up and walked away, drunkenness rolling off his back like BBs off a rhino.

"I think I'm in love," Tavi mumbled, crawled unsteadily out of the bin, and staggered his way to a dispensary for a soberant.

He ate a breakfast of Earthling food—the only kind he could find at K Station—then returned to where his Polybios and East's guerrilla ship were docked. But he found only his own ship.

The guerrilla ship was gone.

Tavi clapped his small red hands over his mouth, but cried out despite himself, "Oh, no. I lost another one!"

Kistraal Ab Seeba at last came into view—first as a dull speck in the starfield, then, as *Laure* drew nearer, the place grew in dimension to its real scale, and Daniel could discern its form.

It was a caravan. Hundreds of ships of all sizes, modern and antique, were docked together, end to end to top to side, in any way they would fit, like a gargantuan chaotic maze for an enormous lab rat. Its sheer size was staggering, and it was rightfully titled a world.

The pirate Kistraalians docked *Laure* to one of the outer ships of the sprawling caravan, and she ceased to be Daniel's ship; she was part of Kistraal Ab Seeba now.

Daniel's first impressions on entering the World Within the Ships were the taste of stale air, uneven gravity, uneven lighting, labyrinthine corridors—and life. The place was alive with children, humans, and great cats—the *volaia*, their pelts glistening like new-fallen snow under a bright sun, their eyes blazing green, their tails lashing like angry serpents. And here too were the invisible Ancient Ones, the ten-thousand-year-old wind beings, refugees of the dead planet Kistraal. Daniel could hear their whispering voices, charged with astonishment and excitement of recognition, calling Niki by his ancient name, still remembering after ten thousand years.

The voices were happy, and so was Daniel. Yet something was troubling him, something wrong, something illogical, but he could not identify what it was just now, and he followed in silence as the *volaia* brought him and Niki before their Leader.

They had come to a dimly lit chamber that was hot and oxygen-rich, where gravity's pull was not so great. The grand matriarch of the caste *volaia* was enthroned at the far end, laden with pirate gold and heavily robed against death's chill.

A bone-white, skeletal hand beckoned the newcomers to her, and Daniel almost turned around and fled when he drew near enough to see her clearly—a shriveled corpse of a woman with black eyes sunk deep in the sockets of a skull face, browless, lashless, her mouth a lipless straight line. A few white wisps of hair like milkweed down hung from the sides of her almost bald head, and when she opened her mouth it could be seen she had few teeth.

Niki walked straight up to her, undaunted, and she reached out an arthritic hand as if to touch his face, but she did not. She trembled and pronounced a name that was legend: "Ni-kiate."

The name echoed on winds throughout the World.

"You are so beautiful," said the living corpse, a wistful girlish note in her reedy voice. "You danced before the world ended. I can still see you dance." And she shed tears.

Daniel was astounded by how her face had changed in that moment. She was not horrible at all. She seemed to him now the Pietà, tearful Madonna, gentle and in no way ugly.

Then she looked at Daniel, and the Madonna was abruptly gone. A face out of a nightmare, malevolent sunken eyes glittering from their depths; here was a Harpy, and Daniel thought she was going to eat him alive.

"An Earthling," she said in anger. "Bring you to me an Earthling?"

A bodiless wind answered her. "He hears our voices. Earthlings hear not our voices."

"This is truth," Leader conceded. Her baleful eyes returned to Daniel, and she spoke. "Then what are you?"

Daniel stammered in broken Kistraalian, "My father is Earthman. My mother born on Aeolis of Earthwoman and Kistraalian man. My caste is *laitine*."

135

"What is Aeolis?" said Leader.

Daniel froze up inside as he suddenly realized what had been bothering him.

Why would the *volaia* be traveling in a wandering caravan of pirated ships when they had a home to go back to? But the last time any of them had seen their homeworld was ten thousand years ago, and it had been a dead and deadly wasteland.

And they had never learned that Kistraal had been restored into a living place called Aeolis.

Oh my God, they don't know! They have no idea!

The nightmare was waiting.

Daniel shook his head in refusal. "No." He could not tell her.

But Niki was there. "Aeolis," said Niki, "Is Kistraal."

And pandemonium broke loose.

III.

The whole World was in uproar. The air crackled and resounded as the report spread from ship to ship—someone had been *born* on Kistraal—until Niki bid them be still, and the World Within the Ships fell silent. Not a breeze whispered. And Niki quietly told them how it came to pass that Kistraal now lived again.

Of course they all wanted to go home. The only problem was that Earthlings lived there.

Daniel was horrified. *What have I done?*

But that did not seem to bother the *volaia.*

"Now I can die," Leader said. "I have a home for my children."

Those of her caste immediately clustered around her. One took her hand. "Do you not want to see it, Mother?"

"No. It will be not like I remember it. What did he call it? Aeolis? The new Kistraal is for those who have never seen it. To see it made alien would break my heart. There is only one thing I require and I will die happy."

"Anything, Mother."

"It is not for you to grant." She waved her children aside and looked past them, her corpse face turned serenely beautiful. "Nikiate, of all things of Kistraal unchanged, will you dance?"

Abandoned at K Station, Tavi was frantically looking for help. He ran up to a dock attendant and grabbed her, crying, "Where's East?"

The attendant looked down curiously at the little Tyi who was tugging on her sleeves. "Who?" she said.

"Silver-haired Earthman. This tall," Tavi said quickly and reached high over his own head. "Came in a guerrilla fighter. Where is he?"

"Oh yeah," she remembered and broke into a smile. She took off her cap and ran fingers through short sweaty curls. "You just missed it. The police came and took him away. It was one hell of a fight. Jeez, that man is quick." She shook her head appreciatively and fit her cap back on.

"*What?*" Tavi cried. "For what? Where did they take him?"

The attendant shrugged. "I don't know the charge, but he's been extradited to Chautaikier."

Tavi's face went white. "Oh no."

"Yeah." She nodded to Tavi's misgivings. "If he can't prove his innocence, you can kiss him goodbye."

Guilty, of course.

East had been arrested, convicted, and sentenced before he could realize that it was for something he had not done. He'd done a lot of things in his life, but this was not one of them. *This.* He was not even sure what he had supposedly done, but he knew he hadn't done it because he had never gone near the scene of the crime, which was on Chautaikier. East had never been anywhere on the planet Chautaikier.

So here he was, receiving punishment. They had put him here in their Labyrinth, a structure as infamous as the old Earth invention of Daedalus. Only there was no Minotaur in this one, just kilometers of glass and mirrored corridors, and God-rest-your-soul-if-you-don't-find-the-exit-before you-need-a-drink-of-water.

East had to find his son. That was the only thing bothering him. Death itself held no terror for him. He was not dragging his heels to join Laure.

Thirst seemed a horrible way to kill a man. But it was a bloodless execution—trial by the gods, it was called, in case Man made a mistake, for there *was* an exit somewhere in this vast tangle of corridors, and if by some miracle the victim found his way out, it was interpreted as divine acquittal and he was set free.

East jammed his fists into his trouser pockets and considered how to proceed. He saw his reflection in one of the mirrored panels (or was it a reflection of a reflection?), and he frowned at his own image. An unshaven face that should have broken all the mirrors, a tall lean frame in rumpled clothing, fierce blue eyes glittering back at him—all in all it was the image of a junkyard dog. He wondered who had arranged to put him in here. He had as many enemies as he had friends.

He turned from the reflection.

Through the clear glass wall nearest him he could see the exit with a guard posted at the door. It seemed if he just rounded the corner he would be free. He tried it and came upon another transparent barrier.

He was not surprised. It had looked too easy.

He returned to where he had begun. The exit mocked him through the glass. So close, so far. One inch separated him from freedom. He wondered how many convoluted passages he would have to go through just to reach the other side of this pane.

He cocked in his leg and lashed out at the glass with a powerful kick that carried all his weight behind it.

It gained him nothing but a suppressed smirk from the guard on the other side.

East leaned against the clear wall and wondered what it was really made of; it only *looked* like glass. It bounced like something else, so there was no use hammering kicks at it. It was not going to break.

He looked up. He had been dropped into the Labyrinth through a trap in the ceiling. It was high up and unpromising, but still it would not do to overlook possibilities. He sprang up and struck at the trap door with the bottom of his fists. The trap did not budge, sealed tight.

The gods probably would not acquit him if he escaped that way anyway.

He again leaned against the glasslike wall that barred him from the exit.

Logic dictated that since he knew this wall connected to the outside, all he needed to do was follow this wall and eventually it would take him to the exit on the other side. Logic also said that logic would let him die of thirst before he made it. More logical men than he had been put in here and never come out.

So much for logic. He switched over to predator instinct.

He smelled death here. Right here. Removed death. He saw countless victims spending the rest of their lives here, beating themselves against this wall like flies against a closed window, trying to get out and unable to pull themselves away from daylight to do it.

East's father had told him once that there would come a time when he would have to walk away from what he wanted most. So he had from Laure once. It was time to go back to her.

He turned away from the exit and murmured one regret. "Son, it looks like you're on your own now."

There was a corridor leading straight back with passages and false passages leading off to both sides all along the way.

139

East could not tell where any of them led—probably nowhere—but he was not going to die like a fly on a window. He was going to take a walk.

He picked a direction—straight back—abandoned hope and logic, and started out with a light heart. "Laure, it's you and me, babe."

Admiral Czals paused to inspect his reflection in a mirror. His muscles were due for retoning. To exercise and sweat never occurred to him. He wanted to *look* athletic. *Being* athletic was vulgar. He also would have to have his teeth tinted again soon. His cigarette holder kept his hands clean, but not his perfect, costly teeth. He touched the hair framing his carefully sculpted aristocratic face. He considered having the white blaze at his temples taken out. He had an aversion to silver after seeing pictures of East with his lupine silver mane.

But East was gone for good, so Czals decided not to be influenced by him. Czals had commended Lieutenant Martin on his disposal of the mercenary. *Leave it to a military man,* he thought with satisfaction. *Scientists do away with aristocrats with cyborg snakes.* But this was perfect—crime and sentence. It had the ring of veracity, and it was so *likely.* No one was ever sure which side of the law East had actually operated on. And the sentence left no blood on anyone's hands. It all appealed to Czals' sense of proportion.

With East out of the way, Czals was still left with the puzzle of how East had known to go to K Station to find his son when no message had passed between them. They had to be in contact somehow. Czals had an idea and was pouring over the tracker's records, till at last the answer appeared, so glaringly obvious he could not understand why he hadn't noticed it before, repeated port after port: LaFayette 0600 *Laure*—

—and rider
—and rider
—and rider.

Daniel had not started out from Earth with the rider, and it was not reported missing with him. So where was it?

Gone back to Earth to fetch East, that's where!

Czals glanced over the records again, wondering how he could have missed what was so clear. Daniel seemed to eat a lot for a single person—even for a teenage boy—and there were many bar tabs for beer and whiskey. Czals smiled in amusement. So the boy hadn't been drinking boilermakers after all; he had a companion. Who had Daniel been traveling with?

Whoever it was, he was trying very hard to stay off the computer record. He was a sly one, but not infallible. Czals went through the records and circled all the evidence for Daniel's unseen companion, then he pushed the records at Lieutenant Martin. "I want an ID on this rider. I want to know where he, she, or it is as soon as possible."

IV.

Daniel lost all sense of time aboard the caravan, but it must have been several days that passed before Niki was ready to dance. Then all the *volaia*, disembodied winds and humans alike, crowded into an immense darkened gutted freighter which they used as an assembly hall, leaving clear only a lit space into which Niki walked; and Daniel was impressed all over again by how beautiful the man was. He wore nothing. His head was bowed, his neck curved to one side. His strong body tapered down from shoulders that were not so broad as to lack proportion to a narrow waist and flat, hard abdomen. Buttocks and thighs were taut, without excess flesh. The muscles of his legs were sharp and defined and fluid as molten steel.

This dance would be very old.

An expectant electricity charged the air in the great hall. Daniel found himself holding his breath in anticipation, his own feelings sucked in and swept along with the rush of emotions of those surrounding him; and a shared excitement set his skin tingling as the music began.

Niki lifted his head with the sound of the ancient beat, sphinx awakening, and, with him, old ghosts and old memories were resurrected. He started with slow steps, as if remembering—or conjuring a memory for others. His eyes were shining as if tearful. Niki would have been a very young man when his planet died, and suddenly Daniel realized that this was it—this was the dance at the end of the world.

Leader and the ancient winds were weeping. Here was what they had seen on the eve of their world's destruction, now on the eve of their return.

Daniel felt, as if possessed, a trauma that was not his own. He had become part of a group entity. Everyone in the hall, even the young, whether they had seen the dance before or not, whether they had seen the world end or not, they *knew* as if by race memory, and all experienced the same. All were held spellbound, unable to look away from the painful and heartbreakingly beautiful dance, feeling horror, joy, and, in the end, triumph. Niki raked them through an ancient fire, and they were astonished and jubilant to find themselves still alive, their survival, their very selves confirmed in the dance. The holocaust was truly over. They were going home. And the dance became an exultation of life, of self; and just to watch it felt like flying.

Then came a moment so ecstatic, so perfect, as if all light in the universe converged into a single point, that there was simply nothing to follow. Niki whirled, reached, and in an instant all sound, all movement ceased.

There was a breathspan's shocked hush in the hall, then everyone broke into thunder, and the shrieking ovation went on forever.

While all around him the *volaia* were cheering, leaping, screaming, laughing, and crying, Niki was frozen still, his eyes glassy, staring, and it was awesome to see someone with so much control overwhelmed.

Then he threw his head back, rolled forward onto the balls of his feet as his legs buckled under him, and he sank down onto his knees. Someone started toward him as if to catch him, but Daniel cried out in Kistraalian, *"Do not touch him!"*

Niki's arms were crossed, fists on opposing shoulders, sweat or tears streaming down his face.

He disappeared.

A day passed—what Daniel approximated to be a day—without sign of Niki. Daniel was very much alone. The kinship he'd felt during the dance had dissolved, and he was an alien among the *volaia* once more.

Leader was dying. Daniel knew when she at last was dead; the cats' weird yowling echoed throughout the caravan in mourning song.

The new Leader announced that the old Leader would be given a funeral in the manner of the Ancients—she would be laid to rest in her native soil.

Daniel was going to ask where they thought they were going to acquire the land for a burial. They did not know what they were up against. He tried to warn them of the danger. "Earthlings live on Kistraal. They will shoot you. They will not go because you come." He was having difficulty making himself understood. They did not seem to realize the hazard—or want to. There had to be some way to get through to them.

Niki, dammit, where are you?

Niki Thea was born of a virgin back when the world was still Kistraal and Earth was populated with men first chipping stones into a cutting edge. The woman who was his mother was human, just a human, with one life, like an Earthling, like everyone else on Kistraal at the time. She wanted a child but did not want to go through what it would take to conceive one naturally. So she volunteered for an experiment.

Being a prototype, there was no guarantee of exactly what the child would be like, but the woman did not care so long as she could keep it and she did not have to touch a man.

So an altered embryo was placed in her womb, and in time the baby was born.

The baby had two human forms identical and independent of each other, and he kept switching from one to the other, not knowing what he was doing.

Then after four years the child discovered he had a third form, his wind form, and he became very contrary, impossible to control, and his mother indulged his every whim or he would disappear.

Thirteen years after the boy's birth his mother discovered men. He walked in and found her with one, doing what she had always painted as the greatest of horrors.

He ran away and never went back. He heard his mother screaming his name as he fled, but he had since forgotten it.

In fact he did not remember his mother at all.

For years he did not count he was a nomadic ungovernable monster. There were no restraints on a being who could turn to wind at will—not when almost everyone around him was a mere single-lived human. He was prototype for a kind of being that did not yet exist in great numbers, so there was no one to hold him. He would throw tantrums, turn to wind, and wreak vengeance on those who tried to punish him.

Somewhere along the way he learned to dance. He was in love with music, and the dance hypnotized him. It was the only endeavor in which he would brook correction—he wanted to be good—until he was better than his teachers, better than anyone around him, and he had no more use for them and they could no longer stand him. He threw one raging fit after another. His physical forms had come of an age when they now terrified him. Irrational feelings and drives tormented him till the chaos within was such that if he stayed human he would go mad. He turned to wind and remained in that form for a long long time.

He stayed away from people; they only confused him. He

144

existed as a wild wind, in constant thought—his thoughts running clearer without his human prison to drag them down and muddy them. Still he sensed a void. He wanted to incarnate again but he would not *let* himself. He who had always defied restrictions felt the need to impose them now, he did not know why. He spent a lot of time thinking about it.

Then he saw his master.

He had ventured among the company of humans as a furtive wind to see a dancer—a man, tall and hard, with total command of his body that was the human form in its perfect glory. Here was a beauty and power the boy had never imagined, and at last he knew what he wanted. He wanted to be like that.

After the performance he materialized out of the air before the dancer. "Teach me to dance."

The dancer knew what this was—one of those new manmade creatures which possessed three lives. He had heard of them. And here now one appeared out of nowhere and asked to be taught to dance. Demanded, rather; the boy had not actually asked.

The dancer considered the male child before him; a pretty creature just stepping out of boyhood, he was going to be a lovely adolescent, with strong limbs and graceful form and a face that made the older man melt from his waist to his knees. The dancer knew this boy would destroy him—and he welcomed his destruction. He could not stop looking at him. "How old are you?"

"I do not know." The manchild had the bearing of someone who had lived awhile and the intense gaze of one who had seen many many things. He was very old, almost mad— or maybe he actually *was* mad. Yet he was like a newborn in ways.

"Do your parents know you have come to me?" said the dancer.

"They are dead." He did not know that. He had killed them in his mind. He did not remember that he did not have two.

The boy barely spoke the language. He had an archaic tongue in his head and was naive about manners and new things, as if he'd just been born out of the wind, an exotic, beautiful, and rare creature.

The dancer took him under his not quite paternal wing.

It began badly. The boy would not let himself be touched—by anyone. His temper was quick and he changed to wind at the least provocation. Finally the master lost his

145

patience. He seized the boy's wrist and laid down a mandate. "You will do whatever I bid you or you will get out of my sight forever."

The first rule was that there would be no more turning to wind; the boy was to live as a human being. Second, if he was to be taught to dance he must allow himself to be touched, like it or not. This was not from desire but from necessity. The boy obeyed.

The day of betrayal came much later when he was physically sixteen and a beautiful boy-man. In a small room that was his, lying on a bed, with no clothes on, he let the pain and tension be massaged from his aching muscles after a lesson. He was nearly asleep. When massage turned to caress the boy was slow to comprehend. He was, by now, accustomed to being touched by this man and never suspected deceit. The man's kisses startled him, and his tongue sliding into his mouth stirred something horrid in his memory—feelings of an event forgotten, a wave of revulsion, memory of horror—and of flight.

He thrust the man away with his foot, got up, and ran into the wind.

He heard the man calling after him the name he currently went by, the one the man had given him. Despite his best efforts he still remembered it.

The first thing he did on reincarnating was spit.

He stayed alone now, as wind or as a human, and he danced. Only the constant self-drill, the dance, and the music in his mind kept him on the near side of sanity.

Then one day he was ready. In physical form he was a fully grown young man. He returned as wind to the place where he had learned to dance. There he saw a broken, aged mortal haunting the back hallways like a crippled ghost.

The boy now grown appeared before the old man and said curiously, "Are you he?"

The old dancer fell to his knees before him and started to cry. He called his prodigy by his old name.

"No. I am someone else now," he said. He called himself Nikiate.

The man was sobbing. He wanted nothing but to look upon the beautiful immortal, a dream materialized in a shaft of light here under the archway.

Nikiate vanished; the light remained. The man cried.

So that was old age.

When the man was dead, Nikiate danced in public for the

146

first time. He was an instant sensation, a young genius sprung full flower out of nowhere.

Then the wars came. The last moments Nikiate was to spend as a human for centuries on end he was running across a mall between fountains with his leading lady, bombs raining out of the sky, exploding all around them. He disappeared. The girl was only human, and she was hit.

The world ended shortly after. Everything organic was destroyed. Only Nikiate and the other winds—the creatures for which he was prototype—survived.

In the ten thousand years of void that followed he came to know the other winds, a brotherhood of survivors. They already knew him. Everyone knew Nikiate.

They talked (if their sounds could be called talking) about what they missed most of being human. Nikiate missed the dance. For others it was physical love. They tried to tell Nikiate that it was not awful. He remained unconvinced.

Then the Earthlings came, and the world lived again as a place called Aeolis. A new name for a new time; Nikiate became Niki Thea and passed among the Earthlings as one of them. His friends among the winds who knew more about computers than he placed his identity in the Universal Bank Computer and gave him ownership of an estate on Aeolis, and the winds dwelled there.

He danced for the Earthlings and became once again a legend overnight.

He met a ballerina. She was light and airy as rising mist in sunlight. Her name was Mercedes. She was only a mortal, a beautiful mayfly, and just once Niki felt a flicker of human love and knew it for something that might kill him. Mercedes had touched him, and it was not dreadful—a touch so gentle and childlike it could not be evil—and he thought that—maybe—someday he might try it—

—maybe once—

—maybe not.

He left her. He had to live. He had to dance.

Until now. Here in a world within ships he had hit his highest. From here he could get no higher, no better. He had touched the sky, where one can stay only a moment, then decline. This was the moment of arrival, the moment of his life, the pinnacle of ten thousand years. Perfection. Where could he go from here? There was nowhere. Everything was here.

Till now he had never questioned the purpose of life, never questioned that to create of the spirit, which was immortal, was preferable to creation of the body, which was mortal.

The body dies. He had never considered that choice. He would dance and live forever. He had always felt special. But one's best only lasted a moment, and now he wondered if he had been cheated.

He thought of the mayfly he loved. Mercedes.

The huge caravan of Kistraal Ab Seeba prepared to mobilize. Daniel was amazed to find that the *volaia* had this great mishmash of ships all figured out so they could actually move the hulking mass in whatever direction they wanted to go.

In one ship Old Leader's body lay wrapped in white funeral cloth—it made such a tiny bundle on the big bed—and one by one all the Kistraalians filed past her in farewell. One of them nudged Daniel as he came by in turn. "Give her something."

"Huh?"

"She is going on her final journey."

A grave gift. Daniel guessed since he would not be there for her burial he was to give her something now. "What shall I give?"

"Something of yours," said the Kistraalian.

There were any number of costly things the lord LaFayette-Remington might give. But something of *his.* . . . He pulled his harmonica out of his pocket. "It is a . . . it makes music," said Daniel.

The Kistraalian made a motion of approval. "She loved music."

Daniel placed it beside the body. "Never stir," he said.

He returned to his own ship and prepared to detach her from the caravan. He became aware that someone in wind form was in the ship with him. He warned in pidgin Kistraalian, "I not going to Kistraal. You get out now or you end up on wrong planet."

The wind answered in whispered flawless American, "Take me to Earth."

Niki. *So there you are.* "As you wish," said Daniel. His ship detached, and Daniel set a fast course for Earth and home.

He needed his father desperately.

V.

East had come to the profound conclusion several kilometers back that there was only so long a man could go before he had to piss. He knew most of a human being's water was lost that way—and East had never sweated much—but there was no holding on to it. So he continued walking down the corridor a few cc's more dehydrated than he was before. It was a long corridor. East had not turned once since he'd started, though there were passages off to every side. If he kept on straight he did not have to come face to face with himself in any of those damned mirrors that lurked at every crook of every passage; his face was not something to be looked at by this time. He had also become possessed of a perverse need to find the end of this wretchedly long corridor. There would be a mirror there, no doubt, and he was going to bash it in if it was the last thing he did.

He knew it probably would be.

Daniel came home, poked his head in the front entrance, and called in, "Dad?"

He walked inside. The house was empty, *felt* empty.

Disappointment sat dully in Daniel's stomach. After such a long absence he had looked forward to a crushing welcome-home hug and a familiar voice. He'd stopped at K Station en route home in faint hope that Tavi would still be there, but Tavi was gone. There was no tracing that one. Only God would know where Tavi was—and then only if He was very lucky. Tavi was good at hiding.

But where could East be?

Daniel went from room to room. "Dad? . . . Dad?"

For no reason he felt dread.

"Dad?"

He went to his father's computer terminal to see if it could tell him where its master was.

He asked; it answered.

149

Daniel fell to his knees, face in his hands. The computer told Daniel his father was dead.

Niki had come to Earth in search of Mercedes. He tried the resident theater of the company he had first stolen her away from, and, sure enough, her name, Stokolska, stood large on the marquee. So she was still dancing after twenty years.

The wind Niki swept inside the theater, wondering how much she had changed.

She hadn't aged a day.

On the stage, practicing alone in the big theater, she looked the same as he remembered her, with luminous eyes and long dark hair and plain/beautiful face; she was slender, almost skinny, swan-light, weightless, ethereal, a sylph dancing on air, more graceful, lighter, and younger than ever.

Time had stood still for the mayfly he loved.

She had waited! She had told time to stop and she'd waited for him. It was miraculous.

He reincarnated, and tears welled in eyes foreign to them.

"Mercedes!"

She whirled and saw him, a naked man in the wings, and she shrank away, frightened, a white flower dropping from her tiara.

Niki stepped into the light of the stage. "Mercedes."

The girl was wide-eyed. "M-my name is M-Marya."

Dull horror crept around him, and jealous time leered at him with the face of a terrified young girl. Time had not been gracious but laughed at a treacherous joke. He knew this story. Time had cast him in the role of a fantasy creature—Peter Pan, was it?

"M-Mercedes was m-my m-mother."

Niki choked on his own voice. "Where is Mercedes?"

The girl backed away. "She died . . . a long time ago. . . ."

"Admiral Czals?"

Czals looked up from his desk. It was the scientist. "What is it?"

"There's a Kistraalian in my laboratory."

Czals was on his feet in an instant. "How did you catch it?" he demanded, escorting the scientist back out the door.

The scientist answered as they made their way back down to the lab. "I didn't. It—he—I think it's a he—came out of thin air. Well, actually he's still *in* thin air. He started talking at me through my radio—he's in the radio—the radio is not on. He speaks English better than I do and *he's volunteering to test the device.*"

"The weapon?" Czals was astounded. "Does he know what he's getting into?"

"I don't know how much he knows. I don't know how he got here or how long he's been here." He opened the door to the lab for the admiral.

"Admiral Czals, I presume," said the radio.

Smartass. "Yes," said Czals. "And whom am I addressing?"

"Never mind. Get on with your experiment," said the radio.

If you insist. Czals nodded to the scientist to proceed, then crossed his arms and tried to quell his anticipation.

The scientist opened the door to a metal chamber and spoke toward the radio. "If you will step—er—move inside here, please. I know it looks dreadful, but there is only a slight risk, and the benefit will be very great."

"I know what your machine is supposed to do," said the radio. "And you are correct—the risk is very slight."

Czals hid a smile behind one aristocratic hand. He liked the creature's attitude. The scientist did not.

There was a rush of air going into the chamber. The scientist closed the door and sealed it, then turned on the scanner. The scanner was a newly constructed instrument based on a theory and, like the weapon, never tested.

"Does it register?" said Czals, nearly tripping over his own heart in anxious curiosity.

"Yes," said the scientist triumphantly. "He's in there." An amorphous gray haze had appeared on the test monitor. "We're in business, sir. If the scanner works, the weapon can't fail. They're based on the same principle."

"Prove it," said Czals. "Kill him."

The scientist activated the weapon in the chamber. There was a low hum, then the device turned itself off after a five-second exposure. That was all.

"Well?" said Czals.

The gray haze was gone from the monitor. "Zero reading on the scanner," said the scientist, checking the instrumentation, not trusting the visual monitor or his own eyes. He moved to the chamber and opened it. There was not a whisper, not a breath of wind.

Czals spoke, "It works?"

The scientist nodded. "It works."

"Very well," said Czals, suppressing extreme pleasure. "Go

151

ahead with large-scale construction of the scanners and the weapon. I want them mounted on satellites. The scanners are to cover the whole planet. The weapons are to be directional to all points on the surface and are to range from a wide field down to laser concentration. Can that be done?"

The scientist smiled and nodded. "The plans have already been drawn."

"Good," said Czals.

Project Eclipse could at last commence.

VI.

The Keeper stood at the exit of the Labyrinth. She was a bored, dark, humanoid female in green uniform. She spent most of her days just standing here swatting yellow flies with her whisk tail.

Today a little red Tyi had come to her seeking an Earthling who'd been condemned to the Labyrinth days ago. The pretty hermaphroditic creature was frantic; he'd been searching the planet for the Earthling for days. It was a pity that he had to come to such a disappointment, and she told him so.

"But he's innocent!" the Tyi cried.

"The gods will decide," said the Keeper. And the gods were very predictable. It was only once in every century or so that they were merciful and a convict actually walked out that exit. The Keeper glanced at her calendar. "Rather, they seem to have already decided."

The Tyi leaned inside the exit and looked at all the mirrors and clear, crystalline corridors and reflections of corridors. He was an optimist—he carried drink with him in a leather skin as if he really expected a rescue. He turned to the Keeper. "What would you do if I yelled in here for him?"

The Keeper smiled. "You may. His time may already be up, and even if he could follow your voice the Labyrinth is very big. He could be kilometers from here. In fact, he probably is. Kilometers."

Tavi stood just inside the Labyrinth, cupped his hands, and yelled, "East! This way! *East!*"

East tried to do something he never did well—sleep. With any luck he would not wake. Thirst was a terrible way to go. He closed his eyes.

She came like a vision, as clear and real as life—dark hair, feral eyes, a smile that could be cruel but wasn't now, white hand beckoning, insistent, as she called him to her, to death. He wanted to go to her. Death looked very inviting, and she was there waiting for him.

153

Then she was blurred, the way wind scatters a sand painting, and her voice changed to—or had always been—Tavi's.

East stirred, opened one dry eye a slit, tried to lick cracked lips with a dry swollen tongue. He lifted his head and listened.

The voice was real. It *was* Tavi's.

And it was coming from *ahead*.

The Keeper was humming a little tune to herself, then she stopped in astonishment

A frightful, black-bearded, silver-maned, desiccated being hung in the exit of the Labyrinth, clawlike hands grasping the lintel over his head to keep himself on his feet.

The Tyi cried out, *"East!"*

East staggered forward and grabbed Tavi's wineskin away from him, too parched even to say his name. He uncorked the skin and squeezed it over his face, his eyes, his mouth. He spat.

When he could speak, the first thing he said in a croaking voice, scowling at the skin, was, "It's water."

"Yes," Tavi nodded. "Water."

"Hell, it was hardly worth it." East put it back into Tavi's hands and walked back into the Labyrinth.

After a startled pause, Tavi ran in after him, threw his arms around the horribly thin East from behind, and hugged him, laughing in relief. "It's good to see you, Mr. East."

"Where's Laure?" East croaked, squinting down the corridor.

"Take it easy, Mr. East," said Tavi.

The Keeper came to them and gave East a bottle. "Drink," she said.

"Is it beer?" said East.

"Not in your condition. Drink."

East took a few sips. It was sweet and went down easier than the water to his shrunken stomach. "What did I do? Go in a circle?"

"No," said the Keeper. "Who told you the real exit was this way?"

Real exit? "You mean that was a fake exit back there?"

"You did not know?" said the Keeper. "Why did you come this way?"

"Because it was the way I didn't want to go," said East, as if it would be obvious to any fool.

"That is the point," said the Keeper. "Thieves do not walk

154

away when they see before them what they think they should have."

"I'm not a thief," East bridled.

"So the gods have said."

"Gods nothing. It was luck." Or Laure calling from beyond the grave—even that seemed within the realm of the possible at this point. East still could not believe he was free. He walked back out of the Labyrinth. "Am I really out?"

"You are," said the Keeper.

East turned to her. "What do you do now that someone knows the way out? What if I tell the galaxy?"

"Go ahead and tell. There are hundreds of people around who claim to have escaped the Labyrinth, each with his own tale of the way out. Why should a thief believe you and walk this way when he *sees* the exit that way? A thief will believe only what he sees." She glanced at the calendar again. "I see you were brought here with a ship. Come, it will be restored to you. Is there anything else you want? Ask and it is yours."

"I want to get the hell off this planet," said East.

"Done," said the Keeper.

Before continuing the search for Daniel, East and Tavi stopped back at East's home in Texas, and, upon arrival, found Daniel's ship, *Laure*, in the underground hangar.

"Hell!" Tavi cried, furious rather than relieved to see that ship again. "I'm going to kill him, Mr. East. He cast me adrift and let me think he was kidnapped by pirates. I am really going to kill him." Tavi's small fingers curled into claws.

"Let's see if he's guilty first," said East, who'd had enough of kangaroo courts. He left Tavi in the hangar and went up to the house.

He found his son dressed in black.

As East walked in the door, Daniel turned with a gasp, stood in the middle of the room and stared and stared, dark-brown eyes wide, a little bit frightened, a reddish forelock hanging in his face making him look like a lost stray. He blinked, looked as if he might cry.

He was taller than East remembered, heavier but without softness, muscles filling out a masculine frame, all traces of boyish build fading. He was really a handsome young man. To see him again pulled at East's heart. *My son by Laure.* He loved him very much in that moment. *Why doesn't he come to me?* East knew that he himself looked frightful—wild-bearded and emaciated—but why did Daniel look as if he'd

155

been stabbed in the gut? But then East could see the boy was in mourning and was not himself. "Whose funeral?" said East.

Daniel shook his head, helpless and bewildered. "Yours!" he cried.

East cocked his head to one side, puzzled, then he was struck by the absurd notion that he was not properly attired for his own funeral. It was one of those moments so bizarre there was nothing appropriate or even sensible to be said. He grinned. "Should I change clothes?"

Daniel ran to him. East grabbed him, held him tight, felt the hard solidity of his body and the crushing strength of his son's embrace. He had known for a long time that he missed him, but was hit with the full magnitude now that he was here again. He pounded him on the back, messed up his hair, and kissed him on the temple.

When he pulled back, his son was crying. "Hey, what's this? I'm not dead."

Daniel shook his head, lips quivered, then he blurted out, "Oh, Dad, I think I started a war!"

By all the gods Man has ever conceived.

Czals watched the monitor with mounting horror.

Ships. All the ships that had disappeared from K Station over the past three hundred years. There they were on his doorstep.

Czals considered Aeolis his doorstep, his domain, even though he himself was light-years distant on Earth, on a Service installation in Nebraska, watching Aeolis on a minitor.

Here was the disaster of all disasters, a whole fleet of creatures possessing the potential to crossbreed with Earthlings and to claim ownership of Earth's most valuable colony. Czals shuddered.

At that moment the tracker came into Czals' office, speaking without looking up from his notes. "Sir, we've located Daniel East. He's by himself; there are no pirates with—oh my heavens." He looked up and sighted the monitor.

Czals turned to the man slowly. "There are no pirates where?" Czals said ironically.

The tracker was without words.

Then Lieutenant Martin entered. "Sir, I have a probable on that rider: the owner of a Polybios—oh my God." He too had caught sight of the pirate caravan on the monitor's screen.

"Forget the rider. Forget Daniel East," said Czals. He had

no more use for them. The sky had already fallen. "Where is that toad of a scientist?" He stalked over to his intercom and bellowed to the laboratory. "This is Admiral Czals. Status! Are my weapon and scanner operational?"

The reply over the intercom was unhurried and unruffled. "Not yet, sir."

"Why not?" Czals roared. Did the man not understand the urgency of this project?

"We will be operational, sir," the scientist said sweetly. "Within the time it takes you to evacuate the Earthlings from Aeolis."

Czals slammed the intercom off. *Gods, how I hate this man.* What the scientist implied was only too true. There was no one Czals could blame for his present inability to act. Even if the weapon were ready at this moment, it could not be fired—not with even one Earthling on the premises. Czals' sole aim was to protect the Earthlings.

He contacted the Aeolian Chief of Police via phase jumper and asked how long it would take to effect a complete evacuation of the planet.

"On what status is the order?" she asked. "Emergency, sir?"

"War status," said Czals.

"Six days," said the chief, shaken at the mention of war. "Sir, is that fleet up there . . . hostile?"

Czals had no time for her question. "Six days," he repeated. "No sooner?"

An entire planet? Sooner than six days? Is he kidding? "No, sir."

Czals pursed his lips and accepted the grim reality. "Commence evacuation immediately," he ordered.

Then he went down to the laboratory in person and took the scientist aside. "This weapon," Czals told him, "I want it under my control only. Can you trust your work crew to arrange that?"

"Voice command, sir?" said the scientist.

"That will do. Yes."

"It will necessitate a control base on the inner moon Kushuh, sir. A voice command to fire a weapon is not exactly the sort of thing you would want bouncing across the galaxy off phase-jumper repeaters."

"Then I will go to Kushuh when the time comes," said Czals. "In six days."

He looked down and set his wrist chronometer for the

countdown. It was presently 0600 hours, 19 May. Barring action by the United Earth Council or unforeseen events, the human race should be rid of the Kistraalian menace six days from *now*.

PART FOUR: Countdown

Eclipse Minus Six Days

It was a strange tandem, a guerrilla fighter docked to a LaFayette speedcraft with a little Polybios ship on top.

East was at the helm of the fighter. He looked like a derelict, too thin, his skin sallow. He had mown his beard, which left his face showing gaunt.

Daniel stood at his shoulder, still dressed in black, though he'd changed to his old navy jacket—which, East noted in passing, had always been big on Daniel. It fit perfectly now.

Tavi was sitting on the deck, feeling like the family pet. Someone had to look after these Easts. They were insane.

East seemed to be piloting them out to the far perimeters of civilized space. He was muttering to himself, "The most valuable colony Earth has, and my son digs up a returning native population. She's going to love this."

Why, then, did Daniel get the feeling "she" was not going to love this?

They were still out in open space, near no solar system, when East switched to standard sublight mode and informed Daniel and Tavi that their destination was within sight.

Through the viewport they could see a squadron of Service ships flanking the oddest-looking flagship there could ever be.

Daniel tried to speak. "It's . . . it's . . ."

Tavi broke in. "It's *plaid.*"

"The *Aberdeen*," said East. "That's the Douglas tartan she's got that thing painted."

Daniel stared over his father's shoulder out the viewport at the ship. "Old friend?" Daniel asked skeptically.

"Old *something*," said East. He hailed the *Aberdeen* and docked with her over strenuous objections from the Service ship's junior officers. They kept trying to tell him he was dead.

Once docked, East strode to the airlock. It opened, and there could be heard from somewhere within the *Aberdeen* the skirl and thrum of bagpipes.

Daniel spoke. "She's kinda Scottish, huh?"

"Trying to be, very hard," said East. "Stay here."

"Can't we come?" said Tavi.

"No," said East.

"Why not?" said Daniel.

"She might start shooting," said East and ducked through the lock into *Aberdeen*.

Commodore Roxanna Douglas sat at her desk, feet up on the desktop, playing her bagpipes. She was not in uniform— not when she could get away with it. And get away with it she could. She was commodore, in command of a squadron light-years from the nearest admiral. She wore a white ruffled blouse, black vest, and kilt in her colors. Auburn hair was held back with gold pins—still those gold pins—they brought her luck. She was not a kid but could still be called young, especially next to East. She had put on weight, but Roxanna had always been too skinny as a junior officer. She looked healthy now. Authority agreed with her. She had never rested easy under other people's thumbs.

Roxanna was one of the twenty-five percent of Service personnel who were not in the Service because they had been sentenced into it for a crime. The Service was her life. She had a promising career ahead of her and a brilliant record behind her, thanks to large doses of gut instinct, luck, and tooth-and-nail struggle.

She looked up with auburn eyes and saw East.

"Oh, no." She took her feet down from the desk. The bagpipes withered to silence. "East, what do you want?"

"No hello for me, Roxy?" said East.

"Hello. What do you want?" said Roxanna.

East swiveled a chair around backward, straddled it facing Roxanna, and leaned his elbows on the backrest. "Do you know what's happening on Aeolis?"

"Who doesn't?" said the commodore, then realization crossed her face and she set her bagpipes aside. "East, you're not mixed up with this, are you?"

"To my teeth."

Roxanna smiled thinly. Teeth. Roxanna had kicked East's teeth in many years ago; the ones he had now were replace-

160

ments—or perhaps replacements of replacements if he had crossed another volatile young lieutenant since then.

"Why should I help you?" said Roxanna.

"I'll tell everyone where you have freckles."

"East, I'm going to bite you where it hurts," said the commodore. "By the way, you look like hell. I know milady can't cook, but doesn't she at least toss a piece of raw meat into your cage now and then?"

East's expression went black. "Laure's dead."

Roxanna blanched; both hands went up to her face. "Oh my God, East, I'm sorry. I wouldn't have said—"

"It's OK, Roxy."

Roxanna rested her forehead on her hand and spoke into the desk. "What is your connection with what's happening at Aeolis?"

East told her the story, starting with his and Laure's discovery of the device in the desert which Laure thought was a weapon, through Daniel's odyssey, to the return of the *volaia* to Kistraal/Aeolis.

Roxanna's expression wavered between astonished and incredulous. "You're trying to tell me Laure was half Kistraalian?" she said. It was impossible.

East shrugged. "I believe it."

"So do I, that's what's bothering me." Roxanna and East had both been there when Laure had summoned up a living hurricane out of the Aeolian skies. "Does anyone else in the Service know about any of this?"

"No," said East.

"Not that you know of," said Roxanna, reserving belief. She sat back and inhaled through her teeth, facing something very difficult. "I'll see what I can do to get this settled peacefully. It's really out of my demesne. And if the same man is in charge of Aeolian Affairs as twenty years ago when we were there—well, you remember what *he* was like. What was his name? No, I got it. Czals. Admiral Czals." She nodded to herself. "He's the one who sent me in there and never expected me to come out."

East could see that Roxanna was spoiling for a fight. He had come to the right person. She was not an admiral, but she would not just file him and forget it as an admiral would. Once Roxanna picked up a sword she did not let go until the battle was done.

"How come you never married, Roxy?"

Roxanna raised an auburn eyebrow. "I did. I am."

"You are?" said East and immediately felt stupid.

161

"That's what I said." One did not say stupid things around Roxanna Douglas and get away with it.

"Is he here?" said East.

"No."

"Why not?"

"Because he's a dashing young commodore like myself and it's in the nature of commodores to be in faraway places." She reached back and turned on a monitor showing a map of the galaxy. A green dot flashed in a sector far from where they were. "That little blip is Mikhail. It's such a damn long way off and such a damn long time."

Her gaze fixed on the flashing dot, and she fell silent.

East knew what she was feeling. He had been celibate since Laure's death, for fear he would forget what it was like with her. But he'd forgotten anyway. All distinct images were gone, the edges of memory blurred, and only longing remained. "Do you play?"

"I haven't," said Roxanna. "Do you?"

"I haven't," said East.

And then neither of them said anything. They stared intently at the walls, their feet, the desk, and eventually their gazes lighted on each other and held a full minute that was slow and thick and bristling with sparks.

There was a tap at the door and two inquisitive heads leaned in, one dark, one red/blond. "Well?"

East cleared his throat, and Roxanna suddenly decided her desk needed rearranging.

East resignedly beckoned Daniel and Tavi into the office and presented them to Roxanna. "This one is Tavi, and this one is mine."

Roxanna looked at Daniel's handsome face and said to East, "Are you sure?"

"He's his mother's son," said East.

"God help us all," said Roxanna.

Investigation into classified records showed Roxanna that Laure's suspicion had been correct—the device she had found was in fact a weapon to be used against the Kistraalian winds. It had very recently been given its final test and was presently being installed on satellites over Aeolis while a planetwide evacuation was in progress under the status of undeclared war. Project Eclipse, it was called.

Eclipse? It's genocide!

With a feeling close to mental panic, Roxanna could hear

162

a clock ticking, marking time to an unknown deadline, leaving her a very limited interval in which to act.

But that much she had expected.

It was something else she found that surprised her, convincing her that Laure was what East said she had been and that the Service *did* know about it—something that sickened, enraged, and horrified.

Oh, East, you have no idea.

But Roxanna was not going to be the one to tell him.

Eclipse Minus Five Days

When Roxanna's squadron arrived into the Aeolian system the *volaia* ships had already begun to mobilize, and the Aeolian horizon guard dutifully destroyed any ship that attempted to enter Aeolis' atmosphere—not that having a ship blasted out from around them would stop the winds from going down to the planet surface. It would, however, prevent contamination of the disease-free planet and it would also serve to make the winds band together. What better way to concentrate one's target than to make them all muster for war?

The winds of all castes were quick to retaliate.

Daniel was staring out the viewport of the *Aberdeen* at the beautiful blue world below when the clouds began to spiral.

"Oh my God," Daniel breathed.

And the clouds twisted into tight, visibly moving living hurricanes, while the skies on the night-blackened side flashed bright as daylight with lightning.

"Dad! Roxanna! Dad! Look what they're doing!"

Roxanna ran into the cabin, stopped, looked, and groaned something obscene.

"*Do* something!" said Daniel.

"The admiral is not answering my calls," said Roxanna. "I'm going to try to go over Czals' head and get the United Earth Council to put someone sane in charge—preferably me—but Danny, it's going to be hard." She gestured to the viewport. "They're hanging themselves."

They think they're invincible, thought Daniel. *Didn't Niki warn them? Where is Niki?*

East was, by then, standing in the doorway. Daniel turned to him. "Dad—"

"Danny, stay with Roxy," East cut him off and started down the corridor.

"Dad, where are you going!"

East was striding toward his docked ship, but it occurred

164

to him on the way that he was dead and did not have an operable ID. So he snagged a bewildered Tavi in the corridor, and the two of them took off for Earth in Tavi's Polybios craft.

East arrived at the Service installation in Nebraska and tried to get to the man in charge. He left Tavi in the Polybios ship. Tavi's ID had gotten him this far. East bullied the rest of his way to the office of the admiral called Czals. He was told that Czals was not in. He stormed in anyway. A pale-skinned blond boy of a man who looked too young to be an officer jumped at East's entrance. This was Czals' aide, and he was reacting as if he'd seen a ghost.

East did not know the lad. The aide knew East and was terrified. East loomed over him, but before East could demand to know where Czals was, the aide blurted out, "I was not responsible for your wife's death. Honest."

My wife. East was numbed in confusion—what was this man talking about his wife?—and then horror came. *My wife.*

The bottom dropped out of the world, and everything that was inside East fell out, leaving him a blank, staring zombie. When sensibility returned, it was not in the form it had been before, but in the form of blinding revelation and inutterable rage.

I was not responsible . . .

Implying: *Somebody had been.*

Any reasoning being would have been suspicious of Laure's *accidental* death simply because of its timing. But East had not questioned it. At the time there had been one thought and one thought only: Laure was gone. Now there was a new thought: *Someone took her.* All the torment, the madness, the loss came back, no less for not being the first time.

He was shaking, his face terrible. He looked mad, and for a moment he probably was.

The aide shrank away from him, babbling, "It wasn't me. Orders are orders. I was only in the spotter ship. I didn't do anything."

Spotter ship? East had not been alone with Laure on the mountain. He remembered the distant lights of a ship in the sky. The ship up there had not been passing, but *watching.* Watching Laure die.

And you didn't do anything. That was supposed to be a defense?

165

The aide backed up till he could back no farther. "Wh-what are you going to do?"

"Nothing," said East. "You are going to kill yourself."

"You knew!" East pounded on Roxanna's desk upon his return from Earth, a trip that had nearly broken Tavi's little Polybios craft apart. Tavi had cringed in a corner the whole way, head between his hands, while this madman possessed his ship.

Now aboard the *Aberdeen* East paced, pantherlike, from one side of the cabin to the other, livid with rage, barely able to speak. Roxanna sat behind her desk and watched. He was going to kill her. But first he waited—and hoped—for her to make a denial. She did not.

"I found out," she admitted quietly.

"And you didn't tell me!" East roared.

Up till this point it looked as if he might recover from the loss of his wife. He had been starting to realize that he was still alive and that Roxanna was a woman. There was a tentative stirring of something new that might have grown, given time and space to breathe. Here it died. He was past Roxanna's reach. All tenderness was engulfed in hatred, and Roxanna was locked outside. She had not told him what she had discovered because she had known he would turn into the irretrievable, rage-driven nemesis she saw before her now.

"No, I didn't tell you," she said. "It would be murder."

"And why shouldn't it be!"

"Hasn't there been enough!"

"No, we're just getting started!"

"Are you crazy!"

"Yes!"

They were screaming at each other. Roxanna was puffed up like a fighting cock, rising behind her desk. Her auburn eyes darkened in angry passion, and her Scottish burr became more broad till she was hardly speaking English.

East, glaring at her from the other side of the desk, was a tall starved wolf, his muscles of steel cable and knotted whipcord, and he planted a fist on Roxanna's desk. "Who was responsible?" he demanded.

"I can't tell you that," said Roxanna.

"Whose side are you on?"

"What you are planning to do isn't justice."

Blue eyes widened an instant. "Who said a damn thing about justice!" Driven by no imaginary sense of Right, simple revenge served East just as well.

166

"You can't do this." She reached across the desk and took his arm with a surprisingly feminine touch. It was both an officer and a desperately lonely woman talking when she said, "East, you go through with this and your life is over."

"It's *been* over!" East shouted. The pain in his voice made Roxanna wince and withdraw her hand. "Yeah," she said softly and sat down.

She had seen them together once briefly while Laure was still a married lady and East her hired bodyguard. Even then there had been no doubt that one could not exist without the other. "I would be an accomplice if I answered your question," said Roxanna.

"Well?" East waited for an answer.

"You're a Neanderthal, East." Roxanna sighed heavily, bowed her head, and rested her brow on her fingertips. "The man you want is Admiral Czals."

"Who was in the spotter ship? Who built the snake?"

Roxanna lifted her face from her hands with a start. "What are you after? Isn't Czals enough?"

"No."

"You want every little button-pushing tech?"

"Yes."

Roxanna looked aside with an air of annoyance and picked up a file—any file—from her desk as if to busy herself with something else, and she assumed an attitude of dismissal. This audience was over. "You find that out for yourself."

"You won't hep me anymore?"

"No." She looked up at him. "I'm going to be the one to arrest you."

Eclipse Minus Four Days

Czals was prowling his office, disturbed, remembering the dead body he had found here—his aide hung from a beam with his own belt. It was grisly and uncivilized—*and in my office!*

It also presented Czals with the annoying task of finding a new aide. He needed someone who was already privy to his secret plans, not an outsider who needed to be briefed and cleared.

He thought of a pilot—one of those two lads he had sent out in pirate's guise to attempt to stop Laure and East from reaching Aeolis. One of them had fallen victim to the unregistered and illegal armament of East's guerrilla ship on that mission, but the other had survived. What was his name? Yanos, that was it, Lieutenant Yanos.

Czals tried to contact the man. But after much shuffling and his call being transferred five times, he was told, "Um . . . the lieutenant has met with an accident. The atmosphere in his ship failed. He's dead."

Czals was given pause. "All right then. Where's that spotter ship pilot? Eurasian girl. Li, Erika Li."

There was a quick check, then a pause, a clearing of a throat and slow answer. "She's dead too, sir."

Czals turned sharply away from the radio, alarmed, indignant, his face dark.

What is going on here?

The *Aberdeen* and its squadron left Aeolian space and headed for Earth. East was not with them. He—with Tavi in tow—had taken Tavi's Polybios ship and departed in grim silent haste.

Daniel grew anxious when the *Aberdeen* began to mobilize. How would East find them again if they moved? He went to Roxanna.

"Where's my dad?" said Daniel.

168

"Gone crazy," said Roxanna. "Let him go."

She was sitting at her desk, hunched over a stack of hand-scribbled notes, trying to memorize the points she wanted to make to the President of the United Earth Council.

There was noise in the corridor. She put her hands over her ears to block it out, her brows knit together in concentration.

Daniel shut the door quietly. He knew that if Roxanna could not get Czals removed, there would be nothing to keep him from activating the killer satellites, and it would be all over for the Kistraalians.

There *was* actually one other possibility, which Roxanna did not mention. In fact, she was trying not to think about it at all, though ignoring it made it no less a possibility. East.

Roxanna was relieved that Czals was not taking any of her calls. She made periodic attempts to get through; it gave her one more thing to tell the president and gave her conscience a half-good excuse for not warning Czals that he was being targeted by a hunter.

Czals would be smugly aware that Roxanna knew that the Kistraalians' time was running out and would be sneering at her efforts to stop it. But he could not know—yet—that his own time was running out as well.

And the real question in Roxanna's mind was whose would run out first.

Eclipse Minus Three Days

The bunker was dark and the Serviceman did not see him at first. No one was supposed to be down here. The Serviceman had come down seeking his hidden store of contraband. The shaft of light slanting in from the overhead hatch caught a glint of silver-white deep in the shadows, and the Serviceman narrowed his eyes to make out the outline of a man. He wondered who it could be. He thought for a moment, with a tightening in his gut, that maybe it was an officer. Then the figure stepped fully into the light, and the Serviceman broke into a broad grin.

He laughed. "Well, look who's here."

A voice from outside the bunker called in, "Who you talking to down there?"

And two men came to the hatch and clambered down the ladder. Then they saw the intruder.

"Who are y—" one started, then gave a wicked laugh in recognition. "Oh yeah. You. Aren't you missing somebody?"

"Where's your pretty wife now?" said the first man.

East said nothing, his head lowered, watching them out of the tops of his eyes. They became uneasy and grinned all the harder to dispel the feelings that were creeping in on them. Half-uniformed subterraneans they were. Three. There had once been five. East spoke. "Where are the other two?"

The first man guffawed, forcing humor, and gestured with his thumb. "Cobalt, he's drunk. Fenerty, dummy, got hisself electrocuted to death a while back."

East gave a hard smile and raised his gun. "Lucky for him." It wasn't cruel and unusual enough.

Czals took the package into his office and closed the door. It was marked Eyes Only. He wondered what this could be.

He lifted the lid, was going to toss it aside, then he saw what was in the box.

He jammed the lid back on and backed away from the box, pale.

How careless. It could have bitten his finger as he undid the catch. *How close.* He stood flat against the wall, staring at the box, horror mounting as he realized just how close he had come.

The box was shut, but still the image remained stamped before his eyes in his mind. Black and yellow. Scanners were programmed to sift out bombs, not valley snakes.

His heart was thudding in his throat.

Be calm. Be calm.

He steadied his breathing, and horror quickly gave way to fury.

That damned scientist.

He went to his desk, opened a drawer, and took out a beam gun. He took aim with the laser sight and shot the box—taking off the corner of his desk with it.

His new aide, Lieutenant Martin, rushed in at the sound. "Sir!"

Czals pushed past him and out the door, gun drawn, determined to shoot that snake-programming, tin-voiced weasel between the eyes.

But as he approached the lab he met stricken-faced lab assistants wandering the hall outside, shaking their heads, quivering and muttering, "Horrible accident. Horrible. Horrible."

Czals leaned in the doorway to see, then backed out, shaken. He ran back up to his office, bellowing for Lieutenant Martin.

When informed of the uncanny chain of deaths, Martin shook his head. "It looks like . . . but that's impossible."

"East," said Czals.

"I had him killed, sir," Martin protested.

"Then do it again, and get it right this time!" said Czals. His gaze had fallen upon his desk where the corner had been blown off. He still saw afterimages of yellow and black.

A dead man walked and stalked. An angry shade without a grave returned to exact vengeance. A sense of the eerie made Czals shiver despite efforts to keep a level, rational outlook.

Damn these Easts and their ghosts! They were as bad as Kistraalians—beings that refused to die. *Why can't these Easts stay dead?*

"Sir?" Lieutenant Martin began, trying not to sound insubordinate. "May I ask how you would suggest I find East if the UBC says he is dead?"

171

Good question. Czals crossed his arms, thinking, trying to figure out how East could possibly be getting around without an operative ID. There was only one answer. He had to be traveling with someone else. "Where is the son?" said Czals.

"With Commodore Douglas aboard the *Aberdeen,* sir."

That discounted Daniel as East's cover. *Who else could he be with?* One possibility came to mind: East and his son's secret go-between. "What about Daniel's rider?" said Czals. "Is he still with Daniel?"

"The Tyi with the Polybios ship? No sir."

"Then find this creature," said Czals. "East will be with him."

And make it very fast, thought Czals, *for my life is at stake.*

Eclipse Minus Two Days

There was little left to do, few people still alive who should not be. East came to the space station between Earth and Aeolis in search of one of the last.

He remembered an eager young man who had wanted to inspect the guerrilla fighter when East and Laure had stopped here on their attempted trip to Aeolis. Only now did East wonder what had made the young man so eager.

He left Tavi and the Polybios ship in a hangar and went to find his prey.

He was not quite sure if the suspect was guilty when he started out, but the jolt that crossed the young man's features when East found him eliminated all doubt.

"You know me," said East.

The young man dropped the tool he had been working with and raised grease-stained hands, declaring innocence. "I never did anything to you."

"What were you hired to do?"

"But I *didn't*." He hadn't found the opportunity to carry out his intent.

But intent and action were one and the same to East, and lack of opportunity was not an extenuating circumstance when attempts on Laure's life were concerned. Chance and luck had spared Laure that one time, not any mercy of this young man.

And, with only one man left to be executed, East walked back to where he'd left Tavi, but he caught sight of uniforms—many uniforms—swarming about the hangar before he got there, and he slipped back into hiding.

He waited, crouched, watching.

In time, a small Service ship arrived and docked in the next bay. A handsome, dark-haired lieutenant marched over to the uniformed men and women about the Polybios craft and gave orders to his betters with the self-assurance of one

173

whose authority comes from a very high place. Uniforms scattered and a search commenced.

East needed a better place to hide. And he saw just the place.

The search did not produce the fugitive East as quickly as Lieutenant Martin had hoped or expected. He contacted Admiral Czals.

"Sir. I have apprehended the Tyi. He's pretending ignorance, and, sir, we can't hold him long. He's threatening to notify his government."

"You haven't found East?" Czals had been so sure East would be with the Tyi.

"Not yet, sir. He has to be here, but the Tyi won't say."

"Bring the creature to me. As a murder suspect it can be held twenty-four Earth hours," said Czals. "And keep searching. I want every ship, every radio signal, every *carrier pigeon* in and out of that station checked." If East was at the station, he could not get out.

And in case he was *not* at the station, Czals would go back to the UBC and find out how to make a Tyi talk in twenty-four hours or less.

Roxanna placed Czals under computer surveillance. Nothing classified would come of it, but it would at least notify her the moment he left Earth. That would signal that she had failed in all her efforts, for he would be on his way to trigger the satellites and kill the winds.

She had succeeded as far as her audience with the President of the United Earth Council, a grave old Chinese woman who promised to put the question of Czals' removal to Council vote tomorrow.

But Roxanna's hopes were not high. The president had only promised a vote, not a decision in Roxanna's favor. Chances were the Duke of Aeolis had bought the majority of Council delegates.

More and more, though reluctantly, Roxanna's hopes rode with East. And those hopes too dimmed when a notice came through the official channel: an all-points had been issued on East. Czals had evidently figured out that East was still alive.

Daniel had by now sensed something wrong and acknowledged the news quietly, almost matter-of-factly. He turned to gaze out the viewport at the planet Earth with the too calm poise of one who has arrived at adulthood early. His hands were clasped behind him without tension; his brow was uncreased, his expression mildly sad—if anything at all. Not to cry; he had already buried his father once.

Roxanna touched his shoulder and silently withdrew from the cabin, leaving Daniel to himself.

She checked on the progress of her computer spy's report, not actually expecting to find anything useful in the unclassified data—beyond the fact that Admiral Czals was still on Earth.

What she did find made her suspect that Czals had discovered he was under surveillance and was toying with her.

What other reason could he possibly have for ordering from New Mexico a whole truckload of free-tailed *bats*?

Admiral Czals had taken to carrying a sidearm. It was distasteful to him, suffused with the taint of a time when all men were barbarians.

He could not sleep when his night cycle came, so he took sleep pills and stayed awake, starting at noises, drawing his weapon at the slightest sound. Try as he might to think of other things—the approaching zero hour—he kept waiting for East.

The search at the space station had not yet produced the assassin. It had, however, uncovered the corpse of Czals' most proficient saboteur. East had definitely been there, whether or not he still was.

The man is insane.

Czals had always prided himself on being able to outthink his enemy—but how does a madman think?

Czals considered perhaps he should play dead, let East think the valley snake had killed him. But Czals strongly suspected that East had not expected that trap to work—and maybe even never meant it to work. Rather the snake had been a threat, a declaration of intent, signature, and justification. It told Czals what was to come, who was doing it and why. *I am East. I am alive. I am going to kill you for taking my wife.* East was not the kind who killed with cyborg snakes; he was a species of cat that torments its victim before the kill.

But Czals was not going to fall to a madman. He'd done a hasty restudy of his adversary. He had with him a holo-image of East that epitomized for Czals all he knew of the man. The image was taken from a news special on mercenaries in which the news recorders had happened to catch a shot of East in the field. It was a recent picture, dating subsequent to Laure's death.

175

In the image there was snow on the ground; East was crouched on an outcropping of rock with others of his kind, as hard-bitten a group as walked on two legs, wary, lean, and wild as a group of cheetahs. Like the others East had a big gun at his hip, angled up like a pseudo-erection. *They and their guns*, Czals thought with derision. Thick silver mane and drab green jacket whipped in the wind that was at East's back. His collar was turned up against the cold. His eyes were cold as the winter sky, blue and narrow underneath thick black brows. The tough hide of his abused and weather-beaten face was marked with scars. Big hands bore knots from past breaks and thick-skinned knuckles of one who used his fists. He was a formidable figure; Czals was not misled by his own contempt. Despicable though they might be, these were survivors. In a nuclear holocaust, like the viruses and the vermin, mercenaries would survive. As Czals viewed the natural world, on the evolutionary scale mercenaries were to be found somewhere between slime molds and stoneworts. Nevertheless Czals kept in mind that some of the most primitive life forms were the most deadly. He had already made the mistake once of underestimating East. Czals did not make mistakes twice.

He shifted his attention to East's accomplice now before him, an impish hermaphroditic alien, an unlikely companion for a man like East. It was probable that the creature had not volunteered for his position but had been conscripted. It shouldn't then be hard to persuade the Tyi to cooperate.

And, as it turned out, Czals needed the Tyi's cooperation, for Lieutenant Martin reported that East was *not* in the space station.

"He's not?" said the Tyi with a bewilderment so believable it almost seemed genuine.

Czals smiled wanly. "You would like to tell me where he is," he told Tavi with quiet menace.

"I would?" said Tavi.

Czals nodded.

"I don't know," said Tavi.

"You don't want to say that," said Czals, friendly as a smiling crocodile.

"I don't?" said Tavi.

With a change in tone that signaled Tavi's last chance, Czals said, "I prepared a little something for you just in case you decided to be difficult. You're not going to like it."

"I believe you," said Tavi sincerely.

"Believe this," said Czals and crossed to a glass door

through which could be seen only darkness. Czals turned a switch beside the door and a light went on inside. Now Tavi could see through the glass to a small room filled with hundreds of bats.

Czals turned to him. "Where is East?"

"You can't do this!" said Tavi, trying to keep panic from his voice. "My government will skin you for this!"

Czals laughed outright. "Who will believe you? You're going to try to tell your government that an admiral of the United Earth Service tossed you into a roomful of bats?"

It was true; such a claim would sound utterly, utterly preposterous. This ploy was as clever as it was bizarre.

Czals gestured to the MPs. "Put him in."

Two husky Earthlings, a man and a woman, laid hands on the Tyi, and Tavi started thrashing and yelling, clawing and biting. He tried to plant his feet on the floor and resist the force dragging him toward the room, but the MPs picked him up and carried him. He kicked the woman in the shin and bit the man's ear. He pulled their hair and flailed in all directions. The dreaded door opened and they tried to shove him through, but he latched onto the doorjamb like a monkey and would not budge.

They pried his little fingers off the jambs and threw him in and were about to slam the door shut when Tavi screamed, "All right! All right! I'll tell you! I'll tell you! I'll tell you!"

And he came flying out of the room and attached himself to the disconcerted admiral's legs like a suppliant, sobbing. He told Czals a location.

Even though some things just aren't said.

Eclipse Minus One Day

Czals deceived was not pleasant. He had sent two MPs in a military ship to the place Tavi had told him. Czals had concluded that Tavi's information was correct when the ship was denied landing privileges; the MPs had been told that the port was closed until tomorrow. That sounded like something East might say. The MPs then reported to Czals via phase jumper that they were going to force a landing anyway. And that was the last Czals heard of them. He sent six more MPs after them, and they too vanished. Finally Czals discovered that Port Lyco, Jarsheno, was a black hole of a city from where no one came out but once a year at the solstice. Czals could not risk an interstellar incident—not another one—getting his MPs out. He did not know what he would do a year from now when they finally emerged from Port Lyco deranged. He would worry about that in a year.

For now he was going to trash a Tyi. He could not waste time on this; he should have been on his way to Aeolis' moon by now to prepare for the termination of the Kistraalian winds. The evacuation of Aeolis was nearly complete and the rampaging winds no doubt thought themselves victorious. In less than twenty-four hours they would be no more.

Czals turned to the two MPs on hand. "Put the Tyi in with the bats, lock the door, and leave him there."

Tavi screamed and fought all the way in. "No! No! No! I hate bats! I hate bats! I hate bats!"

The door shut, and his screams came through the air vent. Little red fists pounded on the glass door that would not break.

Czals watched, impassive. "Where is East?" he said.

A deep voice from behind him said, "Right here."

There was an explosion and a billow of dusty smoke as the room full of bats was blasted open. Gray dust and flapping bats filled the outer room, and it was difficult to open one's eyes, much less see. Tavi was coughing, choking, and shriek-

178

ing until a figure came through the cloud of smoke and debris, hauled Tavi out of the rubble, and smothered his screams against his chest. It was East—at any rate, he smelled like East, felt like East, and carried a big gun like East. The gun was a projectile weapon. Tavi didn't know what he'd blown the room open with, didn't really care, just wanted to get away from the bats. "East, get me out of here!" A bat flapped by his head. "Shoot it!"

"Shut up," East growled. He pressed Tavi's face against him, squinted through the shifting dust, and listened for Czals' cough.

A red dot of light appeared on his arm, and East dove off to one side, taking Tavi with him, as a ray of beam fire from an MP's gun lanced the air where he had been an instant before.

Laser sights. East worked well against guns with laser sights. There was always a split-second delay between the sighting and the pulling of the trigger. East was wary of little red dots, and when one landed on him he knew he had a split second to get himself elsewhere, though none of this went through his conscious mind. It was all reflex action by now.

Tavi was whimpering, and the laser sight quickly found them again. East dodged, then threw Tavi into a cluster of bats. The laser sight pivoted toward the screams, but East was upon the MP before she could fire. The gun flew up and hit the ceiling; an arcking kick cracked the big woman on the side of her head and she collapsed to the floor.

The other MP was already out cold from the explosion, but where was Czals?

The air was starting to clear, the debris settling, the bats scattering.

A laser sight landed on East. He grabbed the MP at his feet, heaved her up bodily, blocked the shot with her, and tossed her husk aside.

Czals was taken aback, sickened. Czals had fired the shot that killed the MP. Not East. That sort of thing could be damnably hard to explain to nosy civilian authorities. They could be narrow-minded that way.

As Czals stood there, stricken, East took aim and fired.

Czals jerked back, unharmed, only startled.

One-way force field. No wonder Czals was standing in the open—or seemed to be.

Czals looked at the dead woman, then at East. *What a barbaric way to conduct a battle.* "You're a savage," said Czals.

"So I am, and so be it," said East and emptied a full round

of bullets into the force field, then he stalked up to it as if he would break through with his bare hands. Czals backed away as if that were actually a possibility. The threat in East's eyes made him believe it. And he gaped, powerless, as if transfixed by some preternatural being, as East stood menacingly on the far side of the invisible barrier.

Rational judgment returned presently, and Czals realized, *Idiot! I have a weapon! Don't just stand here, shoot him!*

He raised his gun, but he was unused to guerrilla combat, and by the time he was in position to fire, East had darted away, snatched up the Tyi, and fled into the hall.

Czals dropped his gun and looked down at his aristocratic hands. They were trembling.

I! Czals! Shaking.

Something in those bestial narrow blue eyes chilled him to the core, like a death mark. It seemed something like voodoo—make one believe he was dying, and he did.

But we are more clever. You can't think an admiral to death. Czals occasionally slipped into royal plurals when thinking about himself.

He sounded the alarm. If East wanted a fight he was going to have to take on the entire Service installation.

East and Tavi were running down the corridor when Czals' voice came over the loudspeakers ordering East's arrest and giving permission to kill if need be.

East set Tavi down on his feet. Tavi swayed momentarily like a newborn foal till he regained equilibrium. East was growling in his ear, "Get yourself out of here and don't look back." He pointed him toward the hangars and gave him a swat to get him running, then East took off in the other direction, yelling and firing shots to announce his location and draw attention away from Tavi.

He only got so far then ran into a team of guards coming from where he was headed, and he ducked into a recess in the wall, his back to a door that would not open. He was trapped.

The guards had stopped and found shelter from possible gunfire in other recessed doorways, and East could hear one of them speaking into an intercom, reporting East's location to the guard captain.

East peered out, then pulled back. No one had time to fire at him. That was a hopeful sign. These guards were not too quick. How much real experience could they have gained while stationed in Nebraska?

East could hear two of them moving in, and he reached his gun round the corner and fired without looking. The guards sprang back for cover, unhurt.

East waited and listened. The guards waited and listened.

East heard some hissing whispers but could not distinguish the words except for the last one: *now*.

And he heard them all creeping in toward him at once. There were six of them.

Six against one. *No way.* East needed help. He saw a possibility.

Over his head two stray bats were hanging from the door trim. East stealthily reached up and caught them both in his left hand—one gnawed on his thumb—and waited till it seemed the guards were about to rush him, then he moved first. He threw the bats at the guards, jumped out of cover, and shot the two men whose eyes did not follow the bats, bowled the other four over like dominoes, and charged past them, through a door into a stairwell. He vaulted over the rail, was down two floors in four bounds and out before the guards could even get to the stairs to see which floor he'd gone to.

"Guard captain. Report." Czals spoke into the intercom. His eyes were watering from the settling dust in the disaster-struck room. He coughed. "Where is East?"

"He's not on the third floor, sir," the captain's voice came over the intercom.

"What kind of answer is *that*? He's not on the third floor," Czals said in irritation. "Where *is* he?"

"My people lost sight of him. He just now changed floors, sir, but we don't know yet whether he went up or down."

Czals uttered an obscenity and picked up his gun again. *If you want something done right.*

Where would East go? Czals tried to deduce. That would depend on East's goal. And Czals was reasonably certain East's goal was not escape. Not just yet.

It is I he wants.

Concluding this, Czals felt immediately vulnerable, even protected behind the one-way force field. Even now, East could be circling around behind it. East knew where Czals was, but the reverse was not true. Czals felt the need for changing his position fast.

He deactivated the force field, crossed soundlessly to the door, and peered out.

181

There was no one in the hallway, not even a guard. Only three flapping bats.

How could they have left me so unprotected?

Of course, the guard captain had said East was not on the third floor. The guards would be looking for him elsewhere.

Czals cursed, feeling deserted on the third floor while a madman roamed lose in the installation seeking his life. He could have wished for a better computer guard network and internal monitor system. The present setup was decidedly lacking. These damned Earth stations presupposed that everyone in them was on the same side.

Czals quickly fled the room before East could return for him. He ran down the hall, stopped in a doorway, felt his heart racing. He had to find East before East found him. He was not accustomed to these tactics—stalking a terrorist in his own station.

He darted to another doorway. Hid. Took his bearings. There were any number of places East could be lurking. Czals had never before realized how many *corners* this place had. He darted to another doorway, alarming a pair of bats, which took flight. Czals refrained from shooting them.

He muttered silently at his mistakes and false starts. *I am a strategist. Not a combat soldier.* Czals was used to moving chess pieces across the board, not being down *on* the board in the front line with the pawns. He was accustomed to viewing death as antiseptic lists of statistics, not seeing it up close before his eyes like the death of the MP he'd shot. He remembered how detached East had been about it. That was fine for East, who'd had time to become inured to battle's horrors. This was all new to Czals.

He shifted the weapon in his hands, gained a better, more natural grip, felt its weight. Movement became easier when he felt for the natural, logical way of doing things.

He'd come to the elevator but was not going to take it. A precarious hanging cage that was. No, Czals was not going to be assassinated in an elevator.

He looked to the stairs. His heartbeat quickened again. East would've had to have taken the stairs if he'd switched floors without the guards knowing which way he'd gone. Czals approached the door to the stairs cautiously. He placed his hand on it, did not open it.

What if East were still in the stairwell, hiding? This could be a death tower.

The alternative was to sit and wait for East to come back to the third floor after him. That option was unappealing.

Czals waited for his heartbeat to calm, then opened the door a crack.

He held his breath, listened, eased his weapon's barrel in through the crack, waited, then opened the door. He stepped inside, let the door close, waited again, eyes scanning and re-scanning all quarters. He leaned over the stair rail, glanced up, glanced down, pulled back, listened.

The quickest, easiest way to go was down. There were more choices to be made closer to ground level. The upper floors offered increased confinement. *Cats are treed, but foxes go to earth.* East would have gone down.

Czals descended gingerly, came to the second floor door, paused, listened.

There was someone on the other side.

Czals hesitated. More than one. East and Tavi? No, it was Czals' own station guards.

Czals spoke loudly before opening the door. "This is your admiral coming through."

He opened the door. Five guns that were pointed at him were immediately raised, and the contingent of MPs snapped to attention.

"As you were," said Czals and moved past.

Now that he was off the third floor and East no more knew where Czals was than Czals knew where East was, Czals, though still alert, allowed himself to relax a little. Now he could think without panic's murky waters and plot a counteroffensive. The thing to do was hide and wait for East to make a false move and betray his position. Then—

Remember your limitations. You're not going to beat a seasoned soldier of fortune in a shootout. Though it was tempting to try.

Czals stopped, alarmed at the turn his thoughts were taking. *Can I possibly be enjoying this?*

Czals was horrified. Hunting, blood lust for a cornered beast, was not something Czals thought he had in him. He had never before seen the thrill in stalking a lower form of life than himself. *I am as bad as he is!* That potential for baseness Czals was not pleased to recognize.

And he was going to see East die for forcing him to face it.

As Lieutenant Martin rounded the corner, his gun was torn from his hands and went skidding down the corridor

And Martin was left facing East, unarmed. His heart sank, sick that he should be dying so young. He drew himself up

183

stoically and waited for East to pull the trigger. Martin was not going to grovel. He knew his end was here, and he would go with dignity.

East shoved past him and glanced around the corner from where Martin had come.

Martin blinked twice, still alive and perplexed to be alive. He had just looked death in the eye and death had turned up its nose at him. He couldn't help blurting out, "Aren't you going to kill me?"

East turned his head back to look at him, cocked an eyebrow as if to say, *Do you want me to?* "Why should I? Did you kill my wife?"

"No. I was the one who put you in the Labyrinth."

East turned fully, angered, but still not aiming his gun at Martin. His wrath was not for the reason expected. It was not vengeance or hatred; East was simply insulted. "Me? You think I care that you tried to kill *me*?"

Martin was thoroughly confused now. All his assumptions and preconceptions were exploding and diving out the windows head first.

East's back was again toward Martin, and he was watching down the corridor for signs of guards. It was quiet in this sector. There were only Martin and East. Martin spoke at East's back. "How did you get into this installation? How did you escape the search at the space station?"

East smiled over his shoulder. "Easily. In your ship, Lieutenant." And a blue eye winked. He was rather proud of that maneuver.

Martin was dumbstruck. How obvious. While Service personnel searched everywhere else, East slipped aboard the one vehicle they would not think to search.

"The last place one looks for the enemy is behind his own front line. Remember that if you're ever an admiral," said East and ran down the empty corridor.

Martin looked back to where his gun lay. He was too stupefied to pick it up.

Me? You think I care that you tried to kill me?

Martin could not imagine Czals saying that. Czals was the only being who counted in Czals' universe.

Given a swift kick in the loyalty, Martin paused for a moment. But still he knew which side he was stuck on, and he crossed to an intercom and reported, "Fugitive sighted on level one, moving into south wing."

And he spat. But the sour taste would not go away.

Czals figured that East would double back on his tracks. Having been announced as heading south, East would now go north. That would bring him to the main compound. From here, there were many options, many directions to go, so he would have to be stopped here. Czals made his way to the main compound to set his trap and wait.

The compound was a huge open area, the hub of the station complex. Where the rest of the building was five levels, there was only one floor here with four levels of balconies and an arched coffered glass ceiling high overhead. A yawning causeway to the control tower led off from the third-level balcony. The causeway was a two-story-tall glass structure of nonutilitarian design, spacious and lined with living plants. The station personnel liked to spend their breaks there. It was deserted now. Czals supposed it wouldn't be possible to station a sharpshooter up there. Though it would be a clear shot from there, East would spot the marksman right away as he came from the south wing; and a trap had to be attractive before it could be sprung.

It was a simple trap. East only *thought* he saw it when he doubled back and came near the compound. Reflected in the polished metal side of a vending machine, he caught sight of Czals lurking ten meters ahead of him, just around the corner where the corridor opened into the compound.

East stopped. As anticipated, he underestimated Czals; he thought the admiral was waiting to spring on him as he entered the compound. Czals had no such intention. He knew perfectly well that East would sight his reflection. Czals was not the trap; Czals was the bait.

East glared at the reflection with cold hatred. He could see his quarry but was not in line to shoot.

The reflection looked back coolly, steel eyes to blue. "Mr. East."

East was half crouched, ready to flee should Czals reach around the corner with his gun. East was in the weaker position and should have retreated, but as expected he did not run. He wanted Czals too badly.

"Welcome to the main compound," said Czals, springing the trap. The intercom was open; guards would soon be swarming in from all sectors—most of them from behind East—before East ever knew his position had been broadcast. All Czals needed to do now was stay alive and keep East here and unaware. "I see you slipped past my guards. They're all running well into the south wing by now. It's just you and

185

I." Czals hoped that wasn't laying it on too thickly. East could get suspicious.

But East was hate-blind. Narrow eyes shifted, looking for a vantagepoint from which to shoot. Perhaps above Czals—but no, the admiral had made sure his overhead was covered.

Czals, in a moment of daring, considering trying to shoot, but sighting in a reflection was tricky at best, and Czals was not expert. One shot would be all he would have, and Czals could not risk East escaping and getting himself lost again. He would be more than doubly dangerous on a second go-round. Czals would only shoot if it were absolutely necessary—if East charged or tried to creep in closer. Ten meters was quite close enough for an uncaged animal to be.

"Set down your weapon and we can talk," said Czals as a distraction, lest East think too much or listen too well to the closing trap.

"You murdered my wife," said East, and that was all there was for him to say.

Czals kept talking to keep East's attention, fanning his anger to blur his perception. Czals felt elatedly in control of this situation, seeing himself in cool handsome contrast to the rugged and ugly beast in the reflection. *You are a stupid brute of a bull and I am the picador.* "Mr. East, there was nothing else to be done. Surely you see she had to be silenced, and surely you know only death would keep her quiet. She was a headstrong woman, Mr. East. It is a bitter coincidence that she—"

Czals stopped talking. East was no longer paying attention. His narrow eyes had abruptly widened as he caught wind of the trap and realized he'd been had.

Czals was immediately on the alert. *Cornered beast. Watch it now, he could do anything.* He'd barely time to think when East shot the vending machine and charged.

East came round the corner shooting, but Czals was gone, having abandoned his position in the instant it took East to get there.

East snarled, poked his gun's snub barrel behind a brick pier, shot, looked. Czals was not there. East turned, kicked over an automaton, prowled the immediate area. Czals could not be far.

East could hear MPs closing in, but he did not take flight. He had only one purpose—to kill Czals before the MPs could come for him.

He hoped Czals would try to shoot. The red dot of his laser sight would tell East where Czals was hiding.

Running footsteps were almost upon him. He took Czals' former position, reached his gun around, and opened fire. That would stall them for a moment.

Then others appeared on the upper-level balconies.

East looked up. The light had dimmed slightly through the coffered glass dome as if a cloud had passed over the sun.

Then there was a loud dull *clunk*, and the guards looked up. It was no cloud. There was something on the dome.

The guards backed away from the balconies as there came a splitting and groaning from the arched ceiling—

—then a crash and rain of glass as a Polybios ship lowered into the compound.

The intercom had told more than MPs where East was.

East was the only one who did not take shelter from the flying glass and the ship with the maniac at the helm. He would not give up his search for Czals.

The ship came low, almost touching the floor, and the side hatch opened. "Dammit, East, come *on*!" Tavi yelled.

East paused, took a few backward steps toward the ship, fired a random spray of shots around the area where Czals had to be hiding, then ran for the ship and dove into the open hatch.

As the ship rose he heard a voice—Czals'—shouting, "You can't fly a ship inside a building!"

Tavi pointed the bow at the glass causeway, and the ship hurtled through like a bullet through a gun barrel and came crashing out the control tower's glass walls.

"Who taught you to fly?" said East, pulling himself up off the deck into a helm seat.

"Your son," said Tavi. "What do I do now?" Breaking out of a military installation did not suggest itself to a tremendous survival rate.

"Stay low," said East, putting a hand over Tavi's on the controls, forcing the ship down.

Emplaced weapons on a Service site were aimed high and at long distance. A low-flying ship would have to be chased with other ships—and without a control tower, pursuit would be slightly delayed.

"Head for the Texas border."

"Where's that?"

"Due south." East cranked the helm around.

Tavi was staring through the viewport as yet another threat appeared, this one in front of them. "American National Guard," said Tavi, pointing at a formation of ships.

"Good," said East.

"Good?"

East turned on the radio transmitter with video, grabbed Tavi by the collar, pointed his gun at his head, and barked, "Back off or I'll shoot my hostage." Then he blacked out the screen.

And the American ships fell back.

There was still no sign of the United Earth military behind them, for the Service did not dare try to shoot them down now that East had called Tavi a hostage on an open frequency. Clandestine torture was one thing, but open killing of an allied alien citizen with no apparent good cause was risking dire repercussions.

The ship crossed into Texan space, and the American ships stayed behind. Then East headed out for space, made a jump, and lost any possible trackers. He set a new course.

Tavi frowned. "East, shouldn't we go back to Roxanna? The whole galaxy is after you now."

"I've got something to do first," said East.

"Haven't you killed everyone already?"

"There's one left."

"But he's back there."

East shook his head. "He won't be for long." He glanced at his chronometer. The Kistraalians' time was up. "He's late for his execution. He's probably underway by now. He may even beat me there. This could be very close."

Tavi grabbed East's arm. "The command station for the weapon! You know where it is?"

East nodded. He'd throttled the information out of one of his late enemies.

"You've got to tell Roxanna!" said Tavi and reached for the phase-jumper transmitter.

East grabbed both of Tavi's hands in one of his and growled, "Radio Silence." He tossed Tavi's hands back at him.

Tavi looked at the heading and became puzzled. "We're not going to Aeolis?"

"Not in this ship," said East. "Couldn't get near it. I'm going to drop you and your ship off." And Tavi's relief was not unmixed when East looked aside at him and said, "The rest of the way I go alone."

Eclipse

The hail of curses from Roxanna when she came out of the Council meeting made Daniel think that the Council had voted against her.

But that was not the problem. Though the Council had not voted to remove Admiral Czals, it had agreed to do the next best thing. The Council ordered an injunction against any hostile acts toward the Kistraalians.

The problem was informing Czals of the decision. He was gone. His ship had left Earth and was either not receiving or not acknowledging attempts to contact him.

"Danny, he's on his way to press his button and I don't know where," Roxanna said helplessly. "Somewhere on Kushuh, but we haven't the time to search a whole planetoid for him." She turned away. "We don't have any time at all."

"The control center is on Kushuh, Dome Six, Annex D," said Daniel, who had not been sitting still while Roxanna met with the United Earth Council.

Roxanna whirled. At the best of times she'd never had access to top-level wartime information. "How could you know that?"

"I bought the President of Texas," said Lord LaFayette-Remington.

"God love you, Danny," said Roxanna, and they ran to the shuttle that would take them to the *Aberdeen*, which was already targeted for a fast trip to Aeolis and its moon Kushuh in hopes there was still time to save an entire race from extinction.

The Polybios ship had come to its final port in Nueva Trinidad unchallenged, for everything on the small moon-sized world was a shade less than legal. There East switched ships. An old comrade-in-arms lent him one of hers. East told her to wait six hours, then report it stolen, so she could both recover the ship and clear herself of a complicity charge.

189

A tough-talking, wiry, petite-framed woman, she gave East a change of clothes from her latest husband's wardrobe, and forced some food and beer down him as he made ready to leave.

Tavi stood around, fists in his pockets and shoulders hunched like a troubled East, and stared at his feet. East was pulling on a drab gray-white jacket. Tavi mumbled, "I can't talk you out of this?"

"No," said East.

"Didn't think so," said Tavi.

East took one last swig of beer and tossed the bottle out into the street. It broke against the shards of many other bottles.

Tavi spoke. "You know, you could've had him back there if you hadn't gotten me out of the bats first."

"I know."

Even though it was East's fault that Tavi had been thrown in with the bats in the first place, it was nevertheless amazing that East had thought of Tavi at all. In his single-minded resolve he seemed to have forgotten everything—the Kistraalian crisis, his son, himself. Nothing existed for him but vengeance.

He slung his gun over his shoulder. He saw Tavi standing by forlornly and paused to crack a smile and ruffle Tavi's hair. "Stay away from guys like me, hm?"

"I'll do that," Tavi promised.

"Now as soon as I'm gone, you go to the nearest policeman and tell him you escaped from me. Then keep your head low till this is all over," East told him.

"What about you?" said Tavi. "How do you get away?"

"I don't," said East. "This is the end of the line." And he reloaded his gun.

When Admiral Czals landed on Kushuh he had recovered from the fiasco at the Nebraska installation. He was on familiar ground now; computerized warfare was more civilized work. He would let others take care of East, and had no doubt they would succeed. The Service would have crack counterterrorists after him now.

Czals proceeded to Annex D, where the weapon controls awaited him. He ignored pages throughout the dome that said there was an urgent message for him; he was certain he did not want to receive it. He suspected it could be a stop order from the United Earth Council. He had a sixth sense for anticipating trouble. Let them order him to stop after he was finished here. Once done it would be done. Council could castigate him, but the Aeolian residents who retained their estates because of him would look after him well.

He came into the control center and turned on the monitors that showed him where the Kistraalian winds were located. The planet was infested with them, amorphous beings that blended one into another like clouds. They had conveniently massed themselves into two large concentrations, one clustering around the estate of the mad dancer Niki Thea—so it was true what they said about him, thought Czals—and one centered on the LaFayette estate. Czals smiled. It was perfect. If he had to destroy part of Aeolis, that would be the estate he would chose.

He took the controls of the deadly satellites and focused them on the two targets. The cloud of Kistraalians over the LaFayette estate would be the newcomers, the pirates Daniel had brought back—the fertile ones. Czals could not afford to miss even one of those.

All the controls worked smoothly. They were the last devices the scientist had designed before he'd . . . departed.

Soon Czals was set. He armed the satellites and adjusted the focus to the shifting clouds. All that was needed now was Czals' voice command to fire.

He heard running footsteps. His sixth sense screamed at him.

He checked over the sights once more, made an adjustment, conferred with the computer.

Roxanna burst through the door. "Stop!"

"Fire."

PART FIVE: Wind Child

Into the deadly frozen silence came again the sound of running footsteps. Roxanna spun around with raised gun and stopped East at the door. "Don't try it, East. It's too late." The red dot of her laser sight rested square between his blue eyes.

East did not move. But his gun was already aimed directly at Czals.

The admiral hadn't had time to draw his own weapon, but he was calm, even smug, confident that Roxanna would protect him, still not really comprehending that threat of death meant nothing to East. He spoke to Roxanna, his eyes on East. "Commodore, do you think you could manage to shoot that gun aside for me?

Roxanna kept her gun leveled at East's head. She did not look aside to answer. "Mr. East is faster than I am and knows it."

East almost smiled. Admissions like that—however true—were rare out of Roxanna. "No matter what Roxanna does, you are dead, mister. At this range I can't miss—even if I'm dead myself."

Czals' upper lip moistened with perspiration. He was beginning to realize that East was suicidal. Czals tended to color his perception of other people's actions with his own motives and values—his own love of living—and so he neglected to see the obvious, that East had no intention of surviving Czals for very long.

Madman.

Roxanna's voice was harsh. "East, drop it. I'll shoot. You know I will."

East did not doubt her. "He will die either way."

"Only maybe," said Roxanna. "If I see a chance I'll kill you first."

Czals started to speak. Roxanna snapped at him, "Shut up."

Czals' head jerked back with disbelief. East half smiled. "Only people with guns may talk."

"Last warning, East. Put it down."

"Roxy, I'm dead even if you don't pull the trigger. I'm a mass murderer, remember?"

"There's always an insanity defense," said Roxanna.

"You know I'm not insane."

"The hell I do!"

East gave a one-shoulder shrug. He wasn't going to argue the point. "For what I've done they'll kill me anyway. It may as well be at your hand with the job finished." He lowered his head slightly, a mannerism that signaled he was about to shoot.

"I don't *want* to kill you!" Roxanna cried in unconcealed anguish.

And East looked at her. He gazed straight into auburn eyes that were filling with tears. He spoke quietly, as if Czals did not even exist. "You're such a pretty woman, Roxy." He lowered his gun and gave it to her.

Czals took an enormous breath of relief and reached for his own weapon. "*Very* convincing, Commodore!"

But when he glanced aside at her, he was staring up the barrel of her gun and there was a red dot on his forehead. "You weren't thinking of doing anything illegal, were you, Admiral?" she said.

"No," he stammered, abandoning his weapon. He cleared his throat and squared his shoulders. "No. He's entitled to due process before he's exterminated."

Roxanna's aim swiveled back to East, and she spoke with a tired voice of defeat. "You're under arrest." And she escorted him out.

Czals glared after her with smoldering hatred. He should have court-martialed her twenty years ago when he had had the chance, when she was still a rude little commander, instead of letting her become the belligerent, swaggering commodore she was now.

He soothed his bruised pride with a survey of his victory. He regarded the monitors. They were blank. The readings had disappeared altogether. Aeolis belonged to the Earthlings.

The winds were dead.

Daniel walked away from his ship, over the devastation that had been the Thea estate, home of the ancient winds. The landscape was charred and desolate as far as he could see. What used to be forest was now black dust all the way down the mountainside to the ocean. He could hear the rush of the mountain river in its deep gorge glutted with black mud, washing the refuse out to the sea.

He sat down under a wide bright sky, weeping, on the remains of brick foundations of the house, the only things not thoroughly disrupted in the two blasts. His eyes were round and could not blink, could only pour out tears.

Oh God. All of them. I brought them here to die. I destroyed my people.

As he sat there staring, an apparition passed into his field of vision. Like a ghost, a white figure came stepping carefully through the ruins. The specter came to a stop, looked down, stooped, picked up a charred piece of something, stood, sighed, tossed it away. He brushed the dust off his immaculate hands. "What a mess."

Daniel tried to speak his name, but no sound came forth.

Niki drew near, his head tilted aside with an expression of a curious child. He spoke gently in a beautifully modulated, oddly accented voice, "What is wrong with you?"

On his third try, Daniel found his voice. "*Niki.* What is *wrong*? They're all dead!"

Niki drew himself up indignantly. "We are not."

"But—" Daniel stuttered, wonderstruck. "What about—" His voice failed again.

"This?" Niki kicked the black dust with the ball of his foot like a prancing horse. "Physical *stuff.* Which we are not."

"But I thought they ran a test. I thought it worked," said Daniel, drying his face with his sleeves. Still the sobs would not subside.

"*I* ran a test," said Niki. "And their machine did exactly what I expected it to do. It made us undetectable."

Daniel was silent one incredulous moment, then broke out into laughter, not untouched with hysteria. The more he thought about it, the louder he howled. Maniacal, half-human sounds rang up and down the mountain and echoed through the gorge.

At last he quieted, sitting on the ground, hugging his knees, rocking back and forth, grinning like a mad thing.

Niki was standing by undisturbed, and when Daniel recovered some sense of himself he asked Niki to explain what had happened.

"It was the auroras that deceived them," Niki began. "They thought that because we cause auroras we must be particulate. We do carry particles; we push them about; but we are not the particles, any more than you are the carcass you inhabit."

"Yeah, except that I would die without this carcass," said Daniel.

"You don't believe in ghosts."

"No such thing."

Niki looked highly skeptical but did not challenge the statement. "I do not know what is the essence of an Earthling. But *we* are not a particulate pest like the *cuyane* to be disrupted by a machine. We are energy." He looked up at the bright sky. "It can kill if one is not ready for it. We were ready. I told them what to expect." He squatted on the ground and traced lines in the dust with his fingertips pensively. "I do not know yet, but I think some of us may have died anyway. We are accustomed to having control of matter. Letting go is sometimes difficult. That is how some of the *volaia* died in the magnetosphere; when they did not let go it tore them to pieces." He let a handful of dust trickle through his fingers.

Daniel shifted. He felt stiff, heavy, and drained. His mouth tasted like ash. He squinted at Niki. "What happens if you use all your energy?"

"Use it?" said Niki. "As in use it and it is gone? Gone where? You cannot destroy energy. We do not entropize. That is the difference between live energy and dead energy."

Daniel shook his head. "I still don't understand. How can you spend energy and still have it?"

"That is the secret of life, and I am not telling."

Daniel smiled slyly. "You mean you don't know."

"That too," said Niki. He stood up. In a strong flowing motion, his whole body in action, he took up a fistful of black ash and threw it into the air. The wind picked it up, swirled it up, and made it dance.

Niki slapped his dusty hands against his thighs. "Now that this nonsense is over, I think your people might like to start discussing a land settlement."

"Can't," said Daniel, sullen, red-streaked bangs in his face. "There's still a jerk in charge."

"Czals? We know," said Niki. "Do not worry about him— since you do not believe in ghosts."

196

Czals made ready for bed amid the costly furnishings of his room. He replaced the stopper on the leather-covered wine decanter, pushed aside his ex-wife's ermine-lined slippers with the side of his foot, extinguished the light, and slid in between the satin sheets and laid his head on the down pillow to which still clung a faint vestige of his wife's musk perfume. He closed his eyes, his mind at peace for the first time in a long time. He could wish that East were already dead, but East was safely under arrest and would be executed soon enough.

Czals sighed and drifted close to sleep.

The wind blew open the French doors and slammed them against the doorstops.

Czals sat up. "Who's there?"

A frosty image like a pale hologram—or a ghost—appeared in the open door.

Laure LaFayette-Remington.

Czals stared. "Are you real?" he said.

She tilted her head to one side, teasing. *Maybe.* Her eyes were laughing, her smile feral.

The wind picked up. Cold gusts swept and eddied into the room.

In the distance an alarm sounded. *Cuyane?* Czals was confused at first.

Cuyane!

He looked at Laure (was she really there?) with sudden comprehension. "Oh no. You wouldn't."

Her smile said she would.

Cuyane. Carried by the wind.

Wind.

Caustic, deadly, windborne *cuyane.* Czals leaped out of bed. He might be imagining Laure, but that alarm was real. "I'm not going that way," he declared and tried to close the French doors. The wind fought him with all its awesome force. He leaned against the wall, panting and sweating. "Gods, you're a ruthless lot. Ever consider working for the government?"

The winds laughed.

He could see the swarm now, spuming into the night sky like a volcanic cloud, blotting out the stars. He knew he was dead this time. There was no Roxanna to bail him out now. The winds planned for him to die horribly. "I won't give you that."

He went to the nightstand, took a gun from the drawer, and shot himself.

Laure's image faded before his darkening eyes, and she went with him, if she had ever been there at all.

The *cuyane* swept away on an updraft. The alarm stopped.

Admiral Czals was found dead of a suicide and no one could say why.

"Of all men to blow his brains out I never would have guessed Admiral Czals. He loved himself more than anyone I've ever known," said Admiral Roxanna Douglas.

The Duke of Aeolis was chagrined with the way things turned out. He regarded the new Officer in Charge of Aeolian Affairs with a combination of intense dislike and implicit trust. She had opened talks with the native Kistraalians, and it looked fairly certain that they would be ceded the southern continent. The northern continent was the larger, but Roxanna reasoned that it was in the Kistraalians' best interests that Earthlings retain a large share of the planet so they would take care to keep the world a paradise and guard against importing diseases. The Earthlings' own selfishness was the best guarantee she could give.

The duke predicted great conflict further in the future when the Kistraalians outgrew their allotted land and wanted the Earthlings' part as well. Daniel murmured a wistful wish. "Maybe the Kistraalians and the Earthlings will just marry each other and have children and live happily ever after."

The duke scoffed. "How naive you are, lad. Humans and aliens cannot have children."

Daniel and Roxanna felt the corners of their mouths twitching and they avoided each other's eyes in silent conspiracy. *Oh yeah?*

But all that was just speculation of events a long way off. Roxanna had a more immediate problem—her prisoner, East.

She went to the *Aberdeen*'s brig, careful not to be observed, and deactivated the force field that contained East. She spoke quickly. "Your guerrilla ship is stocked, armed, and ready to go. I hope the life of a pirate suits you, because after your daring escape from here there's not a planet or port in the galaxy that will receive you."

"Why, Roxanna, I do believe this is the first time I've ever seen you do something dishonest."

"Call it discharging my old debt. Beat it, now; there's not much time before the watch comes by."

"Can I say goodbye to my son?"

198

"Whatever you can get done in nine minutes." She jabbed her gun toward him, hilt first. "Come on. Jump me. And don't forget to lock the cell."

East grabbed the gun, kissed Roxanna, reactivated the force field with her inside, and ran.

The daring escape went off without a hitch. The guerrilla ship detached and sped away into a jump before anyone knew who was in it. The watch officer found Admiral Douglas locked in East's cell and sounded the alarm, but too late.

Roxanna sought out Daniel, found him alone, gazing out a viewport in the direction his father had gone. He was dry-eyed and resigned. When Roxanna came to his side he said, "There's only one thing to do. Get drunk."

"You're an East, all right." She slung her arm around his shoulders, and they went whistling to her cabin in search of spirits. "I've some pretty fell liquor," she warned him.

Daniel had heard. "Are you going to get drunk enough to dance on swords?"

"Drunk enough to eat them. Wait till you see this."

Admiral Roxanna Douglas had the best cache of bourbon and scotch in the Service.

She had.

She stared blankly into the empty hold, then shrieked, "Damn you, East, if I ever get my hands on you again!"

Nine minutes. A lifetime store of booze carted away in nine minutes.

And over the phase jumper a drunken voice could be heard singing between the stars:

"Fifteen men on a dead man's chest
Yo ho ho and a bottle of scotch."

And there came a screaming reply: "You, you, you . . . *space moose!*"

Daniel had the feeling it was the beginning of a wonderful war.

Daniel received a call while he was still aboard the *Aberdeen*. It could only be from one person. Tavi. He was calling from Nueva Trinidad, in tears. He said he'd been grounded by the port authority, and would Daniel come get him?

"Yeah, sure. Hold on, Tavi. Don't cry."

So Daniel set out in his own ship, wondering what Tavi

199

could possibly have done to get himself grounded in a place like Nueva Trinidad—where a person could sell his baby sister and no one would get too upset about it.

When he arrived he found the trouble was not with Tavi himself but with his ship. "My ship died," Tavi whimpered. "It's dead. '

"Well, what exactly is wrong with it?" said Daniel.

"Everything," Tavi wailed and showed him a long list drawn up by the port authority calling the craft an unfit vehicle.

"Looks grim," Daniel agreed. He hired a couple mechanics to look at the Polybios craft and asked what they thought they could do with it.

"Bury it," they said.

Tavi wailed.

"I'll buy you another one," said Daniel, since he was certain it had been his father who had done in Tavi's ship.

Tavi looked ill.

"Tavi, did you hear me?"

But Tavi was not listening, was not looking at him. Tavi was looking past him. Daniel turned.

Ten paces off there stood a Tyi. He—she—stood taller than Tavi, pretty like all Tyi but less distinctive, not so pixielike, with a straight narrow nose and mild liquid eyes. He started to speak in a gentle voice full of concern.

Tavi snapped at him angrily. "In English in front of my friend, if you don t mind!"

The Tyi became flustered and self-conscious, lacking Tavi's gift for languages. He spoke in broken English, eyes shining as if close to tears. "I thought I had lost you. Then I found you again and you were here then there then there. Now I hear you are grounded and sending a message to one Dan-iel. You sounded in trouble. I thought you might . . . need me?"

So this was Tavi's tracker, his betrothed from whom he ran. And since wayward Tavi had fallen in with shady company indeed, this Tyi had good cause to be concerned.

But Tavi was mad as hell. "Stop protecting me! I'm perfectly capable of taking care of myself—and a couple of other crazy idiots besides. Who sent for you? Who asked you? Who *needs* you?" Tavi turned to Daniel. "You wanted to know what was after me; well, here it is. A mother hen."

Liquid eyes blinked, more than wounded, utterly devastated. "I will leave you alone," he said shakily. "I never meant—" He didn't finish, but meekly withdrew.

He looked a small, solitary creature retreating desolately

through the big spaceport. He was almost out of sight when Tavi screamed, ran after him, caught up with him, and threw his arms around him.

Daniel rolled his eyes. He had never cared for sappy love scenes.

And finally Daniel was left alone on Nueva Trinidad. It was a hot night. He walked the boulevard, shoes crushing broken glass, shirt tied around his neck by the sleeves, sultry wind ruffling his hair. It was done now, what Laure had started. He tried to think where that left him.

He was a titled lord, though he had lost a vast part of his land. *Easy come, easy go.*

His best friend had run off to get married.

His father was gone, passed into legend. For years to come there would be a voice that came over the phase jumper in the dead of space, singing old sea chanties and ballads, thick with scotch whiskey:

> "She's bound to the west'ard where the ion winds
>   blow
> Bound away in the *Dreadnaught* to the west'ard
>   we'll go."

And stories abounded of an old pirate with a face like a battlefield, silver mane, and fierce blue eyes, as charming a mass murderer as ever boarded a vessel. He never hurt anyone, and it began to be said he'd been framed. . . .

Daniel never saw him again. Without father or mother it was left for him to chart his own course—and he wasn't too scared.

There were still a few things that needed doing. He would go back to Earth, stay with his grandfather and Maria, finish his education in an American school, and ask Two Braids for a date without making an ass of himself.

And plant a tree over his mother's grave to calm the soul of a restless wind child, and whisper the words, "Never stir."

Rebecca M. Meluch graduated from the University of North Carolina at Greensboro with a B.A. in drama. She also has an M.A. in ancient history from the University of Pennsylvania and a black belt in *tae kwon do*. She has worked as everything from a control clerk and keypunch operator to an assistant in the Classics department at Greensboro, and she has been active in nonprofessional theater. Her other novels, SOVEREIGN and WIND DANCERS, are also available in Signet editions. Miss Meluch lives in Westlake, Ohio.